RED

BLOODED
Red Hot & Blue

Cat Johnson

New York Times & USA Today Bestselling Author

First Edition 2012
Reprint 2017

Copyright © Cat Johnson
All rights reserved.

ISBN-13: 978-1974646302
ISBN-10: 1974646300

ACKNOWLEDGEMENT

A huge thanks goes to Sean Abbott, whose real-life Army training provided the details for the opening scene.

Any mistakes made or liberties taken with the facts are purely my own.

RED HOT & BLUE

TREY

CHAPTER ONE

He waited in the reeds. An RPG launcher rested on top of his shoulder as he watched for the enemy from his hiding place along the road.

His persistence finally paid off. He heard the US force moving toward him. Training gave him the patience to hold until they were dead ahead.

Dead.

He grinned at that word since, for all intents and purposes, they would soon be dead.

Zeroing in on his target, he stood, sighted and then fired. The rocket-propelled grenade cut through the air with a trail of smoke and its unmistakable sound.

The soldiers heard it coming, but it was too late. That tended to be the problem with RPGs. By the time you heard them coming you were as good as gone.

The concussion of the explosion caused the soldiers on foot to fall where they stood. The vehicles behind the ground pounders stopped, the passengers scurrying out. He watched their panic.

Nothing felt as good as a successful mission. He hadn't totally destroyed the force, but he'd done quite a bit of damage with just the one RPG. Enough to teach them a lesson and hadn't that been his goal to begin with? Though right now, it was time to get moving.

He cupped his hands around his mouth. *"Allah achbar!"*

God is great.

That little bit of shouted Arabic had the soldiers scrambling faster than even the incoming RPG had.

Sorry he couldn't stick around to watch the aftermath, he took off running as a spray of gunfire peppered the area where he'd been.

Amid the noise, he heard the scattered orders and curses behind him as the soldiers tried to get their fallen men to cover.

He sped to the next previously selected point of attack, then launched another rocket, this time at one of the trucks. The soldiers would think there were more attackers hiding than there actually were because of the multiple assaults in rapid succession from different locations.

That done, he took off for cover farther away. He wouldn't strike again just yet. Let them think the danger had passed, then he and his team would hit with an improvised explosive device when it was least expected.

A nice IED would shake things up. He was getting bored with the old Russian RPG launcher anyway.

Explosions were much more fun and, when you knew what you were doing, child's play to set up. His team probably had a few in place already.

After reaching a point a safe distance from the strike zone, he hit the ground behind an outcropping of rock. Enjoying a rare, brief moment of leisure, he pulled a bottle of water out of his pack and took a long swallow. He wiped a dribble from his beard with the back of one hand just as footsteps to his right drew his attention.

"Pigeon Two approaching Songbird from the north." The voice came through his earpiece just before his teammate Jack Gordon hit the ground next to him, looking as dirty and sweaty as he felt. "Nice explosions."

"Thanks." His throat dry, Trey Williams took another swig.

"Bull and I set up the IEDs." Jack pulled out his own bottle and took a swallow.

It had been a long, hot day of training exercises for everyone involved and it wasn't over yet.

"How many you set up?" Trey asked.

"A pretty obvious primary in the middle of the road with a secondary one better hidden on the side path just off the main route in case they try to drive around the first one."

Trey scratched an itch on his chin that his sweat-soaked, overgrown beard caused. "They'll see the first one right away."

"Yup." Jack nodded. "And when they're trying to avoid it by driving on the path they'll hit the second one."

"Or they could move backward and fire upon the primary to disarm it," Trey pointed out.

"They could, but they'll back up over the third one we put behind them. Bull's got it hidden so well I'm not sure I could find it if I hadn't been with him when he set it up. Once they've backed up to decide what to do about the one in front of them, Bull will detonate. Then *kaboom*." Jack grinned like a kid on Christmas morning.

Trey shook his head and smiled. "You're evil."

"Hey, why not enjoy ourselves?" Jack shook his head. "I'm kind of sorry this exercise is over after today. I love OPFOR training."

"Hell, who doesn't love it?"

An explosion sounded in the distance and Jack snorted out a laugh. "Those guys who just got blown up by Bull's IED, that's who."

"Bull sets up a nice explosion, even his fake ones." Trey admired the skill. He could set up a decent IED himself, but Bull was a master craftsman at it.

Jack chuckled. "I'm gonna laugh my ass off watching their reaction on the video during the after-action review tonight. This is easier than shooting beer cans off a fence post. A helluva lot more fun too."

"It's definitely more fun playing the bad guys than the

good guys in these exercises." Trey knew well it may be fun, but opposition-force training was crucial. What the soldiers learned today could save their lives when they deployed to regions where the bad guys were actually out to kill them.

All in all, it had been a good day, except for the damn itchy beard he'd grown out so he'd look more like a terrorist and less like a member of Task Force Zeta.

That Trey could have lived without.

CHAPTER TWO

"Vodka tonic, gin and tonic, diet cola, regular cola and a bottle of beer." The bleached-blonde cocktail waitress snapped her gum and read off her scribbled list.

Trey leaned his forearms against the bar rail. Happy to be clean-shaven again and out of the dusty, ripe cammies from the previous day's final exercise, he was more than content to simply sit and watch the bartender work.

After picking up two glasses in each hand, she packed them with ice and then lined them up in front of her on the bar. She poured the liquor with her left hand while operating the soda gun with her right. Not even glancing at the bottles in the speed rack, she just grabbed, poured and then returned them to their proper places.

Leaning on the bar next to him, an also-well-groomed Jack watched her too while shaking his head. "Ooo wee, how can someone look so hot and act so cold?"

"She's not cold. She's just busy." Trey kept his voice low.

Jack laughed. "Oh, believe me, she can get cold as ice. Just ask her out a few times and you'll see."

Trey had seen each and every time Jack had asked this woman out and gotten a *no* in response.

"Hey there, darlin'. Couple of longnecks over here when you get a chance," Jack called out to her.

Trey frowned. "Jeez, Jack. Give her a second. She's got her hands full."

"Vodka tonic has two straws, gin and tonic one straw, diet's got a lemon and regular doesn't." Without even glancing their way, the bartender lined a cocktail tray with the drinks, calling them off for the gum-snapping blonde as she did so.

She turned her back to the two of them, reached down into a fridge against the wall behind the bar and came up with three longneck beer bottles in one hand.

Trey had to admit the view was damn nice from there with her bending over in those tight jeans. No wonder she sold so much bottled beer. Pretty much every guy on the base came in when they were stateside and ninety-nine percent of them ordered the bottled beer strictly for the view.

With an economy of motion he had to appreciate, she popped the tops off the bottles using the bar-mounted opener, letting the caps plunk one by one into the garbage pail positioned perfectly underneath to catch them.

She placed one bottle in the center of the drinks on the cocktail tray. "And there's the beer."

Finished with the waitress, she slapped two cocktail napkins down in front of them and plopped the remaining two beers in her hand on top of them. "And there are your beers, *darlin'.*"

Trey had to smile at the verbal slap aimed directly at Jack until she turned to him next. "And I can do more than one thing at a time, but thanks for your concern."

Just when he'd thought she wasn't listening . . .

Out of the corner of his eye, he saw Jack enjoying his discomfort now.

Trey shrugged. "Looked more like seven things at once to me." He raised his bottle in a mock toast to her and drank.

"Hey, darlin'. Why don't you give in and go out with me? Give up all this cat and mouse. Playing hard to get is fun and all, but I know we could have a lot more fun together." Jack waggled his eyebrows.

Would Jack ever stop trying? His resilience never ceased to amaze Trey.

"Okay. I'll go out with you." She walked over to them and leaned up against the bar, her well-rounded breasts pushing the boundaries of the neckline of her tight T-shirt. "On one condition."

Trey had never seen Jack so flustered before in all the time he'd known him. Jack had been asking this woman out for years now and this was as close as he'd ever come to an actual yes.

Jack swallowed and finally wrestled his eyes up from her chest. "W-what's that, darlin'?"

"What's my name?" She slapped each palm flat on the bar and waited for the answer.

Jack opened his mouth, but no sound came out. Trey paused for a moment himself. She had a good point. They'd been coming here a good two years now and she'd served them most times, but he'd be damned if he knew her name.

Shaking her head, she smiled. "Didn't think so."

She walked away as the waitress returned to give her money for the drinks. Trey watched her glance at them in the reflection of the mirror behind the bar as she opened the cash register and made change.

"Why didn't you remember her name?" Jack backhanded Trey's leg. "Dang it. I was as happy as a puppy with two peters when she said she'd go out with me. I nearly shit my pants. Then she comes up with some stupid question. I didn't think there'd be a test first."

As Jack scowled, Trey shook his head. "It wasn't a stupid question. She's right. We should know after all this time. Besides the team, we probably spend more hours here with her than with anyone else in our lives and we don't even know her name."

Jack frowned and broke his gaze away from watching the nameless bartender. Staring right at Trey now, Jack cocked his head to one side. "What is all this tonight? First it's 'Don't bother her, she's busy'. Now it's 'She's right, we should know her name'. You better not be snooping around my girl. Teammates don't steal each other's women. It's in the code."

Trey rolled his eyes and let out a short laugh. "First of all, I'm not snooping around, as you put it. Second, if she's your woman, learn her damn name."

"I will." Jack banged his bottle onto the bar. He glanced around until his attention landed on the waitress. "Baby cakes, sashay your sweet self on over here."

The willing waitress arrived immediately after his summons in a cloud of perfume mixed with grape gum. She had on so much makeup her eyelashes stuck together when she tried to bat them at Jack.

"Hey, boys. I don't get to hang with you two usually. You're always sitting at the bar instead of at my tables. What can I do for you?"

Jack fielded that question while Trey took another swig of beer. He noticed that while he and Jack had been arguing, the bartender had left briefly. She returned now with a rack of clean, stemmed glasses.

Hoisting the unwieldy item onto the bar with a clang, she started to hang the glasses one by one upside-down above the bar.

Glancing at Jack as he flirted with the waitress, she raised a brow. "Moved on already, has he? I'm heartbroken."

Trey laughed. He considered telling her Jack was sweet talking the waitress in an attempt to find out her name. Instead, without even knowing why he did it, he extended his arm toward her. "I'm Trey Williams."

She looked down at his offered hand and then back to his face. After a moment, she wiped her fingers on a bar rag and took his in a firm, strong grasp. "Carly McAfee."

He smiled and repeated, "Carly."

"Yeah, short for Charlene. Thank God my parents realized I wasn't a Charlene pretty early on and gave me the nickname."

"What's wrong with the name Charlene?" he asked mainly to keep her talking because he was enjoying the conversation.

She glanced at the miniskirt-wearing waitress still talking with Jack.

"I'd have to look like *her* to pull off a name like Charlene." She shook her head. "No, I'm definitely a Carly."

Trey took in her straight brown hair pulled into a ponytail to fully expose a pretty, fresh face. If she wore makeup at all, it didn't scream to be noticed. Her girl-next-door looks sat just fine with him. The centerfold-worthy, shapely jean-clad hips, small waist and even shapelier T-shirt-covered breasts didn't hurt either.

She was a strange cocktail of simplicity mixed with attitude, shaken with killer good looks. More importantly, he could tell there was a brain in that pretty head of hers.

Jack, leaning forward, interrupted Trey's reverie regarding Carly's assets. "Hey, darlin'. I want another chance at this date. Come over here and ask me your question again."

She rolled her eyes and walked to stand in front of Jack. "I'll give you one more chance, but the question has changed."

"Lay it on me, sweet cheeks." Jack grinned wide.

Looking overly confident, Jack leaned back on the barstool and waited for the question. He must have gleaned quite a bit of information from his discussion with the waitress.

Carly covered her eyes with one hand. "What color are my eyes?"

Jack, who never used bad language in mixed company, silently mouthed a vile curse before venturing an obviously blind guess. "Uh, brown?"

"Wrong." She turned, opened the beer cooler and began checking her stock of cold bottles. Scowling, Jack cursed again quietly. "Watch my beer, will you'? I gotta go take a leak."

Trey nodded and Jack disappeared into the bathroom. Eyes still on Carly's back, he whispered, "They're green."

She spun, those beautiful jade-colored eyes open wide and staring straight at him.

Trey knew she was well aware they weren't heading home, but most likely out on an assignment.

There were guys she served who never made it home from their ops. He nodded an acknowledgment for her concern. "Thanks."

On base, he and Jack strode into the meeting room and found the rest of the team already assembled. He was happy they'd only had time for one beer each, because judging by the look on the commander's face something was up and it wasn't good.

"Sit down." The commander gestured to the two chairs still empty at the long table. He looked directly at Jack. "I've gotten a new SITREP. We've lost touch with Jimmy."

At the news revealed in the latest situation report, Trey glanced at Jack as his own stomach sank. Jimmy Gordon was not just Jack's older brother. He was his father figure, his hero and the reason he'd joined both the military and this team.

Jack shook his head with obvious disbelief or maybe just outright denial. "He's deep undercover, sir. He can't be phoning home everyday to ask what's for supper."

The commander nodded his head. "I know that, son. But we've picked up a lot of chatter on the lines lately. Things that make us believe he's been compromised."

"So we're going in to get him. Right?"

Trey could hear the panic in Jack's voice.

The commander shook his head. "No, Gordon. We're not."

Jack stood. "What do you mean no?"

Trey cringed. Jack was upset and coming very close to crossing the line into insubordination.

The commander stood firm. "Sit down, Gordon."

Jack set his jaw and sat, but just barely, on the very edge of his seat.

When he was seated again, if not settled, the commander continued, "We're going to give him some more time to make contact. In the meantime, I want the entire team on standby and ready to leave on an hour's notice if needed. Got it?"

The group nodded, all except for Jack whose eyes were glazed over.

"Permission to be excused, sir." When Jack spoke, Trey could hear the strain in his voice.

The commander nodded and Jack was out the door in a heartbeat.

CHAPTER THREE

Carly took advantage of the slow night to get some much needed organizing and cleaning done around the bar and in the rear storeroom.

There was only one table currently occupied and they had a full pitcher of beer and eyes only for each other. She had a feeling they wouldn't even finish their pitcher before one or the other couldn't take it anymore and they rushed home, or at least out to the parking lot, to have sex.

She was used to women coming in just to hook up with guys from the base. Women made up close to half her business so she really shouldn't complain.

Carly knew she shouldn't judge either. If these women wanted to sleep with men they knew nothing about just because they were in the armed forces it was their choice. Just like it was her prerogative to choose not to date anyone who is, was or was even thinking about being in the military.

Too bad almost every man in her bar was military. That's what she got for buying a bar directly next to a base. A daily buffet of off-limits and hotter-than-hell men who'd love you and leave you lonely in the end.

Glancing out the storeroom door so she could see the amorous couple, she tried not to think of how many of these guys might have girlfriends or wives waiting at home while their tongues were down other women's throats.

Feeling a little bit sick to her stomach at the thought, she unloaded more of the case of cocktail olives onto the shelves when she heard a soft knock on the doorframe behind her.

Turning around, she saw who it was and smiled. "Hi. I'm surprised to see you back here so soon. After both of your phones went off at the same time I figured I wouldn't see you guys for awhile."

He laughed, but it sounded far from happy. "Yup. Me too."

Putting the last of the glass jars on the shelf, Carly completed her task. She glanced at the status of her other customers past . . . What was his name again? She thought she'd heard him called Jack.

Jack. The joking, colorful southern sidekick to the quiet but observant Trey.

Carly pushed aside the image of Trey and his golden brown eyes a girl could get lost in and brown wavy hair just made for running your fingers through. That man was too tempting.

Dark and brooding was exactly her type or had been once. Before her ex.

The man before her now was too damn cute himself as well as far too persistent in his attentions toward her. Southern gentlemen and their trademark drawl always had gotten to her, ever since she'd first watched *Gone with the Wind* with her grandmother as a kid.

You didn't get much more southern than Jack, and he was pretty much the exact opposite of her ex which was tempting in itself.

She shook the thought from her brain. Nope. No more military men. In fact, recently there'd been no men at all. It was safer that way.

Carly had a customer to serve, if she could wrestle her mind off the topic of her pitiful love life, or lack thereof. "I'm assuming you're here for a drink."

He shook his head. "No rush. I can wait until you've finished what you're doing."

A whole conversation without even one darlin'. That was strange.

"It's okay. I'm done." Leaving the now-empty cardboard box in the storeroom, she led the way to the bar with Jack following behind.

When he didn't immediately come out with some colorful comment or start flirting with her, she took a closer look. There was definitely something wrong. He was alone too, which he never was.

Could she ask where Trey was without it looking like she was overly interested? Which she definitely was not.

The suspense of wondering what was up with Jack and why Trey wasn't with him was killing her. The only reason her unsatisfied curiosity didn't actually kill her was because she caved and gave in to it. "You all alone tonight?"

Dammit. So much for self-restraint.

Carly could have kicked herself. She shouldn't care what was up with them because she definitely was not interested in any man in the military. So why did she care where Trey was or what was wrong with Jack?

"Yup. All alone." Jack drew in a deep breath and then let it out slowly.

"Beer?" She turned toward the beer cooler.

Jack stopped her as he said, "No beer tonight, darlin'. Bourbon. Double, straight up and keep 'em coming."

Raising a brow, she poured a long double shot into a glass and then slid a basket full of pretzels in front of him. It wasn't much, but at least it was something to soak up the alcohol.

The problem was he made no move to touch the food. Instead, he downed the drink in one swallow and pushed the glass toward her. She refilled it.

This was going to be bad. She could see that already. Something was very wrong. Wondering what the hell had happened, she couldn't help but move on to consider once again where Trey might be and why he wasn't here.

Every scenario she came up with wasn't good.

If Jack, Trey and their friends were special ops, as she suspected from various clues she'd picked up from being around them for years, Trey could be dead and she'd never know for sure. He'd just disappear one day, after which his buddies would probably get drunk for a single night of silent grieving.

When Jack downed the second as quickly as the first and pushed the glass in her direction again, she feared for the worst.

She covered his hand with hers. "You might want to slow down a little bit."

He gave her a crooked smile. "Don't worry, baby cakes. My daddy was a drunk. It's in my blood. Thanks for worrying though." He pushed the glass closer to her and tapped it again.

Refilling it, she drew in a deep breath, beginning to get really concerned. This was another reason to not date military men—their tendency to get shot at and blown up.

They'd only left her place an hour ago. How could something possibly have happened to Trey in that short a time and so close to base? It had to be something else.

Meanwhile, she had more pressing problems than imagining what had befallen Trey. Jack was downing bourbon faster than she could pour it. She'd better think of something fast or she'd have one messy drunk on her hands, no matter what he said about being able to handle his liquor.

"Um, I have something I have to do in the storeroom. I'll be right back." If she disappeared for a bit and wasn't there to refill his glass, he'd have to stop drinking.

"That's fine, darlin'. Just leave the bottle."

"Um, I can't. Sorry. State liquor law." She was making things up now, but it sounded good.

He smiled. "You're just trying to slow me down. I'm trained to know what people are thinking, but if I don't get drunk here I'll just get drunk somewhere else. I can tell you I'd rather do it here with you than with some stranger."

She sighed, her heart breaking for him. In spite of the

constant flirting, he was a nice guy and he was obviously in pain.

Reaching out, she squeezed his hand. "Then do it for me, Jack. Slow down just a little bit."

He looked at her. Really looked at her for the first time. Not at her boobs, not at her ass, but at her. Then his crooked smile appeared again. "You know my name."

"Yes." She nodded, happy she'd gotten it right.

"Huh. And I never bothered to learn yours. No wonder you don't want to go out with me. I don't blame you one bit." He downed the third shot in one gulp.

Great. Now no matter what had been wrong with him when he'd first gotten here, his current problem was with her, compounded by the self-pity that alcohol enhanced so well.

She'd have to wait for him to go to the men's room and then water down the bottle. Carly knew for a fact that was against the law, but she was running out of options. She could cut him off, but she knew he would make good on his promise to go somewhere else and probably end up in a gutter or in jail. Neither option was a good one.

Watering down the bourbon was probably her best course of action. He was far enough gone he wouldn't notice, but since he wasn't drinking beer it might be a long while until he needed the men's room.

Jack pushed his glass toward her one more time. Carly sighed and then got an idea. "How about a proposition?"

He raised a brow and then laughed. "I never thought I'd hear myself say this, but I'm not really in the mood for a proposition tonight, darlin'."

Sadly, she returned his smile. "I can see that, Jack. It's not that kind of proposition."

"Good, because I would really kick myself in the morning if it were and I said no."

At least he was talking to her. Talking was good. Less time for drinking.

"The deal is a truth for a drink. So for this next shot you have to tell me what's got you in such a mood tonight you wouldn't even accept a proposition from me." She held the bottle in the air as bait.

"No can do, darlin'. You've been slinging beer behind this bar long enough to know everything is top secret 'round here, right down to what time the general takes a dump in the morning. Excuse my coarseness."

She'd heard way worse than *dump* while working behind the bar, but at least now she knew it was something to do with his unit. If it were woman trouble or even a fight with Trey, it wouldn't be top secret and he'd tell her.

He nudged the glass a bit with one finger. She filled it and he downed it. At this rate, he'd be passed out long before closing.

The couple in the booth finally made their move and groped their way out the door without even a backward glance. That afforded Carly an excuse to put the bottle safely away under the bar and go clean off their table. It would buy her a few minutes at least.

To her surprise, Jack followed and sprawled out on the recently vacated and still-warm booth bench.

"Thought I'd check things out over here for a bit." He leaned his head against the red vinyl. "Mmm. Comfy."

Poor guy.

At least he was away from his glass and the bottle. She grabbed the pitcher and dirty glasses and brought them to the kitchen to be washed later.

When she returned, she got a rag from behind the bar. As quietly as she could, she wiped down the table, hoping Jack would sleep off both the bad mood and the liquor.

"You don't have to creep around, darlin'. I'm not sleeping."

So much for her plan.

Leaving the rag on the table, she sat next to him in the booth, thinking how bartending and babysitting were very much alike at times.

She didn't move when he let his head drop onto her shoulder. "Maybe you should get some sleep, Jack."

He rolled his head toward her. "I know you ever going out with me is about as likely as a bull giving birth, but I want you to know I appreciate you pretending to like me tonight."

"I'm not pretending. You're a good guy, Jack. What's not to like?"

"Hmm. I'll have to consider that when I'm a little more sober, but you being nice tonight means a lot. I'm really sorry I didn't know what color your eyes are."

"That's all right. I don't know what color yours are either."

He let out a bark of a laugh. "Then I guess we're even."

"I guess we are." She smiled.

"Carly." Jack sounded sleepier and more southern with every sentence.

"Yes, Jack." She figured he had maybe five minutes left before he was out like a light.

He slid lower and laid his head in her lap. "I really do like you."

She looked down at him. "I like you too. That's not the issue. I don't date guys in the military."

"What if I weren't in the military?" His lids drifted closed.

"But you are." Lightly, she stroked his sandy-colored hair. It felt softer than she expected against her fingertips.

"Yeah, I am, but maybe just for tonight you could pretend I'm not." He opened his eyes, which she noted were hazel and glassy with unshed tears.

She had a feeling the tears weren't over her, but caused by whatever had brought him here so upset in the first place. Because of that, she nodded. "All right, Jack. Just for tonight."

Reaching up, he pulled her head down to his. He gave her the sweetest, gentlest kiss she'd ever been given by any man. Suddenly, she felt more than pity for him.

He cupped her face, ran his thumb over her lower lip and smiled. "That was nice."

Carly swallowed hard. "Yeah, it was."

"Have one dinner with me. In a public place. Nothing more. That's all I'm asking. What d'ya say, darlin'?" His sad eyes showed a glimmer of hope.

Her heart twisted for him. "I'll think about it."

"A maybe is better than a no so I'll take it. Thank you." A small smile curved his lips and his hand captured hers.

He brought her fingers to his mouth and pressed a gentle kiss to them before his eyelids drifted shut again. "I'm just gonna close my eyes and rest for a sec."

"That's fine, Jack. You go ahead."

Almost instantly his breathing became deep and regular. Carly glanced down, helpless. A two-hundred-pound drunk and sleeping man had her pinned in the booth.

Even though it had been a really, *really* long time since a man had had her pinned anywhere, she'd need to get up eventually, especially if customers came in. Not to mention she had to get Jack home somehow and she didn't even know where he lived.

Her gaze caught on a square outline pressing through the denim of his jeans. Sliding her hand into his pocket, she reached for it with the tips of her fingers but couldn't quite get what she hoped was a cell phone out of the tight confines. She pushed her hand deeper and got a handful of more than just phone.

Swallowing hard at the knowledge she'd just basically stroked him pretty intimately without meaning to, she halted all motion. He groaned, moving his hips to press himself farther into her hand.

Stuck between a rock and a hard place, she decided to just go for it and fast. Reaching deep into his pocket, she grabbed and wiggled out the phone.

Holding her breath, Carly watched and waited for his eyelids to open, but he didn't wake. Sighing in relief, she turned her attention to the cell phone.

The phone had been off, which told her he hadn't wanted to talk to anyone. Although he had come to be with her. Of course, she did have alcohol, but as he'd said, he could get that anywhere. She was overthinking things. The man was upset and had come to a familiar place to forget whatever he needed to forget. That was all. She couldn't let herself read anything more into it.

She powered on the cell only to find it required a passcode.

Carly mumbled a curse and hoped for the best as she reached for his hand and pressed his thumb to the cell's front button. Lucky for her he'd had the thumbprint capability enabled. The lock screen was replaced by the home screen.

Fighting the guilt, she hit the icon for his contacts list. This was a huge invasion of privacy, not to mention probably a security breach, but desperate times called for desperate measures.

Scrolling quickly through Jack's saved phone contacts, she found a bunch of names she didn't recognize. Even the names of Jack's teammates she did know from the bar, she didn't feel she knew well enough to call about this.

Finally, when she was about to give up hope, she hit on Trey Williams. Taking a deep breath, she pressed the call button, put the phone to her ear and listened to the ringing.

CHAPTER FOUR

When the commander finally cut them all loose, Trey drove directly to Jack's place. Jack's convertible wasn't parked out front.

There'd been no phone call from him either. Worse, when Trey called Jack's cell it had gone directly to voice mail. He must have turned his phone off even though the commander had told them they were all on standby.

Wherever Jack was and whatever he was doing, he didn't want to be disturbed.

He tried to convince himself his friend was a big boy and could take care of himself. Then he found himself carrying his cell phone into the bathroom with him and laying it on the sink while he showered in case Jack called. He was on standby, he reminded himself so he wouldn't feel foolish waiting around like some girl sitting by the phone after a first date.

Worry squelched any interest in food, but the angry grumble of his empty stomach reminded him he needed to eat anyway. A leftover pork chop in the fridge was just calling his name when his cell phone finally rang.

Trey jumped to answer it when *Jack* appeared on the readout.

"Jack. You okay?"

"Um, Trey? It's not Jack. It's Carly down at the bar. Jack's here with me but he's had a lot to drink."

Trey opened his eyes wide.

Carly. On Jack's phone. It took him a second to shake off the shock.

"You still at the bar now?" he asked hoping—even though he shouldn't be—that the answer was yes and not that they were at her place together.

"Yeah."

"Okay. Keep him there. I'll be right over. And don't let him drive." Trey was already shoving his feet into his sneakers.

"Of course I won't let him drive. He's drunk. How stupid do you think I am?" Her annoyance came through the cell clear as a bell.

He let out a breath of frustration. "I'm sorry. I've just been worried about him. Hang tight. I'm leaving now."

She let out a short laugh. "Oh, believe me. I'm not going anywhere."

Trey didn't understand the meaning of her last statement until the moment he walked into the bar and found Jack passed out in Carly's lap in a booth toward the rear.

He winced. "How long has he been like this?"

"Passed out? Or drunk?" She cocked a brow.

"Uh, both I guess."

"He came in about an hour ago, downed four double shots of bourbon in under ten minutes, then passed out just before I called you. I didn't know what else to do. His cell phone was right there in his, um, pocket. When I found your name in his contact list . . ." She shrugged and let the sentence trail off.

"It's fine. I'm glad you called me." Trey couldn't help but notice how she kept stroking Jack's hair even though he was well past the point of knowing it. For some reason, that really bothered him.

He walked over, squatted down and shook Jack by the shoulder. "Hey, buddy. Time to wake up."

Jack moaned and rolled away from Trey and toward Carly.

He draped one arm around her waist and snuggled deeper into her lap.

Great. That was even worse.

Trey jiggled him harder. He started slapping him lightly on the cheek and then not so lightly.

"Hey, be gentle. The poor guy's having a tough night." Carly frowned up at Trey.

She was right, of course.

Suitably chastised, Trey sighed. "I know."

"Do you know what's the matter?"

"Um, yeah but . . ." The sentence hung, unfinished, as Trey debated what say.

"You can't tell me. Never mind." She leaned down to Jack, stroked his face and said into his ear, "Jack, sweetie. You need to wake up for me."

So it was *sweetie* now. Just great. And of course, sweetie-pie Jack woke right up for her and smiled even though his eyes didn't quite look focused.

"Hey, darlin'." He struggled to sit up, put a hand to his head and then blew out a breath. "This place is spinning like the tilt-a-whirl at the state fair. Oh, hey there, Trey. When'd you get here?"

"Just now." Trey was not in the mood for conversation at the moment. He grabbed Jack by one arm and around the waist. Supporting his weight, he guided him up and out of the booth, pivoting them both toward the door. "Time for bed, Jack."

Unfortunately, Jack wasn't quite done yet. He dug in his feet and spun back toward Carly. "Night, darlin'."

She smiled, an actual, genuine smile. "Night, Jack."

"Trey, we were pretending I'm not in the military. She's a really good kisser."

That little gem of a revelation caused Trey to trip over his own feet.

This ridiculously surreal situation would have been laughable if he weren't so miserable. "That's great, Jack. Thanks for telling me."

Perhaps Jack would vomit in his truck next, then Trey's evening would really be complete.

CHAPTER FIVE

Morning came much too early and soon they were back in the team room, while the commander said, "It has come to our attention our target has a meeting scheduled with an American man suspected of small-arms dealing."

The commander stood at the head of the table as he addressed the six men. The entire team sat a little straighter in their seats at the promise of action, even Jack, who had to be one hurting puppy at the moment.

Trey was surprised to see Jack upright at zero-eight-hundred after practically scraping him off Carly's lap the night before.

He tried to block that image out of his mind. *She's a really good kisser.* Trey gritted his teeth.

"We detained the bastard and his new wife on their way to the meet. When questioned, he said the wife knew nothing about it. She thinks he sells computer software. He brought her along as cover. Says he figured homeland security and customs wouldn't look so hard at a married couple."

"Real sweet guy," one of the team mumbled.

The commander laughed. "Yeah, model husband. Lights out, please."

Someone hit the lights and the commander flipped the photos of a man and woman on the wall screen.

"Meet Mr. and Mrs. Smith. The target is currently unaware his associate is now a guest of the US military and we intend on keeping it that way by replacing the Smiths with two of our own. With some gentle persuasion, our guest downstairs admitted he's never met or spoken directly to our target. They've corresponded only by email. We're now in possession of his computer and all of its files, which back up his story. Although I bet the target has done his research and may have photos. So our replacements should be as close as possible in physical appearance, but at least they don't have to be exact. With only internet contact we won't have to worry about voice matching either. Lights on."

The lights came back on, leaving the images on the wall screen still visible, but dull. "That, boys, is the good news. The bad news is the rendezvous with the target is tomorrow and we need to find our replacements, bring them up to speed and fly them overseas before then. This does have an important upside. The team will be flying over too, putting us in perfect position to gather information about our missing man. At that time we can locate and if necessary extract him."

Jack sat forward at the mention of his brother. "I'll do it, sir. I'll meet with the target." He glanced at the stats of the male on the wall. "We're close enough in coloring and about the same height and weight. I can do this, sir."

"No. Out of the question." The commander shook his head.

"Why?" Jack asked.

"Because you're too close to this, Gordon."

"You can trust me, sir. He's my brother."

"That's exactly why you're not going in undercover, Gordon." The commander turned to Trey. "Williams. It's going to be you. You look close enough and you speak the language. You'll be able to get around the country easier knowing the native tongue in case things go bad. Although you'll have to pretend you don't speak anything except English since that's what our couple's linguistic skills are limited to. All this info will be in the briefing materials. You'll have to review it on the flight over. The couple's plane is scheduled to depart this morning."

Bull, called that because he was as big as one, raised his hand. "Sir, what about the female?"

He'd asked the exact question Trey had been thinking.

"That's the biggest obstacle right now. I've already spoken to Central Command. There's no one they can give us on such short notice who even comes close to resembling this one, even with a wig. We have one hour to get us a trained female who looks like *that*."

They all looked at the image of the hot, shapely brunette on screen.

Trey silently read off the stats listed next to the image. Hair: Brown. Eyes: Green. Height: 5'2". Weight: 120 pounds. 36-24-36.

Shit. He knew someone who fit that description. He kept his mouth glued shut.

"What if Williams tells them his wife suddenly felt ill and couldn't travel, sir? They're newlyweds. He can say she's pregnant or something," BB suggested. BB had come to the team as Billy Bob, but the team had shortened that right quick.

The commander nodded. "That's exactly what he'll have to do, but only as a last resort. We want to cast as little suspicion on this as we can and make as few changes as possible to our guests' original plans. The bastard husband has been bragging by email how smart he was bringing his wife with him to avoid suspicion. The target even commented how much he's looking forward to meeting her. I'd rather have a woman there with him."

"Um, sir? Would you consider a civilian?" Matt Coleman, the communications and computer specialist leaned forward in his chair.

The commander raised an eyebrow, considering. "I guess that depends on quite a few things. Why? You have someone in mind, Coleman?"

Matt nodded. "Call me crazy, but you take that cute little

bartender at the place just off base, throw some makeup and a little hair spray on her and you'd have the spitting image of that woman on screen."

The commander considered this for a moment. "Coleman, run her and make sure she's not a member of some terrorist sleeper cell pretending to be a bartender. I want to know everything you can get and I want it now."

"Yes, sir." Matt, never without his laptop, began tapping keys.

Jack should have had Matt with him at the bar yesterday. He and his computer probably could have come up with Carly's name on the spot. Her eye color too, knowing Matt's skill.

"You know this girl, Williams?" The commander turned to him.

Trey's heart had kicked into double time the moment Matt mentioned Carly. Shit. Had his reaction shown on his face? Or was the commander asking him only because he was the one going in undercover?

"Yes, sir. I do."

"Would you like to elaborate a bit, Williams? Does she really look like this woman? Is she discreet? Is she intelligent? Basically, can she pull this thing off without getting you both killed and losing us Jimmy Gordon in the process?"

Trey swallowed hard and saw Jack watching him wide-eyed. He could lie and say she couldn't pull this off, but he knew she could. Especially with him guiding her.

"Yes, sir."

"Yes to which question, Williams?"

"Yes to all of them, sir. She's perfect, or as perfect as we're going to get from outside the SpecOps community and within an hour." He shot a glance at Jack, who looked like he wanted to kill him.

"Fine. Coleman, what have you got?"

"You're not going to believe this." Matt grinned. "She's military. Separated from the Army shortly after the death of her father, who was also Army. Looks like she used the payout on his life insurance policy to buy the bar just off base."

The commander slapped his hands together. "Well, look here. Something is actually going my way today. Coleman, send whatever information you've got to my email and to the printer in my office. Then, take as many men as you need and bring her in ASAP and by that I mean I want her here an hour ago. You got me?"

"Sir. Yes, sir." Coleman and the others at the table sprung into action.

When Trey and Jack both stood also, the commander held up a hand to stop them. "You two both stay right where you are."

They sat again, Jack looking extremely unhappy, Trey not feeling much better.

"I've got a few calls to make to clear this with the higher-ups. You, Gordon, will sit here and calm yourself down. The only way to help your brother is for you to keep a cool head, and if you can't you'll remain stateside. Williams, you wait here until your new wife arrives." The commander left them and went into his private office just off the meeting room.

The commander was barely out of the room when Jack spun to Trey. "What the hell, Trey? Why did you tell the commander she'd be perfect?"

He shook his head at Jack's question. "I don't know. He caught me off-guard. Besides, what was I supposed to do? Lie?"

"Yes. Taking her undercover to meet the target. Are you crazy? Are you trying to get her killed?"

Trey closed his eyes and took a deep breath. "No, of course not. I have every intention of bringing us both home alive. And Jimmy too, if it comes to that."

Jack shook his head. "You better."

Blowing out a breath, Trey realized it wasn't going to be fun being trapped in a room to wait with Jack.

CHAPTER SIX

Trey was correct in his prediction. They spent the next fifteen minutes in awkward silence until the rest of the team finally returned. He didn't know how they'd done it, but they walked in with Carly in less than twenty minutes and boy oh boy, she didn't seem happy about it.

She entered the meeting room looking pissed off and confused. When she saw him and Jack, she stopped dead, hands on her hips. "Maybe you two will tell me what the hell is going on since these guys wouldn't say a thing when they dragged me out of my apartment at the crack of frigging dawn."

Trey had seen the crack of dawn on many occasions and zero-eight-forty did not qualify. She must have been out of the military for a long time. But running a bar made her schedule pretty much the opposite of his.

He could appreciate her opinion of being yanked out of bed after his own long night babysitting a drunk Jack.

Speaking of Jack . . . He had jumped to his feet the moment Carly entered the room, but before he even had a chance to say *hey, darlin'* the commander was at the door of his office. "Williams. Get in here and bring the woman with you. We have exactly twenty-two minutes before that plane is scheduled to leave."

The commander strode to his desk. He sat and addressed Carly, "Shut the door behind you."

Trey had to give Carly credit. Even though she looked pissed as hell, she silently followed him into the office and closed the door. Then she stood there with her arms crossed, waiting.

He watched the commander appraise her from head to toe. "Not bad."

At that comment, Carly's eyebrows shot up to her hairline. She opened her mouth to speak and Trey jumped in before she could.

"Sir, Ms. McAfee hasn't been apprised of the situation as yet and is a bit confused."

She didn't look any happier he had spoken for her, but at least he'd stopped her from laying into the commander.

"Of course. Ms. McAfee, we're requesting your help in a matter of national security. If you decide to help us, you'll be told as little as possible, your life will be in danger and you can never tell anyone about what you've done, ever. In addition, you'll have to make your decision within the next fifteen minutes and leave for your assignment immediately."

She surprised Trey by laughing. "Well, since you make it sound so tempting and all . . ." She rolled her eyes and then looked at Trey. "Am I necessary for the success of whatever this assignment is?"

Trey considered his answer carefully. "Your presence will increase the chances of the success of this assignment. Yes."

"Increase it by how much? From like ninety percent without me to one hundred percent with me?"

Trey glanced at the commander who answered, "More like sixty percent without you and seventy-five percent with you."

They both watched her carefully as she took a deep breath. Trey knew, or at least hoped, the commander was giving her the worse-case scenario to make sure she was aware of what she was getting herself into and exactly how dangerous it would be because those odds pretty much sucked.

"Why me, specifically?" She directed her question to the

commander.

"Honestly? Mostly because you look like her and we don't have time to find anyone more qualified." The commander slid a print copy of the photo of the woman across his desk.

Carly walked closer, picked it up and studied it. After a moment she glanced up at Trey then back to the commander. "All right."

The commander raised a brow. "That's it? No more questions?"

Her short laugh sounded bitter. "Would you answer them if I asked?"

The commander smiled. "Probably not."

"Then it would be a waste of time, now wouldn't it?" She cocked up one brow.

The commander nodded. "You'll do well I think, McAfee. Williams will brief you on the flight over, but here's a quick overview. You're playing a newlywed American wife. Williams is your husband and as his wife you are devoted, loving and obedient and will do whatever he says."

Carly screwed up her face, mumbling, "Good thing I took that acting class in college."

The commander acted like he didn't hear her, but continued a bit more loudly, "More importantly, he's your field leader on this assignment and as such you'll do whatever he commands, no questions asked. This is imperative. Hesitation could cost lives. He'll be in constant contact with myself and any others who might be working with us. You have to trust him implicitly and without discussion, because you must assume every minute, everywhere, you will be monitored by those who can do you harm. I mean not even a whisper, McAfee. Do you understand?"

"Yes, sir."

Trey noted she was already standing a little straighter and calling the commander *sir*. Military training was just like riding a bike. A person never really forgot it.

"Good. You're quick and you're tough, McAfee. I can see that. You must be to deal with these guys drunk every night. I wouldn't be sending you on this assignment if I didn't think you would succeed. One last thing—" the commander turned to Trey, "—Williams, go kiss your new bride."

It was a test. Trey knew that. A test both for him and for Carly. Keeping his role in mind, he became the newlywed husband who was supplying arms to terrorist bastards.

Without hesitation, Trey strode to where she stood.

More petite up close than she appeared when she was wielding her larger-than-life attitude while mixing drinks behind her bar, in reality she came up only to about his chest.

He tangled one hand in her hair so she couldn't pull her head away, not that she tried. He slipped the other beneath the hem of the shirt where it just met the jeans riding low below her waist.

Her skin felt warm and smooth. He slid his hand higher and let his thumb rest just below the lush curve of her breast.

Trey had to duck his head down to reach her. She stared up at him, her eyes liquid pools of green clearly showing her surprise as he bent and captured her mouth.

Kissing her hard and deep, he parted her lips and drove his tongue between them before he or she had too much time to think about it.

In this particular situation thinking would be bad.

She didn't squirm or pull away. In fact, she actually tilted her head and allowed him greater access to the warm, wet recesses of her mouth.

As his tongue met and stroked hers, he felt a stirring in his pants. There was no way to kiss a woman this attractive this deeply and not have it affect him. He was a healthy, red-blooded male after all, but he didn't need a raging hard-on in front of both Carly and the commander.

When he thought how he and Carly would be sharing a bed as they portrayed a married couple for the duration of this mission his mind went to bad places, and his erection followed.

Trey broke the kiss. Trying to ignore both his pounding heart and his rapidly expanding lower appendage, he dropped his hands from her too-tempting body and noticed her sway slightly as he turned to the commander. "Sir?"

The commander nodded and smiled. "Let's get you two on that plane."

He caught the brief look of shock on Carly's face. They'd have to work on that on the flight over. She couldn't show any surprise in front of the target. It could mean both their lives.

Trey followed the commander out of the office and into the meeting room, guiding a stunned Carly by the elbow until he saw Jack's gaze zero in on his hand holding Carly's arm. He dropped his hold immediately and found himself wiping his mouth and remembering that kiss.

Dammit, he would have to get a hold on himself. If he wanted to get them through this thing alive, he'd have to conquer both the chemistry he felt with Carly and the guilt he had over Jack.

The commander, unaware of the love triangle developing right beneath his nose, continued to brief the team. "Our happy couple here will be flying in a private jet courtesy of our targets' bank account." Trey inwardly cringed at the term *happy couple* and the look on Jack's face.

The commander continued, "The jet has been swept for surveillance and is clean, but count that as the last secure place until this thing is over. The rest of the team will be in a transport just ahead of them. We'll be connected by Williams's earpiece. Let's roll. The team goes wheels up at zero-nine-thirty."

Trey leaned closer to Carly's ear. "Walk up ahead for a moment. I need to talk to Jack alone."

It was killing her already to follow his orders without question, he could tell, but after only a small frown as protest she did as he'd asked. He counted her compliance as another step closer to insuring they'd make their flight home and not in a body bag either.

"Jack." Trey held him back a few paces with a hand on his friend's arm. "I need to know you're okay before I get on that plane."

"No, I'm not okay, Trey. I'm pissed as hell. I'm going to be stuck on the sidelines instead of out there trying to help my brother. And to top it off, I have to watch my best friend play bridegroom to the woman I may very well be falling in love with. If he doesn't get her killed first."

Trey felt his eyes widen at that revelation. Jack had used the "L" word. He'd known Jack had a crush on Carly, but not that he was falling in love.

"This is just an assignment, Jack. It's all pretend." *Yeah, right.* Nothing pretend about his reaction to their kiss. It would also be very real that Carly's warm body would be sharing a bed with him in a hotel room in Kosovo. "You can pick up wherever you left off with her when I bring her back."

Trey hated that thought but that was something he'd have to deal with later. After this op.

"Just make sure you do bring her back." Then Jack surprised him when he reached out and hooked an arm around Trey's neck, pulling him into a quick hug. "Make sure to keep yourself safe and my brother too."

Trey needed no reminding of exactly how many lives he was carrying on his shoulders at the moment, but knowing Jack was still his friend helped ease the burden a bit. He slapped him on the back and they both ran to catch up with the group.

CHAPTER SEVEN

Carly sat in the passenger seat of a rental car as Trey drove them to some private jet at the airport.

The charade had already begun apparently. They drove in a separate car in case anyone was watching so she and Trey wouldn't be seen piling out of the black van that carried his teammates and all their equipment.

She drew some small satisfaction that her suspicions had been dead on. There was no doubt in her mind now that they were black ops, right down to the color of their vehicle.

"I'm scheduled to be off tonight, but I have to call the bar and leave a message so they don't worry about me when I'm not there to open tomorrow."

He handed her a cell phone. "No details."

"I know. I'm not stupid." She added the last part under her breath but he turned to look at her as if he'd heard.

"Do you have your story ready?" he asked.

"Yes." Not really, but now that he'd said it she thought of an excuse for her unexplained absence pretty quickly.

After dialing the bar's main phone number, she waited for the voicemail prompt.

"Hey, guys. Something came up and I have to be out of town for a few days. I'm going to need you to juggle the schedule a bit and cover my shifts. Also, you have to place an order for liquor and beer today or we'll be in big trouble by the weekend. Just ask the distributor to help you put together the order and don't let him talk you into anything you don't think we need. I do not want that orange-flavored creamy tequila crap he keeps pushing on me and if I come home and find it there, I'm going to make whichever one of you ordered it drink every last ounce. I guess that's it. You won't be able to get in touch with me, but I'll call when I'm back."

With nothing else to say, she disconnected the call and handed the cell back to him.

Trey glanced at her. "Boy. I had no idea it was so complicated owning a bar. Then again, I had no idea you owned the bar until today or that you used to be in the service."

Carly sniffed. "One thing the military does well is pry into people's personal business."

So they knew about her time in the Army. She hoped they also knew she spent the entire duration of it behind a desk stateside.

Sure, she went through basic training and yeah she could fire a weapon if she had one, which she didn't so she wasn't at all convinced that skill was going to help in this situation. She could file papers for Trey if the need arose though.

He laid a hand on her knee. "I know you're pissed about being dragged into this, but get it all out now. Yell at me, curse me out if you need to but remember that once we're off that plane you're no longer Carly McAfee and we can't discuss any of this, no matter what you're feeling."

Like she needed reminding he'd put his life into her hands. She decided as long as she had his permission to vent now and only now she might as well get it all out. "What the hell was with that kiss?"

He glanced at her and then focused on the road ahead. Did his brown eyes show guilt? Embarrassment? "You know as well as I that the commander was testing both of us."

"Testing what? How long it took for you to get your tongue down my throat?" She was angry, but more at herself than at him. She'd reacted to his kiss. She hated that thought.

She would like to think it was because of her self-imposed sexual dry spell. Last night she'd let Jack kiss her and almost gave in to his invitation for dinner, though he probably wouldn't remember. Today she'd been ready to crawl into Trey's pants.

Not only was she breaking all her own rules, it seemed to be getting progressively worse. As nice and sweet as Jack's kiss had been the night before, her body hadn't reacted as fiercely as it had to Trey's mind-blowing lip lock today.

Dammit. She didn't want to be attracted to either of them. Not Jack or Trey.

No, it was more than that. She could not allow herself to be attracted. Not since the love of her life had come home from his tour of duty overseas, married and with a baby.

Surprise.

Now here she was pretending to be married to one of the few guys she'd been attracted to since then. A guy who, against all common sense, she was having trouble resisting and of course, he was eyeball deep in the military.

Trey glanced in her direction again. "I'm sorry, but the reality is you and I are either convincingly happily married or dead. Under normal circumstances, my behavior in the commander's office would have been totally inappropriate, but there's nothing normal about this situation. You cannot react to anything I do once we're off that plane or—"

"I know. I know. I know." Her voice rose each time she said it, sounding shriller with each repetition.

"No, Carly. I'm afraid you don't know. We might be under twenty-four-hour audio and visual surveillance even in our hotel room. We have to act married, day and night. No breaks. No downtime."

She whipped her head around to stare at his profile as he drove. "Are you saying I'm supposed to have sex with you?"

His throat worked as he swallowed. "It shouldn't come to that. Hopefully we'll be in and out quick . . . out of the mission I mean. One, two nights maximum."

"What if we're there longer?" she asked.

"We won't be."

"What if we are?"

"We'll figure something out."

Not liking the sound of that, nor the fact her insides had done a total flip at the thought of having sex with Trey, Carly crossed her arms over her chest and stared out the side window.

"Carly."

"What?"

"We may have to get pretty intimate. I have to know you won't react like this during the op if I have to touch you."

"I'll be fine."

"Look at me."

Finally, she turned away from the window to face him.

"Are you going to be okay with all of this?" he asked, his focus on her rather than the road.

"Why don't you have any faith in me?"

"I do have faith in you or I wouldn't have said yes when the commander asked my opinion on your coming."

"Then stop questioning me."

"It's a lot to deal with. You're not trained for this. I need to know that if things get serious you'll be okay."

"Yes, dammit. Once we're off that plane, I'll be the perfect little obedient wife. Okay? But right now, can you please stop talking about this and leave me alone?"

Trey's raised eyebrows were his only reaction to her hissy fit as he finally turned his complete concentration to the road ahead.

She drew in a deep steadying breath. "I'm sorry."

"It's fine. This is a lot to deal with all of a sudden." His voice was kinder, gentler than it had been the entire car ride. He was probably afraid she'd totally break down and start to cry.

Out of the corner of her eye, she watched the well-built muscles flex in his arm as he spun the steering wheel and guided the car into the airport entrance.

Those arms could very well be wrapped around her as they pretended to be married. She pictured them together as they tried to convince the cameras and microphones they were a couple. Need coiled within her and she became very aware of the lower parts of her body.

Trey had no idea how much she was trying to deal with right now.

CHAPTER EIGHT

Inside the airport, Trey pressed one hand against the small of Carly's stiffened back and guided her toward the terminal where the private jet waited.

After her meltdown in the car he took it as a good sign she didn't slap his hand away.

As they waited in line to go through security, he slid his hand up, over her shirt. Cradling the back of her head in one hand, he leaned down and touched his lips to hers, watching her reaction. Her eyes drifted closed, opening again to stare into his when he ended the all-too-brief kiss.

She didn't slap him. That was good. Carly would have to get used to him casually touching her the way a husband would. Better to practice here than in front of the target. If she weren't able to handle this, he would much rather find out now instead of in front of the enemy.

He tried not to think about the fact he just plain liked kissing her. Jack had been right when he said she was a really good kisser.

Trey's stomach clenched and he pushed thoughts of Jack and Carly out of his mind.

This mission required one hundred percent of his concentration. He'd have to deal with any ramifications when they returned, and they would return if he had anything to say about it.

Carly was quiet. Too quiet and a little stiff.

"Everything all right?" He brushed a finger down her cheek.

Her answer was a far-from-convincing nod.

Reaching down, he took her hand and squeezed it. "You're doing great."

She swallowed before answering. "Thanks."

They breezed through the security check with the couple's documents, expertly altered by Matt to include their own photos. The bastard husband had been right about airport security. Even with Carly's nerves apparent, the agents didn't look too hard at an all-American happily married couple traveling together on a private jet.

Trey carried their bag, or rather the single piece of luggage belonging to the real couple they were impersonating, onto the aircraft. They'd have to change into the Smiths' clothes before landing and hope at least something fit well enough to be convincing. Otherwise they would have to wear their own clothes, but the less they deviated from the real couple's original plans and looks the better.

Matt and his magic computer had made sure the pilot was clean. He was actually also a veteran. Trey figured he and Carly were able to feel moderately safe on the flight while they memorized their fake histories.

As they waited for takeoff, she sat in the seat next to him and read the file. She raised an eyebrow. "My name is Candi with an 'i' and I was a stripper before I married you? Oh, that's just lovely."

He laughed. "I can't wait to see what kind of wardrobe is waiting for you in that suitcase."

She scowled. "Just don't expect me to dance for you or anything."

"We'll see."

Carly smacked him on the leg at his little joke. He grinned, happy she was loosening up a bit. Her playful side was just as appealing as the rest of her.

Pushing her appeal out of his mind, he tried to concentrate on his own file. He was having a lot of trouble doing so.

Since he was already thinking about her anyway, he figured he might as well put his arm around her. Strictly for practice, of course.

Without raising her eyes from her file, she commented on his action. "No one can see us here. We don't have to act married now, you know."

"Yes, we do. You still tense up every time I touch you. You have to stop."

Now she did look at him, but not in a nice way. Her brows knit above her gorgeous eyes. "I do not tense up."

He laughed. "Yeah, you do. It's slight, but I feel it."

She rolled her eyes. "Well, if it's so slight no one else is going to notice."

"We can't take that chance."

Serious now too, she nodded. "I know."

"Good." He didn't say what he was thinking, that knowing and doing were two different things. Then he decided to push her a little further, strictly for the sake of the mission, of course. "Kiss me."

With a slight look of surprise, but without hesitation, she leaned in and brushed her lips across his. Then she pulled away. "Ha! That was another test. You thought I would fail, didn't you?" With a humph, she returned to her paperwork, looking very satisfied with herself.

Trey felt like an absolute shit, not to mention a rotten friend, a pitiful soldier and not all that great of a man right now, but he couldn't help himself. He reached out and turned her face toward him again. "I mean really kiss me."

He saw the battle in her eyes. She swallowed hard and dropped her gaze to his lips before closing the distance between them. Then her parted lips were on his and her hand was in his hair.

Acting the aggressor, Carly took control and her tongue met his. His chest tightened and he had to control the groan building inside him.

Trey couldn't stop himself, didn't want to, when his hand brushed the side of her breast and settled there.

She drew in a sharp breath as she kissed him harder. Then she pulled away.

Breathless, her eyelids heavy, she said, "This is just for this assignment. Nothing more."

It was definitely not a question, more of a statement, a demand really.

Why?

Not that he should care. He did not want or need a girlfriend, he reminded himself. Especially not this particular girl who Jack had already begun to fall for.

Still, why was she making rules? Maybe she was falling for Jack too. If so, he should be happy for his friend.

It cut him to the bone he wasn't, not even close.

"Of course." He nodded in response. "Just for the mission."

He leaned against the seatback and continued studying the file until he thought his eyes might burn a hole in the page. He was concentrating so hard on ignoring Carly, the sound of Matt's voice coming through his earpiece startled the hell out of him.

Trey literally jumped in his seat and not surprisingly, Carly noticed.

"What's wrong?" She sat forward, frowning at him.

"Nothing. Go ahead, Matt."

"Just testing it out there, big boy. So, how was that kiss?" Matt's smart ass comment did nothing for his mood and just served to remind him they were indeed under constant surveillance, if not by the bad guys, definitely by the good guys.

He'd been hoping Matt and his magic laptop wouldn't have communications up and running while they were in the transport, but he was wrong.

"Um, hello?" Matt's singsong voice made the word into three syllables rather than two.

"I hear you just fine. This concludes this test." Not only did Trey not want to talk to Matt right now, but he also had to explain what was happening to Carly. She was looking at him like he had lost his mind and was talking to himself.

"Right, you need to get back to that very important part of your mission, I suppose. Can't wait until I have video up and running."

Trey could almost hear Matt smirking.

Shit. This was getting more complicated by the minute.

He turned to Carly and pointed at his ear. "Comm unit."

"I didn't even see it. Wow, it must be really small." Almost in his lap now, she tried to peer into his ear.

She was so close he felt her breath against his skin. An uncontrollable shiver ran down his spine before he could shake it off.

Grabbing her by both shoulders, he planted her firmly back in her seat.

"Put your seatbelt back on. And you can't see it because it's inserted surgically. It's less likely to be detected during undercover ops and if it is, it looks like a cochlear implant."

After hearing that detail she looked especially impressed. Perhaps he should talk about more tech stuff. She seemed to like it. She'd be really in awe when the time came for them to dispose of their files and she saw the patented dissolvable paper disintegrate in the water in the jet's bathroom sink.

"Wow." Her gaze dropped briefly before returning to his face. "What else have you got hidden inside you?"

He laughed. "Wouldn't you like to know?"

Trey wasn't about to tell her he also had a tracking device as well as an encoded identification chip hidden inside him, and who knew what else. It seemed the medical personnel were always jabbing him with something or another during those required physical exams every six months.

"Hmm. I've underestimated Uncle Sam. And speaking of your boss . . . what can you tell me about our *assignment?*"

"Nothing. Read your dossier. There's going to be a test before we land." He wasn't really worried she couldn't remember the facts of their new fake lives.

At the bar he'd seen her memorize a list of drinks a mile long while dodging Jack's advances at the same time, but there was no way he could respond to her question. But it was best to keep her busy so she wouldn't sulk, which he was sure she would do anyway because he wouldn't give in to her.

As if on cue, she screwed up her face in another adorable pout and he found he had to read the same page over again for the third time.

CHAPTER NINE

Carly walked down the much-too-narrow metal stairs of the jet and clutched the railing for dear life.

She could kill Trey. She knew he was walking just behind her, watching her ass in the tight black low-rise leather pants as she tried to walk in the stripper's four-inch heels that were a size too big.

"You're a dancer, remember? Try to be a little more graceful," he whispered behind her.

She shot him a glare over her shoulder. "We're off the plane, remember? No more talking."

He was trying hard not to laugh at her and she was trying harder not to whack him with the stripper's giant leather purse full of the makeup and hairspray he'd made her put on. She looked like a clown, or worse, the cocktail waitress at work.

"Ooo. I hate you right now." Her stomach roiled with frustration.

He made a mock hurt face. "But, sweetheart, I love you so."

Turning away from him, she focused all of her concentration on the downward descent, hoping this assignment would get better, which wasn't very likely.

Finally reaching the bottom of the stairs and the solid

ground of the tarmac, she found it a bit easier to maneuver in the heels.

She hated to admit it, but Trey was right. She'd have to learn damn quickly how to walk more naturally in these death trap stilts or she'd blow it for both of them. How the hell did strippers dance in these things?

Next to her again, Trey draped one arm casually around her shoulders as he pulled the suitcase on wheels behind him.

His clothes were just fine. He got to wear a black silk shirt and fitted gray trousers that made his ass look incredible. She nearly had to shake her head to clear the image of his cute butt from her brain.

This was her own fault. If she hadn't sworn off men, perhaps she wouldn't be finding Trey so irresistibly attractive.

Glancing up, she caught him looking down her cleavage, which was huge and totally exposed thanks to the stripper's taste in tiny tops. Sure, Carly wore the occasional tight T-shirt at the bar. It increased her tips by a laughably large amount, but she never wore anything as revealing as this.

Worse, this was actually the shirt with the most coverage among what she had found in the suitcase. All the others exposed her belly button as well as her boobs.

Carly huffed out a breath. She couldn't even reprimand Trey for looking down her shirt. Playing his happy and horny bride, she should enjoy this kind of lascivious attention.

Actually, on the plane during that kiss she had gotten the horny role down pretty well. She buried the thought quickly. Too bad the ache inside her wasn't as easy to dismiss.

How was she ever supposed to go back to casually serving this guy beer at the bar when she'd never forget the feel of his hand on her breast? She should have said no to this thing.

The commander's words echoed in her head.

Sixty percent chance of success without you.

She couldn't have backed out and doomed Trey to a forty percent chance of failure, possibly death, because she couldn't control her overactive libido around him.

Carly tried not to dwell on the fact the commander had

estimated there was still a twenty-five percent chance of failure even with her there. If she didn't keep her mind on the task that number would probably get even worse.

With all this introspective thought, she'd missed what Trey had just said.

She forced herself to focus. "I'm sorry. What?"

"There's the limo the email said would be waiting for us." He was staring in the direction of a long black car whose driver was leaning against the hood.

Her heart kicked into double time.

The driver walked forward to greet them, taking the bag from Trey. "Mr. Smith, Mrs. Smith. I hope you had a pleasant flight."

The names of the people they were impersonating sounded even more stupid and fake when the driver said them. Carly would bet a year's tips they *were* fake.

The driver continued, "Welcome to Kosovo."

Kosovo? Wow. That explained why the flight was so long and why it looked like it was already night here. She tried to remember anything she'd seen or read recently about this particular hotbed of discontent.

If she ever got out of there alive, she swore to pay more attention to current events.

Carly spotted the bulge of a concealed weapon under the driver's suit jacket. It nearly stopped her dead in her tracks. Only sheer force of will coupled with Trey's gentle nudge kept her teetering onward.

Undercover in Kosovo—when she chose to do something crazy, she sure did it in a big way.

CHAPTER TEN

How Trey loved the way those high heels made Carly's hips sway. If only he could devote all of his attention to just watching her walk.

Instead, he pretended to watch her as he evaluated their surroundings. He visually scanned the rooftop for snipers. His view was limited but things looked clear. He memorized the limo's license plate number to give to Matt later so he could find out who it was registered to.

Of course, he'd noticed right away the driver's concealed weapon as well as his extremely expensive suit.

Trey would bet his pension this was no mere driver, but rather part of the target's most trusted inner circle sent to make sure nothing went wrong. This meet was too important to trust any portion of it to lower-level hired help.

He kept his arm around Carly after they got into the backseat of the car and played with her now larger-than-life hair-sprayed hair. Anything to keep her mind off the driver's weapon, which had nearly toppled her off her heels when she'd noticed it.

Carly sat so close they were pressed together from hip to thigh. She was definitely scared.

They drove the distance from the airport to the capital and pulled up in front of the prestigious Hotel Pristina.

Had Trey been in the dark, he would have been impressed that the target had spared no expense by putting them up in the best hotel in the city. But thanks to the intelligence gathered by Jack's brother Jimmy, combined with Matt's cyber stalking, Trey knew better.

A corporation set up by the target happened to own this hotel. Just one more way the bad guys had figured out how to launder money.

The clerk greeted them in the language of the country, which Trey, as John Smith, had to pretend not to understand.

"We're American. Do you speak English?" He'd responded a bit too loudly in his native tongue, as people tended to do when conversing with those who didn't speak their language.

"Of course." The clerk nodded. "Please, your name?"

"Smith. John and Candi Smith." Trey smiled down at Carly when he said it, knowing she hated her fake name and it would drive her crazy. He nearly laughed as he watched her bite her lip at hearing the name but she didn't say a word.

Laying his hand on her shoulder, he felt her trembling, a visceral reminder this was no game for either of them. He pulled her closer to his side as the front desk clerk consulted a computer. "Yes, I have your reservation here. You have bags?"

"Just one suitcase. It's still in the trunk of the car." No doubt where their host had already had it thoroughly searched. Trey had purposely kept the laptop bag with him the entire time, just as John Smith would have.

The clerk signaled a bellman to retrieve the luggage from the car. He led them up in the elevator to one of the higher floors.

In this case, higher was not better. It only meant they'd have more flights to descend if they needed to get the hell out of there quickly. It also meant escape through the window was not an option.

A chilled bottle of champagne and overflowing fruit basket awaited them inside an impressively large room.

Trey glanced around and quelled his frustration. There was nothing he could do there until Matt set up shop somewhere nearby, hacked into the hotel's security systems and determined whether there was surveillance set up in the room or not.

His instinct told him there would be, but until he knew for sure he was at loose ends waiting on Matt.

Trey took another look around the well-appointed room. He'd been on way worse assignments than this. He really couldn't complain.

Acting like John Smith, he grabbed the icy cold bottle from the bucket and popped the cork, sure his fake wife could use a little something to calm her down. Not enough to get her drunk, just a bit to stop her from shaking.

Carly's eyes opened wide, silently reprimanding him for drinking on the job, he supposed.

"Look, how nice. We can't ignore our host's generous hospitality. Right, baby?"

What was he supposed to do? Judging by what he had learned thus far about John and Candi Smith, they were the type to *pop the cork* in more ways than one. He pushed a nasty thought from his mind at his own sexual euphemism.

Trey poured them both a glass, then walked to Carly and handed one to her. He clinked his champagne flute to hers. "Here's to my beautiful wife."

Watching a blush creep into her cheeks, he let the expensive bubbly slide down his throat.

She was so easy to rattle. It would be fun if their lives weren't on the line. He'd have to get her comfortable with him before the meet tomorrow. If he didn't, someone was bound to notice.

Leaving her behind in the hotel room when he went alone was not an option. If the shit hit the fan he wanted Carly with him. It was his only chance of protecting her.

He was just trying to think of some way to put her at ease when Matt's voice sounded in his ear. "They've got both eyes and ears, Trey. Sophisticated and extremely sensitive shit.

You copy me?"

He covered his mouth and coughed once to indicate to Matt he had indeed heard his less-than-encouraging news. Eyes and ears. Both video and audio surveillance. Just great.

God willing, Carly would remember what the commander had told her during their very brief meeting in his office that morning. *Not even a whisper.*

"You hungry, sweetheart?" When Carly's look told him the last thing she wanted to do was eat, he looped an arm around her neck and planted a big kiss on her champagne-scented lips. "I know the time change is messing with your system but you should eat at least something light."

"Okay." She stared up at him, as if waiting for him to tell her what to do next.

"Why don't you order something for both of us from room service? There should be a menu in here somewhere."

She nodded but didn't move. He needed to knock her out of this deer-in-headlights mode.

"I'm going to hop into the shower quick while you order." Grabbing her shoulders, he lowered his head nearer her ear. "Unless you'd like to join me."

That jolted her out of the sudden stage fright.

"Actually, I'm starving." Pulling away, she walked to the desk and grabbed the room service menu lying there.

If this were any other situation, he would definitely take advantage of how easy it was to ruffle her feathers and enjoy doing it.

Pulling his shirt off over his head while walking toward the bathroom, Trey couldn't help but smile.

CHAPTER ELEVEN

Carly tried to peruse the room service menu but it wasn't until Trey and his well-developed and now shirtless muscles were safely locked away in the bathroom that she actually noticed she couldn't read it.

It must be in Serbian, or Slovakian, or whatever the hell the language was there.

Out of pure frustration, she flipped the menu over and—lo and behold—found the English translation provided for tourists.

American tourists. In Kosovo. That was laughable.

Given all the vacation destinations in the world, why would anyone choose Kosovo?

Maybe businessmen stayed here, though she didn't know what industry Kosovo was famous for. Again, she vowed to be more tuned in to other parts of the world if she got out of there alive.

Glancing at the offerings only raised another question. What did one eat while in Kosovo? She automatically ruled out fish and even meat. Perhaps she was being a typical ethnocentric American, but she wasn't sure what the sanitation was like here. The last thing she needed was E. coli or something.

The ridiculousness of worrying about food poisoning

when most likely they'd both end up shot to death by the gun-wielding limo driver was not lost on her.

Pushing that thought out of her mind, she finally settled on salad and pizza, although pizza in a foreign country was probably more risky than the fish. Hopefully they imported it frozen from the States.

Armed with that illogical belief, she placed the order with an accommodating phone operator who, thank goodness, spoke at least some English.

That done, she began rifling through the one suitcase again. Might as well dig deeper and see what other surprises were in there. She didn't even want to think about what kind of lingerie Candi the former stripper wore.

What she discovered was an embarrassingly small see-through thing she supposed could laughably be called a nightgown in some circles.

She was standing with the item in question dangling from one fingertip, wondering how she was ever going to put this on and sleep with Trey in the room when the bathroom door opened.

The nightie was forgotten immediately when Trey emerged, dressed in nothing but a towel draped low on his hips. Her gaze followed the trail of damp hair that led from his chest, down his belly, directly toward his . . . She swallowed hard.

He walked to the suitcase and picked through the choices left in the bag. He stood so close she could smell the hotel soap and shampoo on him.

Trey raised a brow when he noticed what she still held, forgotten, in her hand.

"Dressing for bed?" He smiled broadly and grabbed a pair of black silk pajama bottoms out of the jumble of clothes. "Good idea."

Without any hesitation, he dropped the towel, leaving a lot more than just his torso exposed this time. As he pulled on the pants she got quite a view before she forced her gaze away.

She rushed to speak and cover for the shock his sudden and total nakedness had caused. "Um, I think I'll wait a bit and get changed after I eat."

Just in time, a knock on the door announced the room service delivery.

"You stay here and finish what you're doing. I got it." Trey, only half-naked now, moved toward the door.

She got his unspoken message. He wanted to answer the door in case there was trouble waiting on the other side instead of room service. That knowledge just added to her already heightened nerves.

When he opened the door and she saw the food cart, Carly could finally breathe again.

It helped that Trey was all the way across the room and not totally nude. She had never welcomed the arrival of a pizza delivery so much in her life, and it wasn't because she was the least bit hungry.

Trey and his bulging pecs returned to her, rolling the room service cart. "You ordered pizza? Wasn't there filet mignon or lobster on the menu? We're not paying for this, you know. We're guests."

"What can I say? I'm a simple girl." Carly shrugged, grabbed a slice and shoved it into her mouth so she didn't continue to stare at Trey's still-bare chest. "Don't you think you'd better put on a shirt?"

He raised a brow. "Why?"

"I just wouldn't want you to get hot cheese on your chest and burn yourself." Yeah, sure. That was the reason.

Trey grinned. "Thank you, sweetheart, for worrying about me."

He grabbed a slice and carefully held a napkin under it while he bit the end off.

When he still showed no sign of covering up, Carly bit into her own slice. It was going to be a very long night.

CHAPTER TWELVE

It was going to be a very long night. Trey lay in the bed next to Carly who was dressed in a scrap of lace that didn't even pretend to cover her.

She was currently rolled on her side, facing away from him and pretending to be asleep. Or maybe she had managed to fall to sleep from sheer exhaustion.

Sighing, he wished he could do the same.

This waiting was killing him. Not that he could do much with the team while he was undercover as John Smith, but hearing at least whether Jimmy had been located would help.

He needed some military action on this op to keep his mind from thinking about another kind of action with Carly. This "sit around and wait" was unbearable.

Trey listened to Carly breathing next to him.

Unbearable.

Although he had to admit things had gone extremely well so far. She hadn't broken character, not even when he'd dropped his towel and changed in front of her.

She looked a little shocked, yeah, but he hoped no one would notice that but him. Certainly not a security guard bored to tears watching them on a tiny black and white monitor in a windowless room somewhere.

There had been one moment he feared she would give

them away. He had walked into the bathroom to find her scrubbing the stripper's toothbrush with hot soapy water. Obviously, she didn't want the used apparatus in her mouth, not that he could blame her.

He hadn't even considered dental hygiene when they assumed possession of the Smith's lives and luggage. Jeez, he'd been on ops where he didn't even see a toothbrush for a week, much less running water, but women were different, he guessed.

Unsure about what to do about her obsessive brush-washing, which was too obvious to ignore, he'd questioned her about it with a casual, "What are you doing, sweetheart?"

He had to hand it to her. She covered for herself on the fly with a plausible excuse when she said, "Some makeup got on my toothbrush in my bag, so I had to wash it."

She'd done well and he'd been free to return to the other room to worry about the next problem. How in the world was he going to avoid having sex with her while still acting like a newly married couple for their observers?

Trey was still considering this when she came out of the bathroom and headed for the suitcase, avoiding eye contact with him the entire way.

He'd gotten up and went into the bathroom to brush his own teeth . . . with John Smith's toothbrush. Trey tried not to think about that fact, but since she had already raised the issue in his mind, he used extra hot water to rinse it first.

By the time he emerged from the bathroom, Carly had already changed into the nightie and was curled on her side and pretending to be sound asleep.

Thank God. She was either really on the ball or just desperate to avoid any more physical contact with him.

Either way, it was the perfect solution to his dilemma. It would simply look like she was tired from traveling and he, being the understanding husband, had let her sleep.

As long as they were here for only the one night as planned, he could definitely get away with it. It would look realistic . . . he hoped.

He'd never been married, but judging by what the guys with wives said, sex got less and less frequent the moment they said *I do.*

Although, glancing at the curve of Carly's body, he couldn't imagine not jumping her every night of the week if they were together, married or not.

Trey sighed again. There was far too much down time, leaving him ample opportunity to think about the one thing he needed to avoid. Sex.

Punching his pillow, he repositioned himself.

What the hell good was the communication device implanted in his damn head if he couldn't even ask them a question without being detected by the bad guy's surveillance?

He'd never felt so cut off from the team in all his time with them. It was with that very disgruntled thought in his mind he started to drift off.

"Trey. Hey, Williams. Wake up."

Trey controlled the urge to sit straight up in the bed as the voice in his ear startled him out of that restless place between being awake and asleep.

He had wanted to know what was going on with the team. *Be careful what you wish for.*

Clearing his throat softly, he let Matt know he was awake and receiving.

"We've got action here, big boy. We found Jimmy. The target has him confined in some sort of holding area right here in the basement of the hotel." Matt's voice radiated excitement.

Trey's heart rate doubled knowing the action was so close to him. Right here in the hotel.

"The bad news is they've worked him over pretty badly and we don't think they're done yet. We've got to get him out, but the area's swarming with the target's men."

His heart fell at that news. Jack must be freaking out and there was not one damn thing Trey could do to help in his present situation.

"We need your help, buddy," Matt continued.

Maybe there was something he could do. Trey waited for Matt to explain and give him his orders.

Trey only wished Carly wasn't involved. He'd kill or die to save Jimmy for Jack, but he wasn't willing to risk Carly's life in the process. She was a civilian under his care. Her safety was his priority at the moment, even over the success of the mission.

"Here's the deal, Trey. They have the surveillance room set up next to where Jimmy is being held. The guards have been sitting around watching the video feed from your room since you arrived. They've taken a liking to your bride. They particularly enjoyed when she changed into that thing she's wearing to sleep in. Even the guy sitting inside watching Jimmy got called in to watch her put that on."

His jaw clenched in anger at that revelation.

"Trey, I need a diversion and I need it now. We're in place to sneak in through the rear and take Jimmy out, but we need every guard in the area glued to the monitor of your room."

Trey tried to control his breathing when Matt said what he was afraid he would say. "You've got to use Carly as a distraction. It's the only way. Do you copy?"

He cleared his throat again.

Oh boy. Just when he was all smug thinking they'd get away from this op fairly unscathed.

CHAPTER THIRTEEN

Trey knew Matt was right. They needed a distraction to get in and out unseen. The team could go in hot with guns blazing but it would be bloody for both sides.

He knew what kind of diversion would keep the guards riveted to the screen. What he didn't know was how Carly would like it.

The different scenarios ran through his mind. It could go a number of ways. He could make a move on Carly and she could break character. Slap him or yell or something. With their cover blown, they would have to use all the firepower they had to grab Jimmy and get the hell out of Dodge.

Or Carly could actually go through with this thing. In that case, he'd have to deal with the fact he'd gotten physical with the girl his best friend thought he might be falling in love with.

Trey would have to find a new best friend and a different place to drink when he got home to base. Neither scenario was very appealing.

Then there was the reality nagging his brain and parts lower that he was trying like hell to suppress. The truth was he wanted nothing more than to be with Carly right now. The idea of giving into the sexual attraction and sinking into her was extremely appealing. Consequences be damned.

He didn't want a girlfriend, he reminded himself again for the umpteenth time, but dammit, he wanted Carly.

Apparently he didn't care how he got her and that made him feel even shittier.

Worse, the fact his teammate plus a room full of terrorists would be watching them together didn't even put a damper on his desire. In fact, it made it all the more exciting. That reaction scared him half to death.

Now was not the time to over-think his sudden desire for exhibitionism. Jimmy was possibly being tortured while he delayed.

Trey had left the bathroom light on with the door ajar so he could see, but he'd need more illumination for his audience's sake.

He reached out into the semi-darkness until his hand hit on the light switch. After turning on the bedside lamp, he rolled toward Carly.

The nightie was cut very low in the back. Actually, in the front too, but he couldn't see that in her current position. Trailing a finger lightly down her exposed spine, he felt the shiver run through her.

Leaning closer, he dipped his tongue into the whorls of her ear.

He slid his hand down under the sheet and along the lace to her thigh where he started the return trip upward.

Pressing against her back with his bare chest, he could feel her start to tremble. He could only hope it was from the anticipation of wanting him and not fear.

The pulse thundered in her neck against his lips. Nearing the point of no return, he could either let her continue to pretend to be asleep and let Jimmy be tortured to death or he could roll her over and give the terrorists a show they would remember for the rest of their miserable lives, however short they may be.

He'd already made the decision about what needed to be done, but Matt's voice in his ear reinforced it. "They're taking the bait, man. They even got up to refill their coffee mugs and make microwave popcorn. They're fighting over front row seats and settling in for the show like it's a damn movie. We're in place, Trey. You keep them entertained and Jimmy will be on a transport to the military hospital in Germany tonight."

That settled it. There was no more internal debating to be done.

Trey rolled Carly over and covered the surprise on her face by pressing his lips to hers. She responded well to his kisses. They'd practiced this. He'd dare say they were damn good at it. It was her reaction to the rest he was worried about.

Dammit. Truth be told, he was just as worried about his own reaction to it. If he sank himself into this woman he was not going to forget it easily.

Trey reminded himself he was a professional. He was supposed to be able to do things like this without any emotional ramifications. They'd all been through psychological training for situations like this one.

They'd been through the prep, but Carly hadn't.

What the hell would this do to her if they had to go through with it and actually have sex?

She was an adult and a bar owner, but this was not some drunken one-night stand she chose to have. He wasn't giving her a choice at all. She knew making a scene could cost them both of their lives.

More importantly, what if she did start dating Jack when they got home? How would Jack feel about the fact his teammate had enjoyed the pleasure of being with his girl before him?

Now was not the time to think about any of that. Matt might as well have issued a direct order. Trey knew the situation and it was in his and Carly's power to help the team get Jimmy out of trouble.

Throwing the covers completely off them, he hoped the sight of Carly in her nightgown would be enough of a distraction to keep the guards' attention off Jimmy.

As he ran his hand over the fabric again, traversing a path from the curve of her waist down to the hem at her thighs, her eyes opened again.

"Mmm." He pressed his mouth against her ear. Knowing the sensitive audio surveillance Matt had told him about would pick up his words, he spoke like John Smith, hoping Carly understood the underlying message. "Candi, baby, I was going to try and let you sleep, but I can't keep my hands off you. I'm sorry."

He'd used her fake name so she knew this was part of the show, not him being a horny dog. Even though at the moment, he totally was.

Shifting her so she lay on her back and he could see the dark traces of her nipples through the sheer fabric, he truly was sorry, but this was necessary. The guilt would be considerably less if he hadn't already gotten aroused from simply thinking about what they might have to do.

His hand reversed direction and started a path up her thigh, pushing the short nightie up her legs until the matching panties she wore were exposed.

Carly's breath caught in her throat. Dare he pull those panties off her? What the hell would she do if he did?

Putting that next move off for a bit until he could gauge her potential reaction, Trey rolled on top of her, hoping the camera wouldn't pick up the nervousness apparent on her face.

Settled between her legs, trying to ignore the erection she no doubt felt pressing against her, he weighed the options.

Could he fake making love to her? Maybe pull the sheet over them and feign the motions?

Would Carly get it and go along with the charade? More importantly, would some movement hidden beneath the covers be enough to capture and hold the guards' interest enough for the team to extract Jimmy?

Probably not.

He was starting to despair when a stroke of brilliance hit him.

"Hey, baby. Get up and dance for me the way you used to."

Her eyes opened wide and he feared she might slap him.

He remembered their conversation on the plane when he teased her.

Just don't expect me to dance for you.

We'll see.

That's what he got for joking around on an op as important as this one. He opened his eyes wider and shook his head slightly. Hopefully his movement wasn't noticeable enough for the terrorists to pick up on it.

"Don't look so mad, sweetheart. I know you gave that life up when we got married, but it turns me on. I really need you to do it for me right now. Okay?"

He could see by the expression on her face she was confused as hell by his request, but had remembered the surveillance and knew she couldn't question him.

The muscles in her throat worked as she swallowed. "Okay, baby. Anything for you. I just don't know how good I'll be. You know, without my costumes and music and all."

She was nervous and a horrible actress under pressure, but he had to believe the guards watching them wouldn't notice once they got a good look at her body in motion.

"The camera is behind the mirror on the wall opposite the end of the bed." Matt's voice in his ear reminded him again just how public this whole situation was.

So why was he rock hard at the thought of it?

Trey got out of bed and, ignoring the tent in his pajamas, walked to where Carly had abandoned the high heels earlier. He picked them up and carried them to where she still lay.

Extending a hand, he took hers and pulled her upright. While she sat on the edge of the mattress he kneeled. Taking one delicate foot in his hand, he drew it toward his mouth and kissed the arch of her instep.

She trembled as he slid one shoe on.

Turning his attention to the other foot, he kissed his way from her ankle to her big toe, before drawing it into his mouth and sucking on it.

Carly drew in a deep breath. If her toes were this sensitive, what the hell would her reaction be if he sucked on a more intimate part of her? That thought had him beginning to tremble too as all his psychological training flew right out the window.

Training. Bullshit. What military genius had thought any red-blooded man could make love to an attractive woman and not be affected in some way by it?

Thrusting the thought out of his mind, he moved this public seduction along and slipped the second shoe on. Then he leaned over to hit the power button on the television. The channel that automatically came on played music to accompany the hotel information written on the screen. He'd discovered that earlier while eating his pizza.

As the soft generic music filled the room, he pulled a chair over to the end of the bed and then motioned Carly over with the crook of one finger. "Come here, baby."

She rose from the bed and teetered over in the heels. He couldn't help thinking how great they made her bare legs look.

Standing her in front of the mirror, he sat in the chair. "There, sweetheart. Dance right there in front of the mirror for me."

She looked a bit frightened, but Trey figured since she was facing him and not the camera, it didn't matter. Hating he'd put her in such an uncomfortable situation, he felt even worse as he watched her hips start to sway.

His body's reaction was clearly visible to both of them. Her gaze dropped to the erection evident in the too-damn-thin silk pajama bottoms.

Instead of it freaking her out, she reacted in the totally opposite way. She lifted her chin a bit, closed her eyes and started to really dance for him.

Turning in time to the rhythm of the music, she spun to face the mirror. Her eyes opened and their gazes met as she watched his reaction in the reflection.

Running her hands over her body, she danced. He alternated between focusing on her reflection and the swaying of her hips right in front of him. All the while his erection was an ever-present sign of his enjoyment of the show. He was happy simply watching her, until she pulled down the top of the nightgown to reveal one breast to him, then wet her finger and circled her own nipple with it.

At that point, he was no longer simply an observer. He couldn't control himself.

This was no longer just a show for the target. Hell, it hadn't been for some time.

CHAPTER FOURTEEN

He pushed down his waistband and began to rub his swollen cock. Not that he had many brain cells functioning at this point, but his thinking was Smith would definitely be the kind of guy who would jerk off as his wife stripped for him.

Second, perhaps if he came while watching her, he could get away with only making Carly strip for the terrorists and not have to go further.

Only making her strip. Ha! There was nothing insignificant about what was happening between them now. Especially not when her eyes caught the reflection of what was happening behind her.

Knowing she was watching him, as well as the target's guards and Matt in the control center, didn't diminish his arousal at all as pre-come seeped from the tip.

His fist moved faster over the rock-hard flesh and, just when he was starting to get really friendly with his own hand, Carly turned to him. Her gaze dropped, observing every motion he made.

His heart pounded faster as she moved closer. Leaning down, she braced herself on each arm of the chair, putting him eye-level with her glorious tits. When she reached out and ran the tip of her finger down the slit of his cock, Trey hissed in a breath.

Her eyes met his and he saw the need in them. If she was into this, he sure as hell was too.

Stopping what he had previously been doing, he released the grip on his cock and reached for her.

With one finger he pulled aside the neckline of the already revealing nightie, just enough to expose her other nipple. Leaning forward, he drew the peak into his mouth and scraped his teeth against it.

She drew in a sharp breath and then grabbed his head and pulled it closer to her breast.

There was no doubt in his mind now. John Smith was definitely going to make love to his wife tonight. Since it was too late to step back from the precipice on which they both teetered, he drew her another step forward.

Wrapping his hands around her hips, he pulled her closer until she was in his lap, straddling him. Then she began to grind her pelvis against his erection.

She lowered her lips to his, devouring his mouth as he kissed her with equal need.

His tongue drove against hers in a rhythm that mimicked what he hoped his very prominent arousal would soon do to her. She rubbed herself against the bulge of his cock.

He heard her breath coming in staggered pants. In another second, she'd probably come just from the contact. If he didn't watch out, he'd come from it too.

Trey broke away. If this was to be the one and only time they'd be together, he wanted it to last a very long time and he intended on enjoying every moment.

Besides, some part of his brain remembered the team wouldn't benefit from his rushing to finish this. They needed as much time as he could give them.

"Turn around. Face the mirror."

Did the pulse in her throat pound faster just from his suggestion? How hot was that?

Swallowing hard from his words, Carly nodded. As her pulse continued to throb wildly, she rose and let him turn her toward the mirror.

This was no simple hook up. They affected each other physically. Chemically.

He couldn't let himself think like that. This was a one-shot deal.

"Spread your legs for me, baby. I want to see you." He sat her in his lap, his hands spreading her thighs wide.

"This is supposed to be a dance for you, remember?" Her voice sounded breathy.

"No reason why we can't both enjoy it." His own voice came out sounding raspy.

Easing aside the scrap of lace that comprised the bottom of Candi Smith's nightwear, he exposed her before both of their eyes. "Look at yourself, baby. You're so beautiful."

Head thrown back against his chest, she stared at her reflection as his hands slipped between her folds. He started circling his finger over her engorged clit.

The first touch had her drawing in a sharp breath.

He scraped his teeth against her earlobe before moving down to nip lightly at her neck. Sliding a finger from his left hand inside her, he stroked in and out while still working her clit with his right.

She began to tremble. It wouldn't be long.

Moving her slightly, he readjusted their positions. He freed his erection from the pants, then slid it between her thighs. She rotated her hips against him, and with every movement his arousal rubbed her wet entrance while his fingers played against her.

Trey watched Carly in the mirror as she sat, shaking, facing away from him, her eyes squeezed closed. Her breathing got faster and then she was crying out and all but bucking out of his lap. He wrapped an arm around her waist and held her closer, but he didn't let up with his fingers as her orgasm rocked her.

Finally, it was obvious she couldn't take anymore. Panting and slumping weakly in his lap as her body jerked sporadically, she grabbed his hand to stop him.

Enjoying the view of her flushed face in the mirror, he

held her as she caught her breath, all the while thinking she better not be done now because he sure as hell wasn't.

That thought was reinforced by Matt's voice in his ear. "For God's sake, Trey. You can't stop now. We've almost got Jimmy out, but we need more time."

Trey closed his eyes for a second, regrouping in his mind. He had become Trey again while touching Carly, but he needed to be John Smith.

Grasping her chin, he angled her face toward his, and then took control of her mouth in a hard, crushing kiss. He unleashed an untamed part of him he rarely gave into, thrusting his tongue into her mouth while he worked her breast roughly with one hand.

When he broke the kiss that had them both breathless, she opened her eyes again. He stared into the sea of green.

"I want you."

She swallowed hard but remained silent.

"I want to fuck you." Purposely choosing those coarse words, he played the role and let John Smith shine through him. It might be the only way to hold onto his own sanity. "Do you want that?"

His gut twisted waiting to hear the words from her lips.

Finally, he was rewarded when she nodded. "Yes."

With two hands around her waist, Trey raised Carly off his lap and set her on her feet before him. He stood too and ran his hands up from her thighs, pulling her nightgown up and over her head. She was there before him, naked except for black lace thong underwear and heels.

God, her breasts were beautiful. He'd really enjoy them in any other situation. Dammit, he was enjoying them now.

He pushed the chair out of the way and led Carly to the end of the bed, trying to reason away the fact he was trembling now too.

Adrenaline. That's all it was.

Sinking into her was going to be a huge mistake. He knew it. Yet he was going to do it anyway for so many reasons, half of them selfish, half not so selfish.

This was for Jimmy, at least partially. He had to keep reminding himself of that, even though he didn't believe one word of his own internal lies.

With both of them still standing, he turned her toward the bed and bent her over the edge of the mattress. No way would the guards leave the monitors with Carly bent over the bed like that.

Trey ran his hands over the warm skin of her perfect heart-shaped ass. He pulled her thong down in one swift move, yanking his own bottoms off next. He wanted her so badly his erection was bobbing with a life of its own.

He'd be fine once he had her. He'd have to be. This was just lust. That's all. That's what he kept telling himself as he stood close behind her and nudged her feet farther apart with his.

With a hand on each of her hips, he glanced at the mirror, saw himself and Carly reflected perfectly, and plunged inside her.

She was so wet and ready he slid into her warmth easily.

He drove into her hard, over and over again, gritting his teeth to make it last as long as possible. Trying to ignore how good it felt, he pounded into her until the cheeks of her ass were pink from the friction.

Carly's breathing got more labored and she began shaking. Pulling out, he turned her around. He wanted to see her face-to-face when she came again. Laying her on the mattress, he crawled between her thighs and poised at her entrance. Her lips were parted and her breath came in gasps as she stared up at him.

His gaze never leaving her face, he slid inside again. She released a shaky breath as he entered her, his own body shuddering from the sensation.

Reaching his hand between them, he connected with her clit and brought her to orgasm for a second time.

The feel of her body gripping his and the sight of her face as she came overwhelmed him. He thrust once more and followed her, coming deep inside as her body milked his.

Totally consumed by Carly beneath him, the sound of Matt's voice in his ear startled Trey right out of his blissful sex haze. "Trey, we—Jack. Shit! You're not supposed to be in here."

He heard the click as Matt disconnected audio and that was it. Still buried deep inside Carly, Trey was left alone with the miserable knowledge the one man who shouldn't have seen what happened between him and Carly, had.

Her body pulsed one more time around him, an aftershock from her lingering orgasm, but there was no joy in it for him.

He pulled out and, squeezing his eyes shut, rubbed a hand over his face to try and erase the misery.

When he opened his eyes again, Carly was watching him. Avoiding eye contact, he retrieved her panties off the floor and handed them to her. As she reached for them, he realized he didn't know if Jimmy was free yet.

Now what?

A click sounded and Matt was in his ear again. Trey said a silent thank you and waited.

"We got Jimmy. I gotta go but you're good, Trey. You're done. We don't need you anymore. Copy?"

Trey cleared his throat to indicate he had heard and understood the message.

Matt signed off with a hurried, "Roger that. Over and out."

His only point of contact on this mission was silent once more. At least he'd gotten what he needed first. Jimmy was out of there and Trey didn't have to prolong this thing with Carly.

She had already pulled her panties back on and had kicked off her heels, all while continuously glancing at him.

After retrieving the nightgown from the floor where he'd dropped it, she crawled under the covers.

The expression on her face told him she knew something was not right. He couldn't explain about Jack because of the surveillance in the room. Nor could he explain the inner turmoil he felt, but that had nothing to do with the bad guys listening in on them.

Trey pulled on the pajama bottoms and shut off the TV and the light. Sliding into the bed, he lay down next to her.

She snuggled closer, seeking contact.

After the intimacy they'd just shared, how could he deny her that? He gave up fighting the urge and let himself pull her into his arms. She felt good there. Too good.

How was he supposed to make love to this woman and then forget about it? Impossible.

Her fingertips brushed his cheek. He didn't move. Her lips met his and he was torn between wanting her all over again and knowing the worst thing he could do was fall into this thing with her any deeper.

The tip of her tongue slid between his lips and she moved closer until the length of her body was pressed against his. Trey sucked in a deep breath.

Maybe just one more time.

The damage was already done. Once more couldn't hurt. It would give him more memories for those long, cold lonely nights when he returned and was supposed to pretend nothing had happened.

She pushed the elastic waistband of his pants down before she stroked his length and his decision was made.

Rolling on top of her, he captured Carly's face in both of his hands. He kissed her hard and deep.

Thrusting one hand into her hair, he slid the other one down, following the curves of her body. Her knee came up and hooked around his hip.

In the dark every breath she took resonated through him. The tiny sound she made in her throat when his tongue tangled with hers sent a tingle straight to his core.

No one could see them now. This time wouldn't be about the mission. It was just about them and it shouldn't be happening.

That thought filled his head even as he pulled her panties off for the second time that night and plunged inside.

CHAPTER FIFTEEN

Trey didn't let himself rest that night. All hell would be breaking loose in the basement after Jimmy's extraction.

He only hoped they didn't connect the team's infiltration to his and Carly's visit. But why should they? The Smiths were simply newlyweds having sex. Nothing suspicious about it.

Though the guards in charge of Jimmy would most likely pay a hefty price for watching the X-rated feed on the monitors instead of their captive. They might even pay with their lives.

His mind circled around and around the possibilities and consequences until just after dawn when he felt Carly slip out of bed. She padded to the bathroom and he heard the shower start.

As the exhaustion began to catch up with him, Trey flung one arm over his eyes. He hadn't slept at all and now, sleep deprived and distracted as hell, he had to be at the top of his game for the meet.

He needed to convince the target to trust him and hopefully build a long-lasting relationship. He also had to try to not get him and Carly killed in the process.

The terrorist they were after was an extremely powerful and very bad man. They didn't want him dead. If they had, Jimmy could have taken him out long ago.

The good guys wanted the target's boss and the best way to locate him was by getting admitted into the inner circle by doing business with him.

Finding John Smith and his computer had been a stroke of luck and the timing couldn't have been better, given the fact their only mole, Jimmy, had been compromised.

Trey told himself he only had to get through this one meet. After that, someone at CentCom should be able to handle all future correspondence electronically. They'd get the info they needed to find the leader.

Hopefully the guy he was dealing with wasn't big on speaking by phone and Trey wouldn't be brought in again unless the bad guy requested another face-to-face.

If that happened, he'd come alone with the team. No way was he bringing Carly here again.

Listening to the water still running in the shower, he pictured it sluicing off Carly's body and remembered the feel of being inside her last night.

Trey relived the taste of her, the scent of her. He had to physically shake his head to rid himself of the memories.

The voice inside, his own this time instead of Matt's, reminded him once again a distracted soldier was a dead soldier . . . accompanied by a dead civilian in this case.

Dammit. Why did this Smith guy have to be such a ball-less bastard he would bring his wife along with him as cover for an arms deal?

Trey was going to have to get his mind fine-tuned again and fast. This was already a risky mission without the distraction of Carly.

Add to that the fact Jimmy had been extracted right out from under the target's nose and their chances for success plummeted. Every bad guy in the vicinity would be on high alert after last night's escape.

Every one in the area would be under suspicion. If only they could call off this meet, but that would only further alert the terrorist bastards.

Where the hell was Matt's voice when he needed it? He

could use a little encouragement and an update about now.

Glancing at the bedside clock, Trey realized Carly had been in the shower for a very long time.

Certain they were still under surveillance, he chose his words carefully. "Baby? You okay in there?"

When she didn't answer his heart leapt into his throat. Had they gotten to her? How? He'd checked the room the best he could, but knowing there were video cameras, he hadn't been as thorough as he should have.

Trey grabbed the doorknob with a suddenly sweaty palm. It turned easily. He opened the door and peered through the steam.

"Baby?" He tried to keep the panic from his voice.

She didn't answer and his pulse kicked into a higher gear.

With trepidation, he pulled open the shower curtain a few inches. Carly stood with both hands and her forehead pressed against the wall with the water hitting her in the back.

She turned her head enough to look at him. "Is everything all right?"

He finally let himself breathe again.

This wasn't something he was prepared for. With all his agonizing about his own feelings, he'd barely considered Carly might be going through something herself.

Guilt overwhelmed him for invading what little privacy she had. The door hadn't been locked because that was one of the rules he'd laid out for her on the flight over. He needed to be able to get to her at all times in case anything happened.

Oh, something had happened, all right. He'd had sex with her not once, but twice. Hot, passionate, emotional sex that broke every rule in this very serious game they were playing.

"I was just concerned about you. You okay?"

"Fine." She paused and swallowed. "How much time do we have?"

"A while. Take as long as you need." He reached out and ran a fingertip down the side of her face.

She nodded and he let the curtain drop back into place. It

wasn't until he'd closed the door behind him he heard the water stop.

They'd deal with this somehow later, but right now he had a meet to prepare for and she was going to have to find an outfit in a stripper's suitcase that would be appropriate for an appointment with a terrorist.

When exactly had this poor woman's life become so complicated? Unfortunately, he knew the answer. It was right about the time Task Force Zeta had walked into her bar.

With a sigh, Trey opened John Smith's laptop and was cruising around in the files when the bathroom door opened and Carly came out in a white robe and a burst of steam.

He thought it best if he left her alone for a bit and tried to instead refresh his memory regarding the emails that had passed between Smith and the target.

Though he found his glance kept straying to watch her move around the room. He wrestled his attention back to the laptop.

The two men never came right out and named what this meet was about in any of their correspondence. That would make things trickier, but Trey knew from the research Matt had included in his folder that Smith had been dealing small arms with some minor players in the terror world.

They also suspected Smith could get his hands on weapons-grade uranium if the incentive was high enough. Trey had a feeling that particular commodity was what this little rendezvous was about.

If only he were here alone, things would be so much easier.

Trey thought he was doing a pretty good job of ignoring Carly and concentrating on the information until she threw the clothes in her hand to the floor with a huff.

"What the hell am I supposed to wear?" She turned and looked accusingly at him, as if it were his fault Candi hadn't packed the proper clothing for a meeting with a terrorist.

He'd done a lot of undercover ops in his years with the team and never once had he gotten stressed out over choosing an outfit, but she was a woman. He had first-hand experience and could definitely attest to that.

All woman.

A really, really hot woman.

Laying the laptop on the bed, he walked over to the suitcase. After a moment of careful consideration and searching, he handed her a short black skirt and one of John Smith's white button-down collared dress shirts. Now for the shoes . . .

His eyes landed briefly on the heels she'd worn last night. Those held way too many memories for both of them. He didn't need further distraction during this meeting.

There must be another pair in there somewhere. Candi was a stripper. Shouldn't she have packed more than that one pair of high heels?

When he didn't find another pair, and boy did he try, he picked up the ones on the floor and thrust them at her.

"Here. Put all that on. You'll look fine."

She looked doubtfully down at the bundle he'd handed her and carried it all into the bathroom.

When she emerged again, she was looking pretty damn hot in the outfit he'd picked. She wasn't supposed to look hot. He'd given her the white men's shirt to cover her up, but somehow with the sleeves rolled up and the top buttons left undone to show a bit of skin, she made the damn thing look sexy.

All he needed was for the target to take a fancy to Carly. Then Trey would be forced to kill him with his bare hands.

That might get him into trouble though since they needed the man alive. He considered that for about a second and then decided if the scum touched Carly, he'd still kill him.

His contemplation of the possible ramifications of going against a direct order and killing the one person this entire operation hinged upon was interrupted by Matt's voice saying, "Trey. Our goose has flown the coop."

"What?" Trey asked Matt, but looked at Carly when he said it in case surveillance was still in place.

She frowned at him. "I didn't say anything."

"Oh, I thought you did. Sorry."

Matt continued, "You heard me right. Elvis has left the building. Packed up, took most of his goons and pulled away in a big limo about ten minutes ago."

Just when Trey was deciding what to do with this information, the phone on the nightstand next to the bed rang. He shot Carly a look he hoped told her to be ready for anything and then moved to answer it.

He put the receiver to the ear with the implant so Matt could record the conversation. "Hello?"

"Hello, my friend." The voice coming through the phone line sounded smooth. Too smooth. The kind of voice that made a person's skin crawl.

"Hello. It's nice to speak with you." Years of training kept Trey sounding calm.

"Yes, yes. You too. I trust you had a good night?" Did the bastard sound smug?

"Yes, thank you. The room is lovely. My wife and I are enjoying it very much." He swallowed hard and glanced at Carly, regretting all over again the bastards had seen them together.

"I'm sure you are." There it was again, an amused, knowing lilt to the bastard's voice.

Trey had no doubt the target had a copy of his and Carly's bedroom escapades in his slimy hand. He hoped that was all he held in his hand at the moment. The thought of him taking physical pleasure while watching Carly on video had Trey mad enough to spit fire.

The target continued, "I must apologize, my friend."

You're no friend of mine.

"Oh? Apologize for what?" Trey asked.

"I was called away suddenly. I'm not sure for how long I'll need to be away."

The coward was running scared. Jimmy disappearing without a trace had made him nervous, made him realize he wasn't untouchable.

It was probably bad for the successful continuance of the mission, but somehow Trey was taking great satisfaction from it.

The fleeing bastard went on talking, "I'll not be able to make our meeting this morning. I'm afraid you traveled all this way for nothing. However, please stay and enjoy the room for as long as you and your beautiful wife wish. Order whatever you'd like from the hotel and whenever you are ready to leave, contact the front desk. They will arrange transportation to the airport."

Yeah, right. Like Trey was really going to get into the limo with that armed bruiser again now the target was suspicious.

He wished the guy would stop talking so they could get the hell out of there. In particular, Trey really wanted him to stop referring to Carly.

"That is very kind of you. My wife and I appreciate it. Will I be hearing from you again soon?"

Come on. Give me something, you schmuck.

"Yes, my friend. I'll be in touch as soon as I'm settled. I look forward to doing business with you in the very near future."

"I look forward to it also. Have a good day." Trey was starting to get itchy.

His gaze strayed to the open suitcase and the clothes all over the floor.

"You too, my friend." The line went dead.

Trey hung up the phone and grabbed the laptop. "Pack the bag, sweetheart. We're going home."

Carly's eyes opened wide, but she didn't question him and did what she was told, obviously as anxious to get the hell out of there as he was.

She packed the clothes into the suitcase so fast, he'd barely gotten the laptop put away and the toiletries from the bathroom and she was finished. She only stopped long enough to rip off the skin-tight skirt and pull a pair of leather pants out of the suitcase.

Good idea. All she'd have to do was kick off those shoes.

Much easier to run in pants should bullets start to fly. Though with neither of them in body armor, he really hoped it wouldn't come to that.

He swallowed and tried not to stare at her ass in the thong as she yanked on the pants right there next to the suitcase. That was another clue Carly was as anxious to get out of there as he was. She'd dropped her skirt while standing in front of him without batting an eye.

In record time, Carly was changed and zipping the suitcase.

Impressed, relieved and feeling so many other things he couldn't begin to put a name to them all, he grabbed the bag and the laptop.

Opening the door, he took one last look around the room, more than grateful to put it behind him.

CHAPTER SIXTEEN

When the elevator doors opened into the lobby, Trey took Carly's hand and led her out onto the sidewalk without looking left or right. Making eye contact with an employee might inspire them to try and help them. There was nothing Trey wanted from any employee of the target's hotel.

Outside, he could feel the anxiety radiating off Carly and kept a tight hold on her hand so she wouldn't sprint down the road, heels and all.

He couldn't blame her. He wouldn't breathe freely again until they were landing on US soil, but every step away from the hotel lightened the feeling of his burden, that burden being getting Carly home safely.

They walked silently for about a block before he stopped in front of none other than a McDonald's.

Quintessential American fast food in the middle of Kosovo. Go figure.

In addition to the chain restaurants, Pristina, like any other capital city, had no shortage of taxis. Trey had no trouble hailing a cab to take them to the airport. Once inside the car, he took out the untraceable disposable cell phone he'd been given by Matt and called the pilot to make sure the jet would be ready and waiting when they arrived.

Trey's feeling of waiting for the other shoe to drop didn't

dissipate until they were on the private jet and in the air. Then the other issue on his mind had time to surface. Carly and the fact this op was over and so were they.

He knew Matt, most likely dressed as a maintenance man, had swept the aircraft and radioed to Trey it was clean so there was no further excuse for him to delay this conversation with Carly. He gathered every bit of professionalism in his being, even sitting straighter while strapped in next to her in the plane's seat.

Measuring his words carefully, Trey focused on keeping his voice even as he said, "We need to go over a few things regarding the op."

She turned and looked at him. "Okay."

"We need to talk about last night."

That caused her to pause a bit before nodding. "All right."

He found himself staring at the magazine in her lap like it was the most interesting thing in the world before he wrestled his eyes up.

Trey cleared his throat. "I need confirmation you're on birth control."

Her eyebrows rose sharply. "Excuse me?"

"I need con—"

"I heard what you said." Gone was the casual demeanor. In its place one angry-looking woman.

"Carly. It's important."

"What was last night about? Really?" she asked.

"The mission." The lie flowed smoothly off his tongue, just like he'd been trained.

"The mission? And that's it?"

Trey nodded. "The mission."

He saw the pain cross her face before she looked away.

Swallowing hard, he tried to clear the lump from his throat. "You didn't answer my question. Are you on any sort of birth control?"

Her head swiveled sharply toward him. "That detail is not part of this mission."

"Yes, actually it is. We had unprotected sex in the course

of this operation."

Twice.

"Just forget it ever happened."

Forget about it. Yeah, not likely.

He shook his head and let out a deep breath. "If you don't answer me now, you'll just have to answer the commander when we return, right before he sends you to Medical."

The look she shot him was filled with hate. "Fine. I haven't had sex in over two years, Trey. So no, I'm not using the pill or anything else for birth control. What would be the point since when I'm not ordered to by the US military, I don't normally sleep around?" She went back to staring blindly at the same magazine page open in her lap since this conversation had begun.

She obviously hated him now.

That was probably for the best. Safer for all involved. Trey could stay professional in the face of anger. If she cried, her tears would break him.

"I'll arrange to have the morning after pill waiting for you when we land."

Carly, still not looking at him, blushed bright red. "I'll take care of things myself."

"Standard operating procedure states in cases such as this—"

She spun on him. "Exactly how long will the military be in control of my personal life from this one favor I was stupid enough to agree to?"

"As soon as we land, we'll go over the mission details with the commander on base. After we get you the pills, you'll be free to go." Trey tried to make it all sound routine, even though nothing felt routine to him right now. "The sooner you take it the better. Matt can arrange to have a prescription waiting for you when we get back."

"Matt?" Her tone had risen high.

Uh, oh. That got her attention. "You knew he was on surveillance for this op. I told you before we landed."

Her eyes narrowed, her seething anger and hatred clear.

"He wasn't just listening to us on that thing in your ear, was he? He could see us too, couldn't he?"

He didn't want to answer that question but he had no choice. "Yes."

Her eyes narrowed further. "Now it all makes sense. *Dance for me. Face the mirror. Spread your legs for me, baby.* You were putting me on display. Tell me, Trey. How many were in the audience for your little lecherous peep show last night?"

There was so much truth in Carly's accusations, Trey felt sick to his stomach. "Too many and I'm sorry, but it wasn't my choice and it was absolutely necessary."

That, at least, was true for the first half of the night. The second half she was totally right about. He was a letch.

There had been no reason for him to make love to her in the dark after Jimmy had already been rescued, except for the fact he'd wanted to.

That was something he could never tell her. He needed to maintain a strictly professional relationship with her, then maybe she'd be able to pick things up in her life, and with Jack, as if nothing had happened.

"Necessary?" Her tone reached a new level that told him exactly how unhappy she was. "Why? Why was it necessary, Trey?"

He hesitated, deciding what he could and couldn't reveal. "We saved a man's life last night, Carly."

She crossed her arms and stared at him. "Forgive me if I don't understand how what we did last night saved a life."

Trey owed her an explanation, even if he was treading a fine line regarding the rules. "This information can't leave this plane, but Jack's brother was being tortured in the basement of our hotel. We provided the distraction that allowed his escape. That's all I can tell you and I shouldn't have even told you that much. I truly hope it's enough."

He watched her react as the expression of her face changed from anger to shock to understanding.

She was quiet for a moment before she spoke again. "Did your commander watch us too?"

"Um . . ." Trey wasn't sure about that answer.

The rest of the team, except for Matt on surveillance and Jack because he was too close to the situation, would have been occupied getting Jimmy out. The commander, however, could have very well been sitting there watching the video feed of both the guards in the basement and their room upstairs.

Good thing Trey hadn't thought of that last night.

"No, Trey." Matt's voice filled his ear. "The commander was on sight with the team."

Carly still watched him, waiting for his answer.

Relieved, Trey relayed that news. "He didn't see."

She still didn't look happy. "Will he?"

"I don't see any reason why he should need to watch it." Unless the commander wanted to see if he and Carly had somehow compromised their cover and sent the target running. Though most likely he ran because of Jimmy's escape, not anything they'd done in their room. Trey couldn't tell her any of that so he left it alone.

"Will the recording of us be shown at the next boys' night out so you can all laugh about it?"

Ow. That one hurt.

"No, Carly. Matt's a professional. We're all professionals." Thinking about his sliding into her the second time for no good reason didn't make him feel very professional.

She let out a big sigh. "If you could arrange for the pills, I'd be willing to take them."

He nodded. "Okay. Thank you."

Matt was obviously still eavesdropping, since his voice filled Trey's ear once again as he said, "I'll take care of it, Trey."

Nothing like living life on constant display.

Trey should tell her the rest too, though he had a feeling it wasn't going to be pretty. "Carly, there's one more thing."

When she spun her head to face him again, he saw the weariness in her. They both needed a good night's sleep. She looked like she couldn't take much more on her shoulders right now and he was about to dump more on top of her.

How he would love to say never mind and forget about the whole thing. Unfortunately, he couldn't. She needed to hear this.

"He wasn't supposed to be there, but Jack walked in and saw the live feed of us last night." Trey felt like he needed to explain and apologize even though there wasn't anything he could have done about it. "I'm pretty sure it was only for a few seconds before Matt got him out of there, but I thought you would want to know. I'm sorry."

She closed her eyes and shook her head. "Yeah, me too."

CHAPTER SEVENTEEN

Carly stepped onto the tarmac and fought the urge to drop to her knees and kiss the ground as relief overwhelmed her.

She'd never been so happy to be on American soil in her life. More importantly, she was one step closer to being free of this military bullshit and Trey so she could get back to her bar and her life and forget any of this had ever happened.

As if she could really do that.

Trey must have seen the need to bolt reflected on her face. He touched her arm for a second and then dropped his hand. In fact, unlike the flight there, he'd barely touched her at all since they'd had sex. Wasn't that ironic?

"You'll have to come back to the base with me to be debriefed by the commander. Then you can go home."

The thought of how Trey had already *debriefed* her in Kosovo flew into Carly's head. A short, bitter laugh burst out before she could control it. That juvenile reaction made her realize she was most likely starting to lose her mind. Either that or she was giddy from lack of sleep.

She glanced at Trey as he raised a brow over her outburst like the staid poster boy for military protocol that he was. His words on the flight echoed in her brain, fueling her anger.

Standard operating procedure clearly states . . .

How could he be so cold and businesslike after the night they'd shared? His quoting SOP to her after what they'd done together had left no doubt in her mind that what she'd been stupid enough to assume was a real attraction between them had been nothing more than a job to him.

Maybe it was her pride hurting more than anything else, which was exactly what she deserved for breaking her own rules and letting herself succumb to temptation.

In any case, he was still waiting for her to say something. "I know I have to go in. You already told me. Believe me, I'm as anxious as you are to have this thing over and done with so I can get back to my life and forget it ever happened."

His calm demeanor didn't crack at her comment or the less-than-nice tone in which it was delivered. No surprise there.

At least she'd been able to change into her own clothes on the flight. That helped her feel more grounded, more normal. She'd had enough of Candi's clothes, especially those damn high heels. They caused too many memories, not to mention blisters.

With the blisters making even her sneakers hurt, Carly limped into the meeting room behind Trey. There she faced five men whose heads all swiveled immediately in her direction when she entered.

Wishing she could crawl beneath the linoleum, she wondered exactly how much they all knew.

From the doorway she spotted Matt and felt her face heat at the knowledge he for certain had watched the whole sordid performance Trey had put on the night before.

That pissed her off all over again until the sight of Jack made her forget her anger and embarrassment took over.

She didn't have long to feel ashamed however, because they were barely inside the room when Jack leapt forward, red faced.

"You rotten son of a bitch." He pulled back his fist and let the punch fly, clocking Trey with a blow that would have leveled a smaller man.

Carly hopped to the side to avoid Trey who took a step back when the blow threw him off balance. The entire team seemed to hold its collective breath, but no one moved a muscle to either help or stop the fight. Carly too stood frozen in place except for the wild pounding of her heart.

Trey's head had whipped back from the hit, but he stayed put and didn't even raise a fist. He stared calmly at Jack as if waiting for the next punch, but it never came.

Instead, Jack stepped forward and grabbed Trey in a bear hug, audibly squeezing the breath out of him. "Thanks for helping to save my brother."

She saw the expression of shock cross Trey's face as he accepted the embrace. When they broke apart, he touched his jaw, working it from side to side. "You're welcome."

Jack came to her next. He forced a small closed-mouth smile. "Hey, darlin'."

Carly returned his smile hesitantly.

How exactly should she act in this situation? This guy had an obvious crush on her and had just seen his best friend screwing her on camera. She'd like to know the standard operating procedure for handling that one.

"Hi, Jack."

He leaned forward and brushed a soft kiss across her cheek. "I'm so glad you're home safe."

The commander stood in his office doorway, watching the whole exchange and not looking very happy. "You three, in my office."

"Three? Me too, sir?" Jack sounded surprised.

"Yes, you." The man turned and walked to his desk obviously assuming they'd follow, which they did.

Carly walked behind Trey and Jack when Matt grabbed her hand and slipped a pill bottle into it. Managing an embarrassed nod, she clutched the prescription in a tight fist.

Could this get any more embarrassing? As she entered the office behind Trey and Jack, she had a feeling it could.

"Close the damn door, McAfee." The commander delivered his order like a man who was used to being followed without question.

"Yes, sir." She did as she was told.

He waited until she had before he turned toward Jack. "What the hell is going on, Gordon?"

"Nothing, sir."

"It didn't look like nothing to me." When Jack remained silent, the commander swung his focus to Trey.

"Williams, would you like to fill me in?"

"No, sir. I mean there's nothing to be filled in on, sir."

"So you're going to tell me you two beat the hell out of each other after every mission?"

Trey kicked at the floor with the toe of his sneaker. "He didn't exactly beat the hell out of me, sir."

The commander raised a brow. "No, I suppose he could have hit you harder if he really wanted to. I'm going to assume your little show out there was a one-time event. Am I right?"

"Yes, sir." Jack and Trey spoke in unison.

"McAfee."

Carly jumped. She had been eyeing the water cooler and deciding if she could take the pill without anyone noticing when he called her name. "Yes, sir?"

"Good job. Go home."

"Sir?" She frowned, wondering what had happened to the debriefing.

"Go home. Williams can handle things here for both of you. If I need you for anything, I know where to find you."

She was being dismissed and she wasn't going to argue. "Okay. Thank you."

He smiled. "No. Thank *you*, McAfee. Oh and remember, not a word to anyone."

A bitter laugh burst out of her before she could stop it. "They wouldn't believe me if I told them. But no, I won't say a word."

She couldn't wait to be on the other side of the door and away from them all. Being the third side in this messed up triangle was more than she could deal with right now.

Glancing from Jack to Trey, she got out of the office as fast as she could. It would feel very good to get home.

Time to start getting things back to normal, though she had a strong suspicion she'd never feel normal again.

CHAPTER EIGHTEEN

Trey gladly handled the mission follow-up without Carly. Having her there would have taken more mental capacity than he had after the night they'd spent together doing everything except sleeping.

Of course, Jack was still there right next to him like the living breathing personification of his own conscience. A constant reminder he'd not only stepped across the line with Carly, but had also trampled all over Jack's toes in the process.

To Jack's credit, following the initial punch he'd thrown he'd acted pretty much normal as he and Trey waited on line with the rest of the team to turn in all equipment they'd been issued for the op.

Then came the paperwork—the bane of the existence of every man and woman in the US military. Trey sat at his desk with a form in front of him and a pen in his hand, but being prepared with the necessary items didn't get the papers filled out any easier.

The task was simple enough. He was going to have to write an account for the expenses he'd charged to John Smith's credit card for things like the rental car and the taxi, but he'd barely filled out his name because he wasn't really there.

Instead, his mind was at Carly's bar as he wondered what she might be doing.

Jack sat at the desk next to him, scribbling away.

Trey looked down at his own nearly blank page. This was going to take a long time at this rate. He sighed.

Jack glanced up at the sound. "That paper's not going to fill out itself while you stare at the wall."

Trey snorted. "I guess I didn't take whatever speed writing course you did."

It seemed he and Jack were just going to forget about the obvious and go back to being friends even though his jaw still hurt like hell. The bruise was already starting to show but it didn't matter if getting it out of his system had helped Jack get over what he'd seen. He owed Jack that much.

"You just need the right motivation, that's all. The sooner I get done, the sooner I can go get a beer."

That captured Trey's wandering attention. No wonder Jack was in such a hurry to finish his paperwork. He was anxious to get to Carly.

Trey bit the inside of his cheek to try to stop himself from asking the question, but it came out anyway. "You going to Carly's?"

"Yup." Jack's single spoken word carried far more meaning today than it normally would. He was in fact telling Trey he was still going after Carly, no matter what had happened in Kosovo.

His stomach clenched. "Maybe you should give her a little time. It's been a tough couple of days."

"Are you going to ask Carly out?" Jack stared at him waiting for an answer.

"Me?" Trey's eyes widened at the question. "No, of course not."

Jack cocked up one brow. "Why not?"

"I don't need the distraction of a girlfriend right now."

Glancing down, he tapped a finger on Trey's blank report. "You look plenty distracted to me already."

For a man who talked like a back country hick most times,

Jack could be really perceptive. He was dead-on this time.

Trey had a feeling his distraction wasn't going to get any better either, particularly if Jack ended up dating Carly. He shook off the unpleasant thought.

"Yeah, well. It's been a tough couple of days for me too." Trey sighed and then dropped the pen. "Look, Jack. I have to say this. I'm sorry. I'm sorry it had to happen and I'm really sorry you had to see it."

Jack shook his head. "I know. You had to. Matt explained it to me. It was his idea and it saved Jimmy, so how can I hold it against you?"

The first time had been Matt's idea and necessary, but the second time? That incident was all Trey and the guilt over it nearly overwhelmed him as he took in the sincerity of Jack's expression.

"I'm fine. We're fine." Jack waved a hand to indicate the two of them. "And I'm sorry I punched you. It's just . . . no stud likes to share his filly, you know?"

Trey wouldn't have worded it that way exactly, but . . . "Yeah, I know."

"Finish that up. I'll wait for you." Arms folded, Jack leaned against his desk.

Trey shook his head. "No, you go ahead. I think I'm going to try to stay out of her face for a while. Things have been a little awkward since we um . . . you know."

Jack laughed. "Yeah, I can imagine. Actually, that's all I can do is imagine, not having experienced it myself."

Trey winced. All may be forgiven, but it was obviously not quite forgotten.

"But it's fine," Jack continued. "One day, when Carly and I are celebrating our wedding anniversary, the three of us will all get together and laugh about this."

Anniversary? Shit. The thought of Jack and Carly married didn't even remotely make Trey feel like laughing.

"Yeah." He forced a smile, even as the iron vise tightened around his chest.

CHAPTER NINETEEN

Carly wiped down the bar. She was so happy to be home and back to her life again, she didn't even care she was tired or that her feet radiated pain every time her sneakers rubbed the blisters on her heels.

Nope. Everything was fine. Good. Back to normal. She'd only grabbed a few hours of restless sleep on the plane, but she'd had to take the shift tonight since no one else was scheduled.

That was okay, though. She was back in her own bar where she was the boss and didn't have to follow anyone else's rules, and she'd already taken the pills Matt had slipped her.

Things were back to normal. Her usual, boring and predictable life looked pretty damn good after the past couple of days . . . until she looked up to see Jack walk through the door.

She held her breath and waited, but Trey wasn't behind him.

Carly tried to deny the fact her heart had just stopped beating as she said, "Hi, Jack."

"Hey, darlin'." Jack's glance swept the nearly empty bar as he perched his butt on a bar stool directly in front of her. "Slow day?"

Slow didn't come close to describing it.

"Yeah, but that's fine. I'm a little jetlagged." Knowing she couldn't tell anyone the truth about her absence, Carly kept her voice low.

She'd told her relief bartender she'd packed a bag and gone out of town to help an old college girlfriend who had an emergency. Since she lived in an apartment above the bar, there'd been no way to avoid someone noticing she was gone.

Pressing his lips together, Jack nodded. "I'm glad it's slow. Not for your business of course, but it'll give us a chance to talk."

Talk? Carly didn't know if she was ready for this discussion right now.

Swallowing hard, she steeled her nerves. "Talk about what?"

"About that *maybe* you gave me the other night to us going out on a date. I'm hoping you've decided to turn that answer into a yes." His slow, sweet smile was enough to melt any woman's heart. Any woman who wasn't fighting it as hard as she was.

"I don't date military guys, Jack. You know that."

Maybe she should have that credo made into a sign and hang it behind the bar.

If nothing else, it would serve to remind her what happened when she gave in to temptation. That she'd seduced Trey in the darkness only to have him act like it was all a job the next day proved she obviously needed reminding.

"I know that, darlin', but you forgot about your rule with me the other night. I may have been drunk as piss, but I remember that kiss and it was real nice. Wasn't it?"

"Yes." She couldn't deny it. It had been nice. Just like Jack was nice and sweet, and kind and funny.

He was just the kind of guy Carly should like, and she did like him in spite of her saying no to all his invitations.

She held firm on her rule with Jack, who was so obviously interested in her. Meanwhile, she'd let herself get attached to Trey, who had no interest in her at all now their assignment was over.

Even so, the thought of Trey took her breath away and made her heart begin to pound. She'd watched the door for him to come in all day.

She craved him like an alcoholic craves a drink. Why? Probably because he didn't want her.

Typical. All of her quoting her rules to any man who asked her out was obviously just crap because she'd gone and let herself get attached to the wrong man yet again.

She was going to have to get over Trey because she had meant nothing to him except as part of his job.

"Darlin'?" Jack touched her hand lightly and brought her attention to the present.

"Sorry. I'm a bit distracted."

Jack raised his brow. "I see that. You're not the only one."

Assuming he was talking about himself being worried about his brother, she lowered her voice as she asked, "How is your brother?"

Jack smiled. "Good. Thanks for asking. He's pretty banged up, but he's alive. You can't ask for more than that. He's still in the hospital in Germany, but they should be transporting him home before too long."

Carly grabbed two beers out of the cooler and popped the tops. She slid one to Jack and kept the other for herself. She needed it after what she'd been through.

"On me. Here's to a complete recovery." *For all of them . . .*

"Amen." Jack raised his bottle in a toast and then sipped the beer. He played a bit with a bead of sweat running down the glass bottle before he raised his gaze to her. "What's with the military-men rule, darlin'? Who hurt you?"

Carly looked at him with surprise. This guy was either really perceptive or she was an open book. She had a feeling it was the latter. "Just some asshole."

He tilted his head. "Some asshole ruined it for all the rest of us? Where is he? I'd like to show him what I think about that."

She smiled. She hadn't had someone want to beat anyone

up for her in a long time, if ever.

"Sorry. He's clear across the country now with his wife and kid." Maybe kids plural by now for all she knew.

"Well, if you ask me, it's a damn shame to throw out the whole pie just because the crust got a little burnt."

Carly laughed. It had been a long time since a man had made her laugh.

Jack smiled. "You should laugh more. I like it."

Contemplating her current situation, Carly took another sip of her beer and let the cold foam slide down her tightened throat.

She didn't date military men, yet here she was, pining over one anyway.

Maybe it was a stupid rule. A doctor or a lawyer or a garbage man could hurt her too. Maybe if she hadn't been living like a nun the last couple of years, she wouldn't have been so affected by Trey after just one night in bed with him.

"Okay."

Jack raised one sandy brow. "Okay what, darlin'?"

"I'll go out with you." She had to laugh again because Jack couldn't have looked more surprised if she had gotten up on the bar and done a striptease.

She quickly pushed the thought of her recent striptease out of her mind.

He'd stopped with the beer halfway to his mouth and just gaped at her.

She pushed the hand holding the beer down to the bar. "Close your mouth before a bug flies in."

A wide smile spread across Jack's face. "When?"

If she was going to do this, then why not make it right away? "I have to work tonight. Is tomorrow night good for you?"

"Hell yeah, tomorrow's good and even if it wasn't I'd make it work." He cocked his head to the side and sobered for a second. "Not that I'm one to look a gift horse in the mouth, but what made you change your mind?"

She laughed. "Believe it or not, I think it was the burnt-pie analogy."

He smiled and raised his beer again. "I'll remember to thank Mama for that one next time I call."

A man who loved his mama. Jack couldn't be more perfect . . . unless he were Trey.

CHAPTER TWENTY

Trey was battling the restlessness he always felt after one op ended and another had yet to begin. Only this time it seemed worse.

He'd decided to try to sweat out the agitation. He and Jack were currently in the middle of a long run. The only problem was it wasn't working. Now he was both sweaty and restless.

"Hey, Jack. You want to come over to my place tonight and watch the game? Or we can go to the bar if you want."

He'd given Carly her space for a day. That should be enough. Besides, he missed the bar. That's what he was telling himself anyway.

"Um, actually, I'm busy."

"Busy? Doing what?" Trey frowned. Jack never gave up an opportunity to go to Carly's bar.

Jack stopped running, so Trey stopped too. "She said yes."

Feeling his eyes pop open wide, Trey hoped he'd jumped to the wrong conclusion as he asked, "She said yes? Carly? To your date?"

Wiping the sweat from his face with the hem of his T-shirt, Jack nodded. "Yup. I couldn't believe it myself but we're going out tonight."

Suddenly sick to his stomach, Trey pressed a hand to his side. He must have run too hard.

He was having trouble wrapping his head around this. He had thought he was safe since she'd been saying no to Jack for about two years now.

Trey couldn't date her, but that didn't mean he wanted to see her dating anyone else either. He supposed that sounded selfish but really, she'd been with him only two days ago. How could she say yes to a date with Jack only two days after she'd been in his bed?

What was that Jack had said about sharing his filly? He'd been right. Trey didn't like it.

He wiped the sweat from his face, still speechless. He should be congratulating his best friend. This was exactly what Jack had wanted for a long time now.

Instead, he paced in a small circle, trying to walk off the sick feeling in his gut.

"You feeling a'ight?" Jack watched him with concern, while he was having trouble looking at Jack at all.

"Fine, just a cramp or something. I think I'm done for the day. I better head in."

"I'll walk with you. I want to get home anyhow. I've got to shower and pick up some flowers before I go get Carly. And I've got to get my bedclothes out of the dryer."

Jesus. Had Jack done laundry so his bed would be fresh for Carly tonight?

Trey bent over, braced his hands on his knees and tried his best not to vomit right there on Jack's running shoes.

~ * ~

Carly couldn't deny that Jack had been an absolutely perfect date. He'd arrived exactly on time. Not too early so she wasn't ready and not too late so she was afraid she'd been stood up.

He'd brought her a beautiful bouquet of white lilies and opened every door and pulled out every chair. He'd chosen just the right restaurant too. Not so expensive she felt obligated to him in any way, but not so cheap she'd think he was stingy either.

So why now, as he walked her to the backdoor of the bar

where the staircase to her apartment was, did she fear what was probably going to come next?

Jack stepped in close and raised his hand to her face. He stared deep into her eyes and smiled. "They're green."

His comment took her by surprise. "Yeah."

He frowned a bit. "Hmm. Why have I never noticed that before?"

The memory of how Trey had surprised her by knowing the color of her eyes the day before they left for Kosovo hit her.

Was that really just a few days ago? It seemed more like a year. So much had happened between them.

And why was she thinking about Trey?

This date was so she could move on and forget him. Although, if that were really the case, she probably shouldn't have picked his best friend to forget him with.

She looked up at Jack. What the hell was she doing?

He lowered his head a bit. "Carly, can I kiss you?"

Her heart rate sped with nervous energy as she nodded.

Jack leaned low and pressed his lips softly to hers.

He was a good kisser, both sober and drunk. His gentle, almost chaste kisses lulled her into a sense of security.

This was fine. Pleasant actually. She could do this. She could like Jack. Though why the hell was she thinking so much? She didn't remember being able to think at all the first time Trey had kissed her, or the second, for that matter.

Jack stepped even closer, his leg between hers now. He wrapped his big hands around her head and tangled them in her hair.

As he kissed her harder, his lips parted and his tongue sought hers. She stiffened at first but forced herself to relax, allowing him to kiss her the way he wanted.

Then he broke away and leaned his forehead against hers with a short laugh. "You're not doing such a good job, darlin'."

"Huh?"

"Of pretending you like me. You're trying, but you're not

really here with me, are you?"

She shook her head. "Jack—"

"Shhh. It's a'ight." He placed one finger across her lips to silence her. "I don't blame you. If I was a woman, hell, I'd be in love with him too."

He was talking about Trey. How did he know? She shook her head again to deny it, but then the tears started and there was nothing she could do about it. "I'm sorry."

"Oh, darlin'." He wrapped her in his arms and rubbed her back. "Let's go upstairs. You put on your favorite pj's, I'll tuck you on the couch under a nice blanket and then I'll make you some tea. We'll talk about you and him and what we're gonna do about it."

Through her tears she grabbed onto the one topic that wouldn't make her cry harder. "You know how to make tea?"

"Darlin', I'm southern. We invented sweet tea, or was that the mint julep?" Jack grinned and took the keys out of her hand.

CHAPTER TWENTY-ONE

Across the parking lot in his truck with the lights turned off, Trey watched Jack kiss Carly then lead her up the stairs to what he assumed was her apartment above the bar.

The fact he was basically stalking them made him realize he was a sick, sick man, both mentally and now physically too. He watched the light go on first in what looked like a living room and then in her bedroom, before she closed the blinds.

He closed his eyes and banged his head against the steering wheel. What the hell was he going to do? Jack and Carly were up there together doing who knew what.

Actually, that wasn't true. Trey knew what.

They were doing what he should be doing with her. What they'd done together in Kosovo. What they could be doing together right now if he hadn't acted like a stubborn ass and pretended their time together meant nothing more to him than a mission.

After a few more bangs of his forehead, he left his head resting there against the truck's steering wheel.

Feeling miserable and exhausted, he must have dozed off in the darkness.

He awoke with a start to the sound of someone knocking on his truck window.

Groaning, he saw it was Jack staring at him through the glass. He was so busted. How was he going to explain this?

Trey lowered the window with what he was sure was a very guilty look on his face. "Hi."

Jack shook his head and laughed. "You two stubborn fools are just incredible."

"I don't know what you're talking about."

"You and Carly, that's what. You're in love with her and either too stupid to realize it or too stubborn to admit it."

Trey sat there, chastised, and let Jack call him both stupid and stubborn. What could he say? It was true. He glanced at the clock. They'd been in her apartment for nearly two hours. What did it matter? Even if he did admit his feelings, to himself and to her, it was too late now.

Folding his arms, Jack twisted his lips into a grimace. "Well? At least admit I'm right."

"I'm sorry, Jack. I really am happy for you two. I know you care about her and you'll be good to her. She deserves a nice guy like you."

Jack shook his head. "Get out of the truck."

Obviously Jack was going to hit him again. That was all right. He deserved it. Getting out, Trey braced himself for the blow.

"Get up those stairs, you fool." Holding the truck door open for him, Jack pointed toward the entrance to Carly's.

Trey shook his head. "I don't . . . Why?"

"Because she doesn't want me, Einstein. She wants you. She always has."

Trey swallowed hard and saw a ray of hope for the first time since Jack had told him about his date with Carly. "You and she . . . You didn't . . ."

"No. Even if she hadn't been bawling her eyes out over you, I still wasn't going to sleep with her tonight. It was our first date, plus it's only two nights after she'd been with you. That's not how I roll, Trey. You know that."

Still in shock, he managed a nod. "I know."

Jack continued, "Besides, when she was kissing me, I

knew she was thinking about kissing you. I'm not willing to be anyone's second choice."

God, Jack really was a nice guy. "But you said you were falling in love with her. You were talking about marriage."

He shrugged. "Hey, I'm a lover. What can I say? I fell in love with every girl on the pep squad in high school too. I'll get over her, but you better treat her right or so help me God—"

"You'll punch me again?" Trey gingerly touched his bruised chin.

"Yeah, only this time maybe I'll actually knock you down." Jack laughed and then got serious again. "You deserve her more than I do, you know."

Trey shook his head. "I doubt it. Why would you say that?"

"She told me how that day, when I didn't know the color of her eyes, you knew. I guess I was always too busy looking at other things."

To be perfectly honest, Trey had looked at those other things too.

Jack grabbed him in a hug and then shoved him toward Carly's door. "Now hurry before she falls asleep. Poor thing's all tuckered out from crying over you."

"Thanks, Jack." Slamming the driver's side door, Trey realized he'd left the key in the ignition and the truck unlocked. Not caring, he ran across the parking lot.

After sprinting up the stairs two at a time, he was faced with Carly's door. Steeling his nerves, he knocked.

"Did you forget some—" she spoke as she pulled open the door, until she saw him standing there rather than Jack. Then her eyes widened. "Trey."

She looked just as Jack had described her—tuckered out with eyes red from crying over him. And he had never been so happy to see her.

"Hi."

"Um, hi."

Suddenly Trey felt like a shy schoolboy who didn't know

what to say to a girl. "Can I come in?"

"Sure." Carly backed up enough for him to step through the doorway.

Once inside, he couldn't wait anymore. He just spilled it all in one big whoosh. "Jack says you're in love with me. Is it true?" She looked horrified, so he rushed on. "Because I really hope it is true. Carly, I'm so in love with you it hurts to breathe."

Her eyes filled with tears as she flung herself against him. Wrapping his arms around her, he buried his face in her hair.

"Is this a yes?" He mentally crossed his fingers, hoping, until she nodded against his chest.

Relieved beyond all comprehension, Trey pulled far enough away to capture her mouth with his in a crushing kiss filled with all the possessiveness he had tried and failed to fight.

She returned his kiss with the intensity of a drowning woman looking for oxygen.

When he finally had to stop for air, she let out a teary, breathy laugh. "That's what a kiss is supposed to feel like."

Confused, Trey frowned. "I agree with you. Why? Was there ever any question about that?"

Carly shook her head. Raising her hands she touched his face as her gaze locked onto his. "No, not really."

JACK

CHAPTER ONE

Jack Gordon leaned in, about to close the deal on what he hoped would be a mind-erasing kiss—because he could really stand to erase some memories right about now.

He was just concentrating on not coughing from the overwhelming cloud of perfume that surrounded her, and now him too, when the blonde's hand on his chest stopped the downward descent of his head toward hers.

He moved back again, almost relieved she had stopped him.

She was right. This kiss was probably a really bad idea. His heart still had the bruise from watching Carly, the woman he'd had a crush on for two years, fall hard for his best friend Trey.

That was in addition to the fact that Darlene, the current near recipient of his impending kiss, worked at Carly's bar as a cocktail waitress.

Darlene held one finger in the air. "Hang on."

Sticking two fingers into her mouth, she pulled out a purple piece of chewing gum. He watched with fascination as she stuck the gum on the doorframe of the back entrance to the bar. Then she grabbed the neck of his T-shirt, yanked him to her and shoved her tongue nearly down his throat.

He was still recovering from that surprise attack when she reached down and grabbed, right through his jeans, what he considered to be his private property.

Jack jumped back, pulling his violated pelvis with him. "Whoa, there. Wait a minute, Darlene. What's the hurry?"

The cocktail waitress ran her hands up and down his chest. "But, Jackie. I've had my eye on you for years and you've never given me the time of day. Now that you've finally come to your senses, I'm not letting you get away."

He backed up, and she stepped closer, pinning him against the railing of the much too small staircase landing.

Her mouth was just closing over his again when he heard someone very loudly and obviously clearing her throat. He pulled back and looked down to see Carly standing at the bottom of the short staircase.

"Darlene, are we already closed for the night?" Carly made a show of glancing at her watch.

Jack felt his face grow hot at being caught sucking face behind the building with the waitress.

Darlene didn't seem to care though. She glanced toward Carly without blinking an eye. "No."

"Oh? Sorry, I assumed since my only cocktail waitress is out back making out with one of my customers we must be closed." Carly waited a beat. When Darlene made no move and still had yet to remove her hands from Jack's chest, she continued, "Darlene. Get inside and back to work."

Darlene rolled her eyes in a move that could probably get her fired if Carly wanted to be a hard-ass boss.

"I'll see you later," Darlene said with a wink at him before she sauntered back inside.

Jack dropped his gaze to the ground, too embarrassed to look Carly in the eye. "Sorry about that."

"It's fine. From what I saw, you were the one being attacked." She stepped up and wiped her thumb across his mouth. "Lipstick."

He rubbed his mouth and tried to ignore the knowledge

that his cheeks were most likely as red as Darlene's lipstick smeared all over his mouth. "Yeah. I can take down a man twice my size in hand-to-hand combat, but they don't teach us a defense for *that* kind of assault in training."

He dropped down and sat on the top step, running both hands over his face.

Carly sat next to him and bumped her shoulder against his. "What's wrong, Jack?"

Jack glanced sideways at her. "What makes you think something's wrong?"

She shrugged. "You just don't seem yourself lately and I never in a million years imagined Darlene was your type."

He smiled sadly. She wasn't. His type was sitting right next to him—and she belonged to his best friend.

Jack decided to change the subject before that still-raw wound opened back up. "What are you doing back here at the bar on your night off? I thought you were over at Trey's place."

"I was. Then I remembered tomorrow is the first of the month and I forgot to pay the bills. Figured I better get back here and on my computer to do it quick. I guess I'm not used to having a man in my life. It gets in the way of things like paperwork sometimes."

Jack raised a brow. Was she unhappy? And what if she were? Trey was head over heels for this girl. Jack could never pursue Carly knowing that.

Could he?

Against all logic, his heart began to beat faster as hope he shouldn't have—couldn't have—started to creep into him.

"I heard Trey asked you to move in with him. He told me you said no." Jack mentioned it casually, thinking a bit of investigation into this situation couldn't hurt. Strictly for Trey's sake, of course.

Elbows on knees, Carly rested her chin on one hand. She tilted her head toward him. "You heard right."

Jack tried to control his heart rate. Even though he had

buried them so deep it would take a backhoe to find them, Jack still had feelings for her.

Could she possibly have feelings for him too? Could they both be denying what they felt because of Trey?

"Carly, I need to know something. The reason you won't move in with him, it's not because of me, is it?"

She pressed her lips together with what? Pity?

Great. He regretted the question and his stupidity immediately.

She reached out and squeezed his hand. "No, Jack."

The pity part sucked, but besides that, her answer didn't hurt him quite as badly as he'd feared it would.

This was progress. There might be hope for his poor heart to recover yet. In fact, he felt a bit relieved. He didn't know what the hell he would have done if she'd said yes.

No man should have to choose between his best friend and a woman.

He laced his fingers with hers. "Then what's the problem, darlin'?"

"It's me." She sighed. "I'm so damn afraid of being hurt again that I'm going to end up driving away a really good man."

Jack shook his head. "I wouldn't worry about that if I were you. A stampede couldn't drive Trey away. I know that for a fact. Just like I know he would never willingly hurt you."

She looked up at him with glassy eyes. "And what if he has no choice in the matter? What if he goes away on one of his mysterious assignments and just never comes home? I was with you guys on one of your missions, remember? I know what happened to your brother Jimmy. I know what could happen to Trey."

The fear of every military wife, mother and girlfriend.

Jack breathed in deep and considered his answer. "Well, I reckon it will hurt just as bad if that happens whether you two are living together or not. The only thing you can do is try to live the life God gives you to the fullest with no regrets."

She smiled in spite of the tears making her eyes glisten. "How'd you get so smart?"

Jack smiled back at her and wiped the single teardrop from her cheek. "My brothers wouldn't agree with you, but thanks for the compliment, darlin'."

Still looking incredibly sad, Carly blew out a breath. "You're all so secretive. Would they even tell me if something did happen? Or would he just disappear and I'd never know why?"

Secrets were a part of military life, but especially so in his particular unit. Carly was correct in that. It added yet another difficulty to the already staggering challenge of trying to maintain a relationship.

"I'd never let you wonder. I'd tell you as much as I was allowed. I promise."

"Thank you." Eyes filled to brimming with tears, she leaned over and hugged him.

Feeling awkward being this close, he still couldn't resist dropping a light kiss on the top of her head. He breathed in the fresh scent of her shampoo. As he felt his heart tighten, he squeezed her once and then released her.

When he raised his eyes, he saw Trey standing at the bottom of the stairs, his expression less than happy.

Carly glanced up at Trey and wiped her eyes. "Hi. I'm sorry. I didn't even get upstairs to the computer yet to pay my bills. I'll do it right now. I'll be quick, I promise." She hopped up, planted a quick kiss on Trey's mouth and then jogged up the staircase to her apartment above the bar.

Trey pursed his lips and put one foot up on the bottom step. "So."

Jack raised a brow. "So?"

He could see the inner turmoil written all over Trey's face.

"So I know it's crazy, but I'm jealous as hell of you sitting here talking with Carly."

Jack broke out laughing. Wasn't that ironic? Trey was the

one who had Carly in his bed every night and he was jealous of Jack for sitting on the steps next to her? "Trey. There's nothing going on. You know that. She loves you. She wouldn't cheat on you."

"I know that. Besides, we're at it so often she wouldn't physically have the energy to cheat on me. Sex is not the problem with our relationship."

Jack covered his face. This was way too much information.

He looked up through his hands as Trey continued, "I'm jealous she talks to you when she doesn't talk to me. Not about the important stuff anyway. Not even to give me a reason why she won't move in with me. It's damn frustrating."

"Ask her again."

"What?" Trey frowned.

"Go upstairs and ask her to move in with you again. I think she might say yes."

Trey's eyes opened wide with hope, then he frowned suspiciously. "Why? What did she tell you?"

Jack shook his head and stood. He already seemed to be deep in between them, and he wasn't digging his own hole any deeper. He grabbed Trey by the shoulders and steered him in the direction of Carly's door. "Go."

Trey glanced back and then smiled. "Thanks, Jack. Oh, and by the way, you've got a red smudge right by your mouth."

That little reminder made up Jack's mind about what to do next. He had considered going back into the bar for another beer, but the thought of Darlene in hot pursuit sent him in the other direction, into the lot to where he'd parked his convertible.

Once safely in his car, he took a napkin out of the glove compartment. Frowning at the lipstick smudges he saw on his face reflected in the rearview mirror, he wiped hard.

The damn stuff was nearly indelible, but after he finally

got himself fairly clean, Jack fired up the engine and headed for home where he could wallow in his lonely misery in private.

At least Trey and Carly were happy. He'd work on getting himself happy later.

While driving, Jack considered the best way to do that.

Tomorrow, he'd go to the commander's office and ask to be assigned somewhere, anywhere. A little life-and-death action would do wonders to take his mind off Trey and Carly until the scar on his heart finally disappeared completely.

CHAPTER TWO

Things had been too slow lately with no missions. Not even a damn field training exercise since the team had returned from Kosovo. Maybe the commander would have an assignment for him if he asked.

The hope for some excitement carried Jack through a restless night and to the next morning as he got ready to head to base.

That was when his cell sounded with the text alert. The commander was calling the team in. He was finally about to get his wish for some action.

More than ready, Jack grabbed his keys off the hook by the apartment's door and headed outside. As his Mustang's engine roared to life, Jack's spirits rose.

His good mood lasted all the way until he walked into the meeting room, where the stormy look on the commander's face was not at all encouraging.

Jack sat and waited in silence with the others already in the room until the entire team arrived. Trey was the last one in, looking like he'd just rolled out of Carly's bed.

Great. That was an image he didn't need burned into his brain. Scowling, Jack swallowed the bitter taste of envy burning the back of his throat.

Only when everyone was seated and quiet did the

commander draw in a breath and say, "Well, boys. The pencil-pushing heads-up-their-asses idiots from Central Command have come up with yet another scheme to mess up our lives. It seems we haven't been using enough of our leave. So these idiots have decided to institute a forced furlough period for our 'mental health'."

BB Dalton frowned. "Furlough, sir?"

"Extended leave, Dalton. Three weeks to be exact. They'd wanted six weeks but I managed to talk them out of it."

Jack had to agree with the commander. Three weeks away was bad enough, but six would have been ridiculous. They all knew that skills began to degrade after a month of disuse. It was why they constantly trained to keep sharp whenever they weren't actively on a mission.

There was a general grumbling among the team, except for Trey, who leaned forward and whispered, "I'll gladly take the time. You were right last night. Carly agreed to move in with me. I want to get her moved before she changes her mind."

Wonderful. Not only was Jack not getting in on any action to take his mind off things, but he would probably end up using his three weeks of forced leave helping Trey move Carly into his place.

That was just what he needed, to carry a box full of her unmentionables into Trey's bedroom. He had to do something about this.

Jack raised his hand. "What about any assignments that come up, sir? Who will take care of them if we're all off?"

"Well, that will just teach those bastards, won't it? CentCom thinks they can stagger the different teams' furloughs and reassign anything that comes up. I think they're wrong."

Matt Coleman peered up from behind his ever-present laptop. "Obviously, sir. What if the target from Kosovo requests another face-to-face meeting with Trey? They can't reassign that. Not after the guy's already seen him on video and spoken to him on the phone."

Jack really didn't need to be reminded of Trey's last

undercover assignment. He'd never forget the image of seeing Trey and Carly together. It was seared into his brain.

"Agreed, Coleman. I'm actually hoping something exactly like that comes up to teach these assholes they should stick to pushing papers and leave the commanding to those who know what the hell they're doing. But until they learn, you boys are free for the next three weeks. Oh, and don't make yourselves too accessible. I want you all off the radar. Go home. Visit Mom. Take a transport to Fiji and soak up some sun. I don't care. Just let the guys up at Central know they really are up the creek without a paddle if they need us on short notice during this furlough. Dismissed."

Trey looked like a kid on Christmas morning as he stood. "That's it then. I'm on my way to the Exchange to check the dumpster."

"The dumpster? Um, why?" Even in his miserable and distracted state, that still caught Jack's attention.

"For some sturdy cardboard boxes to pack Carly's things in. I figure either the Exchange or the commissary probably tosses out boxes all the time. Carly's got a couple of liquor boxes in the storeroom at the bar but not nearly enough for all her stuff. You wanna come?" Trey asked, looking way too excited.

Since Trey was serious, and seriously happy about his little field trip to the dumpster in the North Carolina heat, Jack tried not to laugh in his face. "No, thanks though. Maybe I'll meet you at the bar later."

"All right. See you." Once Trey had said his goodbye and sprinted out the door in search of used boxes, Jack stood and headed in the opposite direction.

He knocked on the doorframe of the commander's open door. "Sir. May I speak with you?"

"Gordon. Come on in. I've been meaning to ask you how Jimmy's doing."

"He's doing good. He's home with Mama recuperating. He says she's driving him batty with all the mothering."

The commander smiled. "Good to hear. So, what can I do

for you, Gordon? Why aren't you already off enjoying your *furlough*?" He said the last word like it left a bad taste in his mouth.

"That's what I want to speak to you about. Is there any possibility of being assigned to another unit just for the three weeks?"

The commander raised his brows. "May I ask why?"

Jack searched for a valid reason. "I . . . need to be busy."

The commander seemed to look deep inside him. The man had the uncanny ability to do that and used it too often for Jack's liking. It was probably what made him a good leader, but it was still annoying.

"I know something's up with you, Jack. I'm not as blind as everyone thinks I am."

"No one thinks you're blind, sir." Sometimes they hoped he was, when they were bending the rules. But unfortunately for them, they always found out he wasn't.

"Yeah, sure. Anyway the problem is this is a direct order from higher up and there is no way around it. Go home, Jack. It's just a few hours drive to your hometown, right?"

"Yes, sir."

"Then go. Enjoy your mama's sweet-potato pie you're always bragging about. Spend time with Jimmy. Get away from your friend Williams, his girl and her damn bar. I think it'll do you good."

Jack tried not to let his surprise show. Were his feelings that transparent? He'd have to work on that. "Yes, sir. Thank you."

"And, Jack . . ."

Jack paused at the door and turned back toward the commander. "Sir?"

"It wouldn't have mattered if I *had* put you undercover with her in Kosovo instead of Williams. I saw them together. She was already half in love with him before they left for the mission."

The commander wasn't lying when he said he wasn't blind. In fact, Jack was starting to wonder if he was psychic, or maybe he just eavesdropped on their communications implants when they didn't know.

In any event, what the commander said about Carly and Trey was true. Deep down Jack knew that.

He blew out a breath and embraced what he'd known for a while now but had refused to accept. "Yeah. I know."

CHAPTER THREE

Driving into the city limits of his hometown after being away for a while was bound to be a strange experience. The wind in his face glanced off the sunglasses he wore as he slowed the convertible to the local speed limit and took it all in.

Jack supposed it was to be expected, but a wave of nostalgia hit him hard as he passed the high school. Good memories there. He'd been MVP of the football team the year he graduated.

Tapping the brakes, he reduced his speed further at the hairpin turn where he'd lost control of his truck and wrecked it just two weeks after getting his driver's license.

He smiled when he saw the parking area by the river where he'd lost something else with Mary Sue Barton.

But mingled with the usual hometown sense of belonging was the realization that he was a totally different person from the boy he'd been when he'd left years before. He'd seen and done so much since that time when this small town had seemed like the center of the universe to him.

Maybe the commander had been right. This little furlough trip home would be good. There were no reminders of Carly and Trey in Pigeon Hollow like there were back at the base, and it had been much too long since Jack had seen his mama.

There was an underlying homesickness living deep inside him he hadn't been aware of, but it hit him hard as he drove down the magnolia-lined drive to the house he'd been born in.

He was so happy to see his old home that his eyes got a little misty.

Damn, when had he become such a pussy? He pushed aside the thought that his emotional instability had begun just about the time he'd fallen hard for Carly, which happened to be the same time his brother had gone missing in Kosovo.

Both of those things were over now. Time to move on.

Perhaps three weeks mental-health leave would put everything in perspective and get his emotions back on track.

Jack parked by the barn, and then put up the roof before he turned off the engine. It could go from sunny to pouring rain in just minutes in the South. He'd learned the hard way not to leave his convertible top down. Not even to just run into the diner for a quick bite.

He grabbed his duffle bag out of the trunk and turned in the direction of the house, but a new colt running after its mother in the paddock just off the breeding stable caught his attention.

Jack paused to admire it. That was one thing he missed about home besides his mama. The horses.

The mare came to the fence where Jack stood watching her. She was probably hoping for an apple or carrot. He had neither, so he rubbed her nose instead.

He didn't recognize her, which made him realize he had been away too long. There was a time when he knew every horse on this property. That time had passed.

"I don't take too kindly to strangers handling my stock."

Jack spun around at the sound of his younger brother's voice and smiled. "Jared. Damn, little brother. Did you get bigger?"

All dimples, Jared grinned back. He looked broader than usual as his muscles strained the confines of his T-shirt. "Nah, I think you just shrunk some. Whatever you do all day at that super secret spy job of yours can't build muscles the way unloading and stacking two hundred bales of hay can."

"I told you, I'm not a spy." Jack dumped his duffle on the ground and hugged his younger brother hard.

"Whatever." Jared slapped him on the back before pulling away. He visually sized Jack up. "And I'm only three years younger than you, so get off the *little* thing, will you?"

Jack had first left for the service when Jared still seemed like a boy, but before him now was a man. They'd been eye level for years, but now Jared seemed as wide and broad as the barn they were standing next to.

Where Jack had followed in his older brother Jimmy's footsteps and joined the service, Jared had stayed to run the breeding stables with Mama. If he hadn't, there was no way Jack could have left his mama and the farm without help.

As much as Jack loved horses, Jared lived and breathed them. He had since before he could walk. It had been a chore just getting Jared to go to school most days. He hadn't wanted to leave the stables. He'd sleep there too if a mare was close to foaling.

It was because of Jared's dedication that Jack didn't feel guilty being away so much.

Still, he should try to get home more often. It was obvious from the tightness in his chest he missed the place more than he realized.

Jack pushed the serious thoughts aside and hooked a boot heel on the bottom rail of the white painted fence. "This new mare's a beauty and the colt looks like a real winner."

Leaning on the fence, Jared mirrored Jack's pose. "Yeah. Good stock, this one. Not that you know winners. If I remember right, you always bet the underdog."

Jack smiled. Always betting the underdog had won him a few sizeable payoffs. He didn't tend to remember all the times he lost.

"So what brings you home?" Jared turned and picked up Jack's duffle for him. As Jack followed, Jared carried it toward the house.

"The head shed got the bright idea that we all needed a few weeks off to recharge or something. But I've been wanting to check up on Jimmy anyway. How is he?"

"Miserable. Old Doc Jackson won't let him do much of anything, which is killing him. I keep finding him sneaking down here to the stables when Mama's not looking."

Jack laughed. "That sounds like Jimmy."

Jared nodded. "Of course, his sudden interest in the horses might have something to do with the new hand I just hired. She's a looker and man oh man she's hot enough to heal what ails you. Quiet though and real secretive. Can't get anything out of her, including where she's from. But she's real good with the horses. That's all that matters to me."

His brother's description of this new hire raised Jack's suspicions immediately. He'd have to meet this elusive beauty and figure out what she was hiding and why.

He nearly tripped over his own feet as that thought made him realize a few things. First off, he'd been in special operations too long if he was suspicious of everyone, even a woman he'd never met.

Second, he obviously wasn't over Carly yet if his only goal regarding this supposedly sizzling hot woman was to get information out of her instead of getting her out of her clothes.

Jack followed Jared to the back door and sighed.

Time. That's all it would take to move on. Just time.

Then he caught a whiff of something incredible baking. Maybe time *and* some of his mama's pie.

Speaking of Mama . . . She screamed when she saw him, rushing forward to fling her arms around his neck before she pulled back and slapped him hard on his arm.

"Why didn't you call and say you were fixin' to come home?" She frowned even as she hugged him again. "Sit down. The pie is just out of the oven."

He laughed. That was Mama. Not that she was really angry with him for not calling before he came home. But even if she had been, she still would have fed him pie.

"Thanks, Mama. I was dreaming about your pie the whole drive here." He sat in the same chair he'd sat in to eat for as long as he could remember and glanced back to where she stood at the counter, knife poised to impale the golden brown piecrust. "So where you got Jimmy stashed? I'm sure he's drooling by now. It would be just plain cruel not to share with him."

"*Jimmy* can fend for himself. Thank you."

Jack looked around to see his Jimmy standing in the doorway, smiling and speaking of himself in the third person. His face still showed the yellow tinge of healing bruises, but he looked good. Way better than he had the last time Jack had seen him, half-dead on a backboard being strapped into a military transport heading for the hospital in Germany.

Standing, Jack hugged his older brother hard. Too hard, he realized when Jimmy's breath whooshed out.

Jimmy winced but tried to dismiss the obvious pain with a crooked grin. "Coupla' broken ribs."

"Jeez, Jimmy. I'm sorry."

Slapping Jack hard on the back, Jimmy proved he was okay. "No problem. Bones heal, little brother. We both know that. Now where's that pie I've been smelling for the last half hour?"

Jimmy walked with a slight but noticeable limp to the table, pulling out his usual chair before easing himself into it. Maybe he was still hurting more than he let on. But he was home and safe and that was good enough for now.

Jared had already grabbed forks and plates for them all and was sitting waiting for their mother to cut the pie.

Jack sat between his two brothers at the same oak kitchen table he'd eaten at since he was born. While his mama slid a piece of her famous sweet-potato pie onto one of his grandma's china plates, he decided the commander had been right. This visit home might be just what he needed.

CHAPTER FOUR

Nicki leaned against the fence, watching the newborn in the corral with his mother. She sighed and tried to pinpoint what she was feeling, finally deciding on a single word to describe it.

Contentment.

Finally, for the first time in a month of being on the run, she felt moderately safe, without the weight of heart pounding fear riding her twenty-four-seven.

Although she feared she would never be truly safe again—not as long as the man she was hiding from still lived and breathed—at least she could allow herself to relax just a little bit here at the farm.

She was about as far from New York as she could get. Who would think to look for her buried away here in the Deep South on a small horse-breeding farm? Certainly not the thick-necked imbecile she'd run from.

As long as the Gordon family accepted her without question, and continued to pay her in cash and give her a place to live, she was set. She could drop off the radar indefinitely.

The colt walked slowly up to the fence and nuzzled her hand. She ran her fingers over him. "You are such a sweetie."

"Why, thank you, darlin'."

The deep voice caused Nicki to startle. She let out a squeak of fear, spooking the colt. He took off running for his mother.

She spun to look at the stranger, heart thundering until she saw his face. He was so much like the other two Gordon brothers, right down to the way he stood and talked, she knew who he was immediately.

Relieved, and feeling a little silly for thinking her enemies could have found her, she smiled in greeting. "You must be Jack."

He raised a brow. "I must be. It seems you know me, but who might you be, darlin'?"

Mmm, mmm. How she loved the way southern men talked. So much nicer than the horrid accents she'd grown up around in New York. The accents from the five boroughs of New York City and Long Island made her cringe. But a southern man could practically make a girl's panties fall right off just by talking to her.

She nearly shook herself to regain her senses. She was in hiding. This was no time to be thinking about romance, or sex, or whatever this feeling was that Jack caused deep inside her in places long dormant. Besides that, this particular Gordon man was only here temporarily from what she'd heard.

Good thing too. He was much too yummy and tempting to have around for very long. She sure did like the way he called her darlin' though.

"I'm Nicki." She offered him her hand.

His handshake was warm and slow. But then, everything in the south seemed warm and slow. Nicki imagined what else might be warm and slow with Jack.

"Nicki . . ." He apparently wanted her to elaborate.

She scrambled to provide the false name she'd settled on when she'd first come to the farm. "Camp. Nicki Camp."

The guilt of the lie hit her hard.

Did it show as obviously on her face as it felt on her tongue? If it did sound like a lie to him, the expression on

Jack's face didn't show it.

He was still holding her hand in his big, strong one when he crooned, "Nice to meet you, Nicki Camp."

Slightly shaky, she pulled her hand back and then glanced up at his face again. His hair was golden brown like his brothers, but Jack's hazel eyes had more green in them and flecks of gold.

Stop it, Niccolina.

She had to remind herself she was in no position to be checking this guy out. No matter how cute and charming he was.

"So what brings you here to our little town of Pigeon Hollow, Miss Nicki Camp? Because you sure don't sound like you're a local girl."

Nicki considered her answer carefully. She didn't think she had a typical New York accent. As a teenager, she'd worked damn hard to make sure of that. It had been important to her then because she'd wanted to sound more sophisticated.

It was even more important now. It was a matter of life and death that no one knew where she was from. But Jack was right. She didn't sound like someone born south of the Mason-Dixon line. She didn't think she could pull off sounding like a native southerner no matter how long she worked down here.

"Oh, you know. I'm just traveling around. Seeing the country." Yeah, that didn't sound too lame.

He took one step closer, and she resisted the urge to take a step back as he towered over her.

"Well, I sure am glad you decided to settle here for a bit during your travels." He smiled, his eyes twinkling.

Nicki felt her cheeks warm at the attention. Another few minutes of this onslaught of charm and Nicki didn't know what she'd do.

Thank goodness, Jared chose that moment to interrupt them. Otherwise, she might have swooned like in all those old movies where the southern gentleman made the belle of the ball faint from sheer charm alone.

"Steer clear of my help before you scare her away." Jared shot Jack a stern look, and then smiled and winked in her direction.

She decided to make a joke of her own and get the hell out of there before Jack wedged her any more between him and the fence. "Not much scares me, except my boss finding me loafing around not doing my job. I better get back to it."

Jared laughed. "Yeah, I'm such a tough boss. But actually, I do have something I'd like you to take a look at. One of the boys just told me old Bucky is lying down in the pasture and won't get up. He said he noticed Bucky limping for the last few days. I was just on my way out there if you want to come with me."

Old Bucky was an apt name for the animal. The horse had to be thirty-five if he was a day, but he was sweet. Nicki hated the thought that anything might be wrong with him.

"I learned how to ride on Bucky." Jack joined them as they started walking.

She could see by the concern on Jack's face that he loved the horse as much as his brother did.

"We all did, even Jimmy. But he's old now, Jack. We have to face the fact it might be time . . ." Jared let the sentence trail off. No one there needed him to spell out what it might be time for. "I haven't called the vet yet. I want to check him out for myself first."

They reached the pasture and found Bucky lying right out in the middle under the hot sun. Nicki approached slowly, speaking softly to him. She saw him watching her out of the corner of his eye, but he didn't make a move to get up.

She leaned down and stroked his neck. "What's wrong, old guy?"

The whites of his eyes were showing. He wasn't happy about the three of them hovering over him, but he wasn't getting up either.

Nicki dropped to her knees and noticed the two men hanging back, watching her.

If they were testing her to see if she knew what she was

doing when it came to horses, she had nothing to worry about.

Her daddy raised racehorses on a farm on Long Island. She'd spent every weekend and every summer in his barns or at the stalls at the racetrack. She didn't know much about a lot of things, but she knew horses.

Nicki leaned low and pressed her ear against Bucky's side. She listened and then straightened up. "I'm hearing plenty of belly noises. It's not colic or an obstruction. Jared, you said the guys saw him limping?"

"Yup." Jared nodded.

Nicki ran her hands down each of Bucky's four legs, all the while under the watchful eyes of the three males—those being the two Gordon men and Bucky. She got to the last foot and stopped.

She drew in a breath of relief. "His hoof has a hot spot. I'm betting it's an abscess. It hurts him to stand. That's why he's down and it would explain why he's lame."

Standing, she brushed the dirt from the knees of her jeans. Jared walked over, bent and felt the hoof for himself.

He shook his head as he squatted down to pat Bucky's neck. "I thought it looked like that new blacksmith cut his hooves too short."

"Yeah, I didn't like the way he handled the horses either. The infection will have to work its way out, but at least you won't have to call the vet to put Bucky down."

Jared stood. "You're right about that. That makes you employee of the day." He grinned. "You just earned yourself the rest of the day off."

"Thanks, Jared. That's really not necessary." What would she do with a day off? It's not like she had friends to visit. Or even a car to go anywhere. "I would like to see if we could get him up and in a stall though. He'll be more comfortable out of the hot sun."

Nicki was trying to ignore the fact that Jack was standing just off to the side, watching her much too closely. Cute or not, this Gordon was a bit too observant for her liking.

As if he knew what she was thinking, he wandered closer. "You know your stuff. Where'd a northerner like you learn so much about horses?"

Shit.

Deciding offense was the best defense she cocked up one brow. "First of all, who said I was a northerner? Second, there are horses in other parts of the country besides the south, you know."

With that, she escaped any further discussion into her background.

Coaxing Bucky into getting up worked well to distract them all. It took all three of them, along with lots of shouting and butt slapping—Bucky's butt, not hers—to get him up and moving, though slowly, toward the barn.

Once they settled him in the stall, he lay down on the fresh wood shavings Nicki had put in that morning after cleaning the stalls.

Jared made one more offer for her to take the remainder of the day off and this time she agreed. She needed to get away from Jack and his probing stare.

She asked to borrow a truck and headed into town with the excuse that she had errands to run. But her main errand was to avoid Jack.

CHAPTER FIVE

Jack watched as Nicki sped out of the drive in one of the Gordon Equine pick-up trucks. She was a cute one, just like Jared had said, and she was also lying.

Oh, yeah, she knew horses all right. Her performance with Bucky had proven that. But it had been pretty obvious that was exactly what she'd been trying to do—prove herself by performing for them both.

She'd also successfully avoided answering any of Jack's questions about why she was there and where she'd come from. Her accent screamed northerner to him, most likely New York, although she tried to hide it.

He would bet the farm that Nicki Camp was not her real name. She was not only a liar. She was a darn poor one at that. The way she hesitated before answering his questions. Her avoidance of direct eye contact. Her evasiveness. It all screamed deception.

At least it did to Jack, who'd been trained to not only lie, but to spot lies in others.

The worst part was Jared didn't seem to notice or care.

A horrible thought struck Jack. "Jared, what do you think about this Nicki?"

Jared turned from where he'd been setting up a fan to blow into Bucky's stall so the flies wouldn't bother him. "I think she knows her stuff and I'm damn lucky to have her. Why?"

"You, ah, into her? On a personal level, I mean." It was bad enough to have someone who was so obviously hiding something working for his family and living on their property to boot. But if his little brother had a thing for her, it would be even worse when they found out what she was hiding.

Jared's brow furrowed. "Why?"

Jack breathed out in exasperation. "Can't you just answer a question?"

"Can't you?" Jared glared back.

Jack bit the side of his mouth to stop from laying into his annoying little brother. He regrouped. No use getting Jared upset now. Jack could investigate this girl on his own, then tell Jared about it later when he found out what was what.

"A man doesn't steal his brother's girl." Jack smiled at his brother and lied through his teeth. "I just need to know where you stand when it comes to Nicki. I'm going to be here for a few weeks. A man can make a lot of progress in that time."

Jared broke into a wide grin. "Well, it's about time you showed some interest in a nice girl for a change after some of those cheerleaders you dated back in high school. Thank God you didn't marry any of them. No, I'm not interested in Nicki that way. I decided the day I hired her that it would be wrong to date an employee. Besides, there's a little filly in town I've been um . . . *seeing* lately."

Jack smiled, happy for his brother and his *filly*, but even more relieved that Jared hadn't fallen for Nicki. "What about Jimmy? You said he's sneaking down here a lot."

Jared shrugged. "You'll have to ask him about that. Could be he just has cabin fever from being cooped up for so long. Go for it with Nicki if you want. You've got my blessing. Just don't do anything that'll make her quit on me. She's too good to lose." He turned back to Bucky and shook his head. "To think I was ready to put him down and it's only an abscess."

Jack was grateful about that too, but even more resolved

to get to the bottom of this as soon as possible.

He stepped out of the barn while Jared stayed inside talking to one of the men.

Outside and out of earshot, Jack pulled out his cell phone. Scrolling through his contact list, he found the name of the one man most likely to deliver the answers he needed and fast. He hit the button and listened to the ringing and the eventual, "Hello."

"Hey, Matt. How you doing?"

Matt replied with a groan. "I'm bored as hell on this damn furlough, that's how I'm doing. What about you?"

"I'm home at my mama's place and I think I've got something that's right up your alley, oh god of the computer world."

"Lay it on me, brother." Matt's excitement radiated through the cell phone.

"I need everything you can find out about a new employee my brother hired, but I gotta warn you, I don't have much."

"That's okay. I love a good challenge. Give me what you've got."

Jack fed Matt what information he could and texted him the photo he'd snapped of Nicki while she'd been busy with Bucky. Cell phones with built-in cameras came in handy at times like this.

"How long do you think it'll take?" Jack asked.

He could hear clicking as Matt typed on his ever-present computer keyboard. "Well, I can tell you right now you're right about her name. There's no Nicki Camp. It's fake. I don't know how long. The photo should help, and the fact that you're pretty sure she's originally from the northeast. I'll get back to you when I have something."

"Great. Thanks, Matt. I really appreciate this."

"Thank *you*. You might have saved me from going insane during my mental-health leave."

Jack laughed. He and Matt said goodbye and hung up.

He knew his teammate well. If there was something to be found on this girl, Matt would find it, no matter how deep he had to dig.

With that thought in mind, Jack headed inside the house to feel out his older brother about his opinion regarding Nicki. A pretty young thing like her would be real tempting to a man recovering from what Jimmy had gone through. Jack really hoped he was wrong about her as he knocked on Jimmy's open bedroom door.

"So, little brother, you've got the hots for Nicki?"

Jack stopped dead in the doorway and stared at Jimmy. "What?"

From his position on the bed, Jimmy grinned. He waved his cell phone at Jack. "Jared just called me from the barn."

"Great." Jack rolled his eyes. "I'm glad to see you two are putting modern technology to such good use. I guess you're too busy gossiping like a couple of old washwomen, so I'll leave."

Turning toward the hall, Jack pretended he was going to leave.

"Don't you dare go." Jack paused in the doorway until Jimmy said, "I'm sorry. I'm just bored and you and Nicki together would put a little excitement in my sad life."

He pivoted back with an exaggerated sigh. "Oh, a'ight."

Coming back into the room Jack flopped backward into the upholstered chair next to the bed. Jimmy lay on top of the covers with a book open in his lap. His left foot was propped up on a pillow. That was the ankle that had been broken by the bastard terrorists while they'd had Jimmy in captivity.

The memory of that twisted Jack's gut. He glanced at Jimmy's face and the fading bruises there angered him all over again. "How much longer did the doc say he wants you laid up like this?"

"No idea. It has something to do with my spleen." Jimmy shook his head. "The broken bones, I can handle. The bruises, who cares? But this internal stuff . . . there's nothing I can do about that but just wait it out, I guess."

Jack nodded and decided to bring the subject back around to Nicki, but on his terms this time. "While you're waiting it out, aren't you a little tempted by Nicki yourself?"

Jimmy's room overlooked the barns. He'd have a great view right here from his bed of Nicki's jean-clad ass sauntering around all day long as she did her chores.

Jimmy shrugged. "I guess I haven't been feeling all that romantic lately. It's gonna take a bit of time before I'm back in the saddle again. Besides, she's a bit on the young side for me."

Being cooped up while on his medical leave obviously hadn't done Jimmy's mental health any good. Jack was going to have to speak with the doc himself, privately, and see just how bad Jimmy really was.

Maybe it would be all right to take him out for a drive or something. A change of scenery might do him good as long as it couldn't do any damage to him, physically.

What the hell did a spleen do anyway? Jack didn't know, but damaged spleen or not, Jimmy had managed to get himself into the kitchen for pie today.

Mama's pie was strong motivation, no matter what the consequences. Hopefully that little trip hadn't done him any harm.

"Jack, if you're holding back because of me, don't." Jimmy interrupted Jack's thoughts on pie and mysterious organs. "Go for it. I give you my blessing with Nicki."

"That's what Jared said." Jack held in a sigh.

He knew his brothers well enough to realize he'd have both of them hell-bent on fixing him up with a girl he was only pretending to like so he could secretly investigate her. And he'd only been home a few hours.

The next few weeks should be mighty interesting.

CHAPTER SIX

Nicki spent two days trying to avoid Jack. The man seemed to be everywhere.

Not that he wasn't adorable, because he was, and sexy. Hell, he practically melted her every time he came up, actually snuck up, behind her with a *hey, darlin'*.

The problem was his constant questions.

The other two Gordon brothers had been easy to lie to. They took her and her story at face value, never pushing for more.

Not Jack. He must have made a thousand subtle inquiries, all purred out in that sexy southern drawl of his.

Maybe being on the run had made her paranoid. Maybe Jack was only interested in learning more about her because he liked her.

That would have been welcome attention at any other time in her life, but not now. Now secrecy was the only thing keeping her safe.

Bad timing, that's what this was. If they had met at any other time, in any other situation, she would have flirted her butt off with him.

Flirting. Maybe that was still a good idea.

If she could blind him with her sex appeal, maybe he'd stop prying into her past. She glanced down at her mucking boots, sunken ankle-high in mud and manure, and laughed at that ridiculous idea.

Sex appeal. Yeah, right.

She dragged the heavy hose behind her and refilled the water tub in one of the far paddocks where the stallions were turned out. She doubted Jack would follow her all the way out here and she could use a few minutes away from his prodding.

"Hey, Nicki."

Hearing the male voice suddenly close behind her made her jump. Turning, she breathed in relief to see it was a Gordon brother, but not Jack. "Jared. Hey."

"So, now that I've got you alone, what do you think of my brother?"

Jeez. Could she never get away from Jack, even when he wasn't there? She decided to play coy. "You know I like Jimmy."

Jared grinned. "You're a smart one, Nick, and you know very well I wasn't talking about Jimmy. What do you think of our Jack?"

"I think he's not going to be around here long enough for me to think anything about him. That's what I think." She hoped that would end this line of questioning.

She'd thought she was safe with Jared. Who knew he was a matchmaker? And was the question Jared's idea to begin with?

What if Jack had put Jared up to this because he really did have a thing for her?

If Jack wasn't suspicious, just interested, she didn't know what to do because the facts remained the same. She was in hiding. Making romantic connections, opening up to anyone about her past, getting tied down to one place and one person, was not an option. Even if she did wish it were.

Jared continued to watch her as she devoted more than the necessary attention to filling the tub.

She finally couldn't take it any longer. "Was there something else, Jared, besides your interest in my opinion of your brothers?"

He smiled broader and shook his head. "Nah. That was pretty much it. Oh, and Bucky's abscess broke through. He's up and standing in the stall again."

Thank goodness he was back to talking about work. This she could handle. "That's great. I'll turn him out into the paddock when I'm done here."

"Do that later. The new mare I bought is in heat and ready to be bred. I'm fixin' to bring the lucky stud over to her." Jared hooked a thumb in the direction of the paddock containing the stud in question. "Since this mare's an unknown, I wouldn't mind an extra hand around in case she's a kicker."

Nicki raised a brow. "So you *are* here for something besides bothering me?"

He grinned while slipping open the gate. "Yup, but bothering you is so much fun I decided to do that too."

Jared hooked the lead rope she hadn't noticed him holding to a beautiful black Arabian's halter and led him out of the paddock. Nicki secured the gate behind them, then ran to shut off the water to the hose.

When she caught up with him and the stallion, Jared glanced sideways at her. "So, you like Jimmy more than Jack then."

She couldn't help but laugh at his persistence. "Whose side are you on, anyway? Jack's or Jimmy's?"

"I'm on my own side. I figure if I can marry you off to one of my two brothers, you'll never quit on me *and* I won't have to pay you anymore."

Nicki laughed again. She didn't have plans to marry anyone at the moment, but she did like it here. She only hoped she could stick around for a while.

CHAPTER SEVEN

Jack had been helping out in the barns since his arrival home for two reasons. First, he truly did miss being around the horses when he was away. Second, and most important, it was where Nicki usually could be found.

Matt was taking longer to find information on her than Jack had expected. While waiting for Matt's call—and boy, did he wish Matt would hurry the hell up and call—Jack had figured he could do a little digging himself.

He'd have to be more careful though. He'd noticed Nicki was starting to avoid him. He was pushing too hard.

Maybe he'd lost his touch when it came to flirting. Usually women fell at his feet. Well, all women except for Carly. She hadn't, but that had been a special situation.

Sighing, Jack was about to start feeling sorry for himself again when he spotted Nicki and Jared walking across the field with the stud horse Jared had been going on and on about for days.

Jack's heart kicked into high gear at the sight of Nicki. Damn, she looked good in those jeans. It was a darn shame she was most likely hiding something.

"Hey, darlin'," he greeted her when they were close enough.

Jack noticed Jared smirk at him as he continued into the paddock with the stallion. When Nicki went to follow him in,

Jack stepped forward and stopped her with a hand on her arm. "Stay out here where it's safe. There's plenty of men in there already. Jared doesn't need you too."

She didn't seem to like that one bit. Her brow furrowed as she shook his hand off her arm. "He asked me to help."

Inside the paddock, Jared handed the stallion off to two farm hands. "Jack's right, Nicki. Stay there for now and I'll call you if I need you."

She screwed up her pretty mouth in a pout and leaned against the rail, leaving a good few feet between herself and Jack. He closed that distance fast enough and leaned next to her. She pretended not to notice, but she did. He saw her body tense even as she pretended he wasn't there.

As a second lead rope was hooked to the antsy stallion's halter, she watched, wide-eyed. Two men held him now as the horse, who knew something was up, started to rear.

The mare was still locked up in the barn, but it was very obvious the stud horse could smell her from out here. He was, understandably, becoming more spirited, not to mention visibly excited.

Was she blushing as she stared at the impressive stud? As much as she knew about horses, it seemed she wasn't all that versed in the breeding process.

Jack asked, "You ever see a mare bred before?"

She didn't look at him, but shook her head. "We always used frozen transported sperm and artificial insemination on our mares. We never had to deal with the stallion."

He had to contain his excitement. She'd just spilled a whole lot of clues he could give Matt. She must have worked on a breeding farm, and a pretty big one too, if she knew about artificial insemination and transported sperm.

"And who's *we*, darlin'? What farm was this?"

She glanced at him then looked away just as fast, shaking her head. "It was a tiny farm. I'm sure you've never heard of it."

"What's the name? Maybe I have."

"It was so tiny, it didn't have a name. Just an old farmer

with a few mares, that's all." She dismissed his question with a wave of a hand that was meant, he supposed, to look casual.

Another lie. At ten thousand bucks a pop minimum, there was no way some old farmer on a little no name farm was using artificial insemination to breed his mares.

He didn't have time to pursue this latest fallacy, since just then Jared brought the mare out on a lead, but kept her on the other side of the fence. He walked her past the stallion who was doing what he could to get to her in spite of the two farmhands holding him and the fence separating them.

Nicki had definitely not been lying when she said she'd never seen breeding done the old-fashioned way. Her eyes widened at the sight.

"What Jared is doing is kind of introducing the mare to the stallion. That's also how you can tell if she's really in season. It's called teasing. If she is in heat and is going to accept him, she'll show for him." Jack narrated the amorous equine action for Nicki. As if on cue, the mare sashayed her butt in front of the stallion and lifted her tail, holding it to one side. He watched Nicki blush darker as he continued, "Just like that."

Jared brought the mare into the paddock.

"He's going to keep a hold on her so he can pull her away if necessary. Since he's never bred her before, he's not sure she won't kick at the stallion instead of stand for him. But he's already pulled off her rear shoes just in case. If she kicks, she won't do as much damage." Jack glanced down at Nicki. "She could also strike out forward, toward the person holding her on the lead rope, so Jared has to watch out for himself too. That's why neither of us wanted you in there until you're used to the procedure."

She glanced up at him and then quickly toward the action in the paddock. It was starting to really heat up. He watched Nicki's eyes drop to the ground as the stallion mounted the mare and began thrusting.

It was over quick enough, but Nicki looked like she was ready to crawl into a hole by the time it was done. Jack had been watching horses being bred for as long as he could remember and never thought twice about it.

Meanwhile, Nicki reacted as if she were watching the filming of a porno movie.

The two men brought the stallion back out to the far paddock, Jared led the mare to her stall and it was all over.

Nicki mumbled something about having to get Bucky and left Jack to consider all he'd learned and wonder. She was a strange mix of city girl and horsewoman . . . and where the hell was Matt with his answers about her past?

Jack pulled out his cell and dialed. Maybe if he kept pestering Matt, he'd get working a little harder on this.

Matt answered the phone after the first ring. "I was just picking up the phone to call you. I've got her." Jack's heart pounded faster as Matt said,"Niccolina Campolini. Born in Brooklyn, New York to Nicholas Campolini, who trains racehorses on Long Island."

Jack let out a long, slow whistle. "Wow."

Little old farmer, his ass. He'd heard of the Campolinis. They trained at Belmont racetrack and had a few champions come out of their stables.

"And get this," Matt continued. "It seems someone filed a missing persons report on her about a month back. A classmate of Niccolina's called the police after she missed her final exam for an equine vet class she was taking at night school. When the police questioned her father, he told them she was fine. He said she was away on some family emergency, so they dropped it."

"So what's really going on? Why is she here mucking stalls and using a fake name?" Jack's stomach clenched as a sick thought struck him. "Do you think her father was messing around with her and she had to run?"

"I don't know, Jack. But from what you've said about her not answering any questions, it seems she doesn't want to be found."

"That rotten, cowardly, son of a—"

"Jack, I recognize that tone of voice. Do not even think of going to New York and dealing out justice yourself. First of all, you don't know that her father did anything wrong. Second, this Campolini has got mob ties. That might not mean much to a southern boy like you, but take it from a New Yorker. You don't want to mess with those guys."

When Jack didn't answer, Matt said, "Jack. I want you to promise me you won't do anything."

"Sure. No problem. Thanks for the info, Matt."

"Why am I not convinced?" Matt sounded skeptical.

"Because you're a suspicious bastard?" Jack asked.

Matt laughed. "No, because I know you. Let me make you a deal. You don't do anything on your own without talking to me first. If you're going to do something stupid, you might need backup."

Jack smiled. "You really are bored."

"No. Well, yes, but I'm more interested in preventing you from starting a war with the mob."

"A'ight, I promise. That good enough?" It wouldn't hurt to humor Matt for now. Jack could decide if he was going to proceed on his own or if he really did need backup later.

"It'll have to do. I'm checking in with you every day and I think I'll be calling you on your mama's house phone from now on. Make sure you're actually where you say you are."

Matt, his friend and teammate, didn't trust him? Even if he was planning on going off on his own to handle this thing, Jack still frowned at that thought. "You don't have my mama's house phone number."

"Jack, really, you insult me. I'll talk to you tomorrow. Say hi to Jimmy for me." Then the line went dead.

He shook his head and walked toward the house. Matt was right. Finding a listed phone number was no challenge for anyone, but particularly not for Matt the computer god.

Besides, Jack wouldn't put it past Matt to resort to using his implanted GPS tracker to locate him if he had to.

He needed a few minutes and a cold glass of sweet tea to mull over this latest information. Nicki's lies took on a whole new color now that he'd learned more about her.

Suddenly, she went from wearing a black hat to a white one in his mind.

As his natural instinct to protect her kicked in strong, the questions remained. How did he protect her without letting her know he'd investigated her? And would she even let him help?

CHAPTER EIGHT

It was hot. Not just normal hot like it got at home in New York in the summer, but beastly, sauna kind of hot. It felt like she'd stuck her head in a pizza oven.

Nicki let out a breath, but even her own breathing seemed to raise the temperature.

She leaned against a fence in the shade and wiped the back of her hand over her forehead, ignoring the fact she'd probably just left a lovely dirt streak there.

"How you doing?" The deep sultry voice came from behind her.

Speaking of hot . . .

His hotness didn't overshadow that Jack had managed to sneak up without her hearing him once again. It was like the guy walked on air.

"It's hot," she complained, not in the mood to hide her discomfort and pretend she was happy with the climate in the south.

Jack laughed. "Oh, darlin', by the calendar it's not even summer yet. What're you going to do then?"

"Die. Or get a job in the frozen-food section of the grocery store in town."

He shook his head. "Nope. I can't let you do that. Jared

would kill me if I let you quit over a little heat."

"A little heat?" She glared at him for that understatement.

Though he didn't look uncomfortably warm at all. Thin blood, she decided, from living here his entire life.

He reached out and grabbed her hand. "Come on. I know how to cool you off."

She dug in her feet but lost the battle as he pulled her along behind him. "Wait. Where are we going?"

It wasn't that she didn't trust him. She did. Over the last few days, they'd settled on a kind of unspoken truce. He'd stopped with the questions, and she'd stopped avoiding him. But since this heat wave had hit overnight, she honestly was too hot to move.

"You'll see."

"Is it far?"

He shot her a glance. "No. And don't look so miserable. You're not going to melt from the heat. I promise."

They crossed the field beneath the brutally hot sun until they were beneath a stand of pine trees. She was happy to be in the shade again and even happier when they broke out through the trees and she spotted Jack's destination.

He stopped in front of a big, beautiful and, most important, cool-looking pond shaded by a giant willow tree.

She took another step forward. "It's like heaven."

He smiled down at her. "And it's fed by an underground spring, so it's always cold."

That information nearly sent her running into the water fully clothed. She wouldn't do that but taking off her boots, hiking up her jeans, and wading in far enough to get her feet wet was definitely an option.

She'd just turned to thank him when she noticed Jack stripping off his shirt while kicking off his own boots.

"I don't have a suit," she said.

He grinned. "Neither do I, but don't worry. We're not formal around here."

Her eyes widened. "You don't mean . . ."

Surely he didn't intend to jump in naked. Did he?

He paused with his hand on the top button of his jeans and looked at her. "Don't tell me you've never been skinny dipping before?"

"Okay, I won't tell you." She kicked at the dirt and tried not to notice the muscles of his bare chest. Swallowing hard, she forced her gaze back up to his face.

He paused, then bent and retrieved his discarded shirt and boots. "Okay. I'll give you some privacy." He turned back toward the way they'd come when she put one hand on his arm and stopped him.

The sun glinted off the sheen of sweat on his face proving he wasn't as immune to the heat as she'd thought. It wouldn't be fair to make him leave. He was just as uncomfortable as she was, and it was his family's pond.

"No. You don't have to leave." She hesitated, then asked. "So, you do this a lot? Skinny dip?"

He cocked his head to the side. "I was swimming in this pond naked before I could walk."

"With girls?"

"Yup." He shrugged. "Just another rite of passage. It's really not a big deal around here. Now going to the local drive-in for a first date with a girl—*that's* a big deal."

She looked toward the water and could practically feel it against her skin, cooling her right down to the core. "Okay. Let's do it."

He smiled. "Good for you, darlin'. You really haven't lived 'til you've jumped into a cool pond on a hot day."

She kicked off her rubber mucking boots that made her sweaty feet feel as if she'd stepped in a swamp and paused with her hands on her jeans' button.

Jack pulled his pants off. While she stood frozen in shock, he stood in nothing but his boxers.

"Um, Jack?"

He raised a brow. "Yeah?"

"You are a gentleman, aren't you?"

He laughed, a sound that started deep in his chest and kind of bubbled out. "Darlin', I'm southern."

With that he pulled off the boxers and she got quite a view of his white ass cheeks as he ran for the pond. With a whoop, he dove in head first, naked as the day he was born.

She couldn't help but be jealous of the sheer abandon of the move as he swam, smooth as an eel under the water.

Hoping there were no actual eels in there she stripped naked and dove in herself while he wasn't looking.

Nicki broke the surface and shook the wet hair out of her eyes. "This is amazing."

He swam circles around her. "Told you so. When are you gonna start trusting me, darlin'?"

She treaded water and spun to follow his motion as he moved slowly around her. "I do trust you."

Her words had come out softly but he'd obviously heard them. He stopped swimming and just bobbed. "You do?"

Uh, oh. When had this gotten serious? "Of course. You've never given me reason not to. Your entire family has taken me in as one of their own. Why wouldn't I trust you?"

He looked like he wanted to say something more, but instead he just shrugged and starting swimming around her again.

"Um, Jack?"

"Yeah?"

"How do we dry off so we can get dressed again?"

Tight jeans and wet skin did not mix well.

He stopped swimming and grinned. "Sunshine, darlin'. Sunshine."

"Oh." She'd been afraid that might be his answer.

CHAPTER NINE

Jack gazed at the twinkling, star-filled sky. He never saw night skies quite like this back on base. Too close to the city lights.

Only in the country could a person see stars as clear and bright as these.

He glanced up and noticed the light on in Nicki's room over the barn and thought back to their little dip in the pond. How they'd lain next to each other in the grass afterward.

Being a gentleman, he'd kept his gaze on the sky. Well, most of the time. He smiled at the memory of the expanse of smooth pale skin he'd glimpsed when she'd bent to retrieve her clothing off the grass.

He didn't get views like *that* back at the base either.

That image of her had Jack walking in the direction of the barn. He climbed the exterior stairs to her door and knocked, then realized he probably should identify himself too so he wouldn't scare her.

If she were on the run, which it was pretty clear she was, a knock on her door in the dark could scare the hell out of her.

"It's Jack." He heard her throw the locks before the door swung open.

"Hey, Jack." She stood in the doorway wearing nothing but a tank top and short shorts.

Her black wavy hair was damp. She must have just showered, unless she'd snuck back to the pond for another dip. He liked the thought of that.

He peeked past her into the room and saw she had a fan in the window. At least that would keep it from getting beastly hot in there, but it was still not cool by any stretch of the imagination.

Jared needed to buy her an air conditioner for that window.

He'd mention it to his brother tomorrow. Tonight, he had other plans. "I've come to take you out, darlin'. The show starts at the drive-in in twenty minutes."

Jack still hadn't decided what to do about her situation back in New York. Hell, he hadn't even determined exactly what that situation was. He'd made up his mind. She was safe for now working here.

He would most likely tell his brother about what he'd learned before he left. Jared would make sure her identity stayed secret while keeping an eye out for her.

For now though, the least Jack could do was try to make her life here a little bit happier. His plan seemed to be working. She broke into a gorgeous smile that made her blue eyes twinkle.

"I thought you said taking a girl to the drive-in was a very big deal around here." She planted a fist on each of her hips in challenge.

She was a beauty, even when she was pretending to frown at him like she was doing now.

He grinned and kicked at the doormat. "Yeah, well I meant it *was* a big deal, back when I was sixteen."

"Oh? So it's not a big deal now?" She put on a pretty pout.

Was she flirting with him? He hoped so.

Jack smiled. "You caught me lying. It's still a big deal to me and if you say no, I'll be crushed. So what d'you say?"

Her gaze dropped. "Okay, but I have to get changed first."

He shook his head and laughed. "It's the drive-in in

Pigeon Hollow. Believe me, you're overdressed."

She frowned so deeply it told him she'd likely never gone anywhere in New York in cut-offs and a tank top with no bra underneath. He noted that last detail happily.

"All right. I'll just put on some shoes." She shoved her feet into flip-flops, then grabbed her purse from the hook on the wall beside the door. As she pulled the door closed, Nicki met his gaze. "So, um, is the drive-in the place where you went as a teenager to . . . you know?"

Figuring out pretty quick what she meant, Jack laughed. "No. The drive-in is for the warm-up. I save the other part for later while we're parked by the river."

At his wink, Nicki widened her eyes. "Oh."

As they walked down the stairs and toward his convertible, he considered his plan of action.

Maybe he should put the car's roof up when they got to the drive-in. The way Nicki looked tonight, they might need a little privacy later.

CHAPTER TEN

Nicki glanced sideways at Jack and then back at the larger-than-life outdoor movie screen. She'd never been to a drive-in before. The experience was nothing like the eleven-movie multiplex theaters back home in New York.

Jack laid an arm around the back of her seat and shot her a grin. "Having a good time?"

She nodded and then had to stifle a yawn. Shocked at her own appalling lack of manners, she covered her mouth. "I'm so sorry. It's no reflection on you or the movie. I'm just a little tired."

And wasn't that the biggest understatement of the century? She hadn't really slept in a month. Not since she'd been on the run.

"That's all right, darlin'. It's late. They can't start the movie 'til after sundown and that comes pretty late this time of year. You wanna go home?"

She shook her head. "No. I'm enjoying being out. I'll be fine."

"Come here." He pulled her closer until her head leaned against the hard bulk of his shoulder. "Rest for a bit."

As if she'd ever be able to rest this close to him? Since their little trip to the pond, every time she closed her eyes or even let her mind wander, visions of a naked Jack swam through her head.

Even so, she must have fallen asleep because the next thing she was conscious of was Jack brushing a soft kiss across her forehead before he said, "Nicki?"

She opened her eyes. "I'm sorry. I fell asleep. Is it over?" She saw the screen filled with an ad for the snack bar.

He smiled, his face close to hers. "The first one is over. It's a double feature, but the second movie is some horror flick. I would have just driven us home, but you're on my right arm and I need it to shift."

While apologizing, she started to move away, but his arm around her shoulder stopped her from going too far.

"Don't apologize, darlin'. I liked it. You're so cute while you sleep. I hated to wake you up."

He leaned in a little closer, or maybe she did. Either way, she found herself in the position where there was a choice to be made. Pull back and save herself from the temptation, or move forward and succumb to what she'd been thinking about so much lately, pretty much non-stop.

Jack.

His sexy, low voice washing over her body. His thick southern drawl that almost seemed to cling to her like molasses.

Jack, the man whose mouth hovered temptingly above hers. He truly was a southern gentleman. Their lips were just a breath apart, but he didn't move in.

It was as if he waited for her to move first. But if the look in his eyes was any indication, he wanted this kiss as much as she did.

Licking her lips, Nicki dropped her gaze to his mouth, leaned in and then lost herself in his kiss.

She heard his quick intake of breath before his other hand moved to cradle the back of her head. Her hands found their way up his rock-hard chest, and then down the V to his narrow waist and hips.

He nipped at her lower lip before tilting her head and sliding his tongue inside her mouth.

She melted. Eyes closed, a small whimper of pleasure escaped her throat.

At hearing the sound, he leaned back and smiled down at her. Thankfully, he didn't stay away long, but moved in again, this time to tease her earlobe with his lips.

His breath in her ear sent tingles straight to her core.

She wanted more from him. Wanted his shirt off. Her hands on him. His hands on her. His mouth all over her . . . then she remembered they were in a convertible in a public place.

Nicki drew in a deep, shaky breath and released it. "Jack."

He pulled back enough to look at her with heavy-lidded eyes. "Yeah, darlin'?"

Swallowing hard, she gathered her nerve. "Take me to the river."

His eyes widened for a second, before he dropped his hold on her, turned to face the steering wheel, and had the car started and on the road so fast she wasn't quite sure how he'd done it.

Jack left his hand on her knee, only removing it occasionally to shift gears.

She tried not to let herself get nervous on the drive to this infamous parking spot. All too soon, they were at the river.

He pulled the car beneath a tree, put it into park and pulled up the emergency brake.

Before he turned off the car, Nicki touched his hand. "Put the roof up, Jack."

Her heart thundered harder as he did what she asked. Then he turned in his seat and faced her . . . that's when she attacked him.

There was a jumble of limbs, interrupted by car parts, punctuated by the bruising of limbs by car parts.

Somehow Jack wiggled into the passenger seat. He ended up beneath Nicki as he sat her in his lap facing him.

He tugged her tank top up and over her head—not an easy task since her head was pressed against the roof of the car.

Bare from the waist up, she felt the thick, southern summer press against her exposed skin. But the heat of the air didn't scorch her the way Jack's mouth did as he captured her nipple and worked it with his tongue.

Arching her back, she shuddered as his teeth scraped over her nipple. He ran his palms up her sides, burning a path over her skin with his touch.

His hands were so broad that his fingertips reached the center of her back while his thumbs brushed the sides of her breasts.

He released one heavily teased nipple and moved to torture the other with his mouth. He worked it until she pulled back and leaned low to crash her mouth against his. Her tongue tangled with his as he cupped her ass with both hands and held her close.

She broke the kiss long enough to yank his T-shirt over his head, then went back to kissing him.

Indulging a fantasy she'd had since meeting him, she ran her hands over his bare chest and finally got to feel the hard muscles beneath her fingers.

She'd been picturing his chest ever since their swim. The reality was better than the fantasy. He felt even better than he looked.

His tongue plunged in and out of her mouth in an erotic dance, making her wish he were plunging something else inside her.

Pressing closer, she tried to get as much of her skin against his as she could, in spite of the heat and the fact that they were both becoming slick with sweat.

He pulled her pelvis closer to his and she could feel the evidence through his jeans of exactly how aroused he was.

Shameless and well past the point of no return, she ground herself against him and moaned. His bulge pressed against the seam in her cut-off denim shorts and rubbed her just right.

Jack breathed faster. She began to tremble, craving the release that hovered just out of reach.

She rotated her hips harder and faster against him.

"Jack. Oh, God." Nicki couldn't get out any more words as the orgasm rocked her.

The thrusts of Jack's pelvis match the rhythm of his cries before he clutched her tighter and groaned, the sound muffled as he pressed his mouth against her throat.

They clung to each other, Nicki still panting so loudly, still so thrown by what had just happened, she barely heard the *tap-tap-tap* on the windshield.

Then the sound repeated louder and she heard Jack mumble, "Ah, crap."

Pulling back, she twisted to try and see what was making the noise.

Once she did, she had to agree with Jack. *Crap.*

CHAPTER ELEVEN

Two things hadn't happened to Jack since he'd been a teenager.

The first was being with a girl and coming before he even got his pants off. The second was the local deputy sheriff busting him with that girl while they were parked and half-naked.

Yet here he was, reliving his teen years.

Jack reached for his T-shirt and draped it over Nicki's bare breasts before the deputy leaned down and peered into the open passenger window—they had always been considerate about giving those couples caught parked by the river a few seconds to cover up.

"Jack? Jack Gordon, is that you?"

The flashlight was blinding, but Jack recognized the voice. Frowning, he shielded his eyes against the glare with one hand. "Bobby Barton? You're with the sheriff's department now? You got to be kidding me."

The light switched off and Bobby leaned a forearm on the open window. "Yup. Got hired as the deputy sheriff a few years back. What're you doing back here? You home for good?"

Jack overcame the surreal feeling of having a conversation with an old school chum while holding a topless Nicki in his lap, all the while ignoring his own now warm, wet boxer shorts. "Nah, I'm home on furlough for a few weeks."

Bobby nodded. "How's your mama? And Jared and Jimmy? I heard Jimmy got a bit banged up."

"Yeah, he's recovering. Everybody's fine." Enough with the chit-chat. Jack had a girl in his lap, but it was as if Bobby hadn't noticed.

"So, who's your friend?"

Or maybe he had.

"Um, this is Nicki Camp. Jared hired her to help around the farm. She's great with the horses."

Bobby extended his hand. "Nice to meet you, Nicki."

"You too." Nicki had to clutch the T-shirt to her chest with her left hand while pulling back from Jack far enough to shake Bobby's hand with her right.

Yeah, this wasn't too weird at all. Even so, Jack had to smile. Nicki was a real trooper. Not all women would take this sort of situation in stride the way she was.

"It was good seeing you again, Jack. I'll radio to the other car and tell them to give you two some privacy."

Thank God, Bobby was finally wrapping this up.

"Thanks, Bobby, but I think we're about to head home anyway." Privacy or not, Jack wasn't about to continue anything with Nicki here now.

Bobby nodded. "All right, then. Night, Jack. Night, Nicki."

Nicki nodded back as Jack answered, "Night, Bobby."

When the sheriff's car pulled away, Jack let out a long, slow breath and dared to glance at Nicki.

He felt her shaking but he couldn't see her face well in the dark. It took a moment before he realized she was silently laughing . . . and then not so silently as she laughed out loud.

Jack joined her. The more he thought about it, the funnier it seemed, until he had to wipe his eyes.

Finally, he caught his breath enough to speak. "I was going to ask if you were all right, but I guess you are."

With the back of one hand, Nicki swiped at her own eyes.

"I'm sorry. I shouldn't be laughing, but this is the craziest thing that's happened to me in a long time."

He ran a hand up and down the bare skin of her back. "Don't apologize. It's good to see you laugh. But besides good old Bobby, are you okay with . . . you know. What happened between us?"

She nodded, more serious now. "Yeah. That was pretty crazy too, but I'm fine. Are you okay with it?"

"Besides performing like an untried youth—" and really needing to get out of his boxers, "—yeah, I'm fine. I usually do have a bit more finesse in that department. I promise."

"You'll have to show me some time." Her soft voice affected him like no other female's had.

Jack smiled. "With pleasure."

Nicki leaned in and planted a kiss on his lips and, just like when he was a teenager, Jack was hard as a rock again.

Enough with making out in the car. She had a whole apartment above the barn all to herself with a bed in it.

Jack decided it was time to go home and hopefully get naked, in private this time so they could get to know each other a whole lot better. "Come on. Let's get out of here."

"Okay."

Reaching out, he grabbed Nicki's tank top from where it had landed on the dashboard. He held it out to her, exchanging it for his T-shirt that she handed back to him.

They pulled their respective shirts back on and Jack worked his way out from beneath Nicki and back over to the driver's seat.

He started the engine and put a little distance between them and Lover's Lane, as the locals had always called this spot.

It had been a hell of a good night so far, but he was old enough now to appreciate the qualities of a good mattress and the privacy of four walls and a door with a lock.

The closer they got to home, the more he anticipated all the pleasures that would await him with Nicki there.

He drove a bit over the speed limit and was just about to

turn onto the road that led to his mama's farm when his cell phone rang.

It had to be after twenty-three-hundred hours. The only calls that came that late at night were bad ones. He pulled the cell out of the console and saw Jimmy's name on the read-out. His heart nearly stopped. What the hell had happened at home?

As fast as he could safely manage it, Jack steered to the side of the road, shifted into neutral and yanked up the emergency break. He flipped open the phone. "Jimmy, what's wrong?"

"Now, Jack, it could be nothing, but my sixth sense kicked in and I wanted to run it by you right away."

He finally breathed again. At least the barn wasn't on fire or something, but Jimmy's instincts were rarely wrong. He'd been on too many missions with his brother to ignore one of Jimmy's gut feelings.

If Jimmy's warning bells were going off tonight, it wasn't good news.

"Okay. What's the situation?"

"Two thick-necked bruisers in cheap suits stopped by. They spoke like the guys in the mob movies. They were asking about Nicki."

Jack's training kicked in and he started formulating a plan while he turned off the car lights. Cradling the phone on one shoulder, he pulled the car back onto the road.

He kept a bug out bag in the trunk. He could disappear with her if he had to, but he could not take her home now.

"What exactly did you say to them?" he asked.

"Nothing. I told them I'd never heard of her. Something's not right. Who the hell comes knocking unannounced this late? Besides that, I didn't like the vibe I got from them. I've been out of action for a little while, but I'm not stupid. I know Nicki's hiding something. I figured she was just running from a bad relationship, but if these guys are any indication, she's in big trouble and needs help."

"I'm on it. I'm heading for the old hunting cabin. I'll call

Matt and Trey. They're both still at the base. They can be here in a couple of hours if they drive fast enough. You get a hold of Jared and explain things. And see if you can get Mama out of the house without scaring her. Send her to Aunt Lydia's for the next few days."

Jack remembered the physical state his brother was still in and added, "And you go with her, Jimmy."

"No freaking way." Jimmy sounded adamant.

That was the exact response Jack expected from him, but he was prepared for it. "Jimmy, they're probably watching the house. I don't want Mama driving alone and getting picked up by them."

It was true, but also a way of keeping Jimmy out of harm's way.

He heard Jimmy huff out a big breath. "All right. Keep in touch."

"Jimmy."

"Yeah?"

"Take your gun with you," Jack reminded.

Jimmy snorted. "Are you kidding me? I strapped on my holster the moment I closed the door on those assholes. I only wish I had my body armor here."

Jack was feeling pretty naked himself without the benefit of at least some Kevlar and his weapons. "I hear you. Talk later."

"Later."

As he wrapped up the call with his brother, Nicki was practically vibrating next to him in the car. An obvious reaction to the half of the conversation she'd heard.

Taking a deep breath, Jack forced himself to ignore her for the moment and stay focused on the task at hand. He'd get to her soon, but now he had a call to make.

While driving he hit the name in his contact list to call Matt.

His teammate answered after the first ring. "Jack. What's happening?" Matt's voice came through the phone sounding wide awake in spite of the late hour.

He could always count on Matt to be wired for technology at any time of day or night.

"It's come to a head. Two men came to the farm looking for her. We're safe for now, but I need you, and Trey too if possible, down here ASAP."

They discussed logistics for a minute, then Jack ended the call.

This time of night Trey and Matt could break a few speed limits and hopefully cut the drive time down to an hour and a half, barring any speed traps and state troopers.

Two New York mobsters against two, soon to be four, highly trained special operatives. Jack liked the odds. What he didn't like was the risk for collateral damage. Nicki, his mama and both his brothers were in danger.

He glanced sideways at Nicki. She was watching him wide-eyed. He sensed her trembling increase.

"Jack," she whispered. "What's happening?"

"That's what I need you to tell me, darlin'. All of it."

He said a quick prayer for her sake as well as his own that what she was about to reveal wasn't going to be too bad. He'd let himself get attached to her, and he didn't think his heart could stand another break soon.

CHAPTER TWELVE

Nicki's stomach clenched. She feared she might lose it out the car window as Jack sped down the dark road with the lights turned off.

It wasn't his driving making her feel ill. There was enough moonlight for him to see the road and he seemed to know where he was going. It was that they had found her somehow. How?

She'd made one call to her father from a pay phone she was lucky enough to find before she even met Jared and started working on the farm. Did they track her from that?

It didn't matter how they got here. All that she knew was she was no longer safe. Maybe she never had been.

Things were bad. Very bad. And not fifteen minutes ago she had been happy in Jack's arms.

Time to tell the truth, before her lies got Jack's entire family killed.

She took a deep breath to steady her stomach.

"My real name is Niccolina Campolini. My father breeds and trains racehorses near Belmont Park in Long Island. You've heard of Belmont, right? It's the third leg in the Triple Crown after the Kentucky Derby and the Preakness Stakes."

He glanced at her like she was a babbling imbecile, so she continued, "Sorry, of course you've heard of it. Anyway, this guy was putting pressure on my father to throw a race. Tell the jockey to pull up, make the horse lame . . . whatever. He didn't care, as long as this horse didn't win the race. My father was pretty tired of being a pawn for these guys. He'd owed them some money, but he'd paid it all back plus a ridiculous amount of interest. In his mind, his obligation was done, but they kept demanding favors. He decided to end it there and then and his horse won."

"And they weren't very happy with him," Jack guessed correctly.

"No, they weren't. They took me as collateral . . ." Nicki paused as her voice started to shake. She drew in a breath and blew it out before she continued. "I was leverage so my father would have to do what they said. And I guess it was also to teach him a lesson for crossing them."

Jack took his eyes off the road long enough to look at her for a few seconds. He put one hand on her knee and squeezed. "Go on, darlin'. Tell me what happened."

In the dark, she could see the firm, angry set of his jaw as he waited for her to finish. "The head guy had always liked me, so he decided he would make me his woman, then he would have control over my father forever."

She glanced at him. The next part was going to be very hard to say, especially to him. Particularly now, after what had happened between them. "I—I was under constant guard until one night when he summoned me to his bedroom. The bastard dismissed the guards for the night, so we were alone."

Her heart pounded just remembering it. Jack squeezed her leg again. "Don't, darlin'. It doesn't matter what you had to do. You got away. That's all that matters."

She shook her head. "No, I need to tell you this. I went along with him until he was . . . in a vulnerable position. Then I bit him. Hard. Down there."

Cringing, Nicki remembered too vividly the metallic taste of his blood in her mouth.

The car jerked a bit as Jack, obviously surprised, turned to look at her.

She continued with the sordid tale. "He didn't have a chance to call the guards before I grabbed the brass lamp next to the bed and smashed him over the head. I don't know if I killed him. I didn't check. I didn't care. I just wanted to get out. I'd spent my time memorizing the location of the security cameras and where the guards were usually stationed. I managed to slip out of the house unnoticed. I ran until I couldn't run anymore then I walked after that. I made it to town and stole a woman's purse. I'm not proud of that, but I had nothing with me and I was desperate. I got to the train station and bought a ticket with cash."

Jack turned onto an unpaved, very bumpy and winding path, not even a road. He flipped on the lights again and slowed the car to a crawl. She assumed they were nearing their destination.

"I ended up in Pigeon Hollow with nothing but the clothes on my back and a few dollars in a stolen purse. I was about to spend the last of the money on food when I heard your brother in the diner saying he wanted to hire more help on his horse farm. So here I am." She shrugged with the completion of the story.

Jack brought the car to a stop behind an old cabin that looked like it had seen better days. She doubted they'd be found here and that was good enough for her.

He yanked up the parking brake and turned in his seat to face her. Reaching out, he pulled her into his arms. "I'm so sorry, darlin'. But you did good. You were very brave."

"But they found me and now your family is in danger because of me. I should have told you all the truth sooner. I shouldn't have stayed in one place for so long. I meant to keep moving, but everyone was so nice here. Then I met you . . ."

He pulled back and held her face while he gazed at her. "Shhh. Regrets do nobody any good. I'm glad you stayed. I can help you."

She was about to protest again when he silenced her with one finger on her lips. "Listen to me now. This is what I do for a living. I fight bad guys and I'm darn good at it. And with my friends on their way here to help, those guys after you don't stand a chance. Trust me. Okay?"

Her eyes filled with tears making it even harder to see his face in the darkness. "I do trust you."

"Good." He smiled and kissed her, quick and hard, before pulling back too soon.

Jack got out of the car and then jogged around to open her door. Grabbing her hand, he led her to the cabin.

The door creaked open and she was hit with the musty air from within the dim interior. She didn't care if it was a bit run down and smelled like it might not have been aired out in years.

It felt safe. Or maybe it was just being with Jack that made her feel safe.

The problem was, she knew the feeling was only temporary. As long as they were after her she'd never be safe again.

CHAPTER THIRTEEN

"So let me get this straight. The one guy's name is Paulie the Pudge and the other guy's name is Vinnie Don't Know?" Trey's wide-eyed gaze moved from Jack to Matt.

Another call to Jimmy right after he'd arrived at the cabin had provided Jack with enough of a physical description of the two men for Nicki to identify them.

Now Jack's quickly assembled team had names to go with the bad guys chasing Nicki, but he still didn't know how they'd finally been able to locate her at his family's farm.

"That's what Nicki said." Jack nodded before once again checking his cell phone for any updates from Jared on the farm or Jimmy on the road with their mother.

"Yeah, but you gotta say it like you're from Brooklyn. *Vinnie Don' Kno'.*" Matt, being from New York himself, had mastered the proper pronunciation of the ridiculous nickname.

He'd arrived at the cabin toting his laptop plus a bunch of other electronics and was currently tapping away on the keyboard. Hopefully finding something they could use against these guys to get Nicki away from them for good.

Trey let out a long breath. "This is like a really bad movie."

Jack glanced over to make sure Nicki was still lying down

171

on the cot in the corner of the cabin. Poor thing had been so exhausted she'd been barely able to stay upright When he finally convinced her to just rest for a bit after Matt and Trey had arrived, she'd eventually given in.

Judging by the look of her now as she curled on her side, breathing deeply, she'd fallen asleep. Jack kept his voice low as he asked, "Matt, what have you got on Vinnie and Paulie's boss? This Tony guy."

"It looks like he recently dropped out of sight." Matt glanced in Nicki's direction before saying, "After what you told me Nicki did to him, I'm sure he crawled away to lick his wounds in private. No mobster is gonna want that story to leak out."

"Yeah, no shit." Jack grimaced at the thought of the wounds Nicki had inflicted on Tony. Not that the bastard didn't deserve that plus more.

Matt continued, "But she definitely didn't kill him. Word would have gotten out if he'd died. He's too big a name for it not to."

Too big. Great. Why couldn't Nicki's father have pissed off a small-time gangster instead?

"So we can't just make him disappear is what you're saying," Jack guessed.

"As much as we'd all like to, no. He'd be missed. But I have an idea on that front. If you agree, Jack. This is your deal." Matt waited a beat.

Jack accepted his role as leader of this operation with a nod. "A'ight. What've you got?"

"I've hacked into Tony's accounts. Ridiculously easy. I thought mobsters would have better tech guys, but apparently not." Matt shook his head.

"They hire guys like Paulie the Pudge and Vinnie Don' Kno' and you think they're going to have state-of-the-art internet security?" Trey raised a brow.

"Okay, you got me there. Anyway, he's got his fingers in businesses all over Long Island. There's a paper trail of dirty money and how he launders it a mile wide. All I have to do is drop an anonymous tip to the IRS and FBI and this guy is going away on tax evasion and racketeering for life."

Jack frowned. "I don't want anything that can be linked back to Nicki. Those guys can do damage even while behind bars."

"There's no way he can trace it to Nicki or her father. In fact, I can bounce it from his computers so it looks like one of his own men turned on him." Matt's face glowed with satisfaction beneath the light of the kerosene lamp.

Jack considered Matt's solution. Non-violent. It couldn't be traced to Nicki and it would give this guy what he deserved—life in prison. "Do it."

"All right. Now for some fun." Matt rubbed his hands together, bent lower over the screen and started tapping away again just as Jack's cell phone vibrated in his pocket.

He pulled it out and saw Jimmy's name on the display. Jack answered but didn't bother with a hello. "Jimmy, where are you and Mama?"

"I pulled some strings with a friend and she and Aunt Lydia are spending the next few days on a riverboat, wining, dining and gambling. I figured they'd be safer in a public place than at Aunt Lydia's house way off in the country. Jared and the boys are hiding in the barn, well armed, in case these idiots get any ideas about getting to us by hurting the horses or burning us out."

Shit. Jack hadn't even considered the safety of the animals in his worry about Nicki and his family. "Good thinking. Where are you now?"

"I'm driving around town with the two New York idiots tailing me. I lost them on the way to drop off Mama, then I picked them up again on the road in front of the farm."

"What?" Jack ran a hand through his hair in frustration. Why couldn't Jimmy just do as he'd asked? "Why didn't you stay with Mama where it's safe?"

"And miss all the excitement? Hell no. Besides, these guys are fun to mess with. They really think I haven't made them. So far they've followed me to the drive-up ATM, the diner for some coffee-to-go, and we even pulled up outside the late show at the drive-in theater and watched the movie for a bit. What do you want me to do with them now?"

Jack rolled his eyes. These gangsters did seem too dimwitted to be much of a danger against a trained operative like Jimmy, but he wasn't willing to risk anyone by betting on that.

Not to mention that Jimmy was still recuperating. The doctor would definitely not approve of this latest activity. "You're supposed to be resting, not acting as bait for two mobsters."

Jimmy laughed. "Yeah. Two of the stupidest mobsters on earth, so don't worry. Just tell me what to do. Are you guys set up? Do you want me to lead them there to the cabin?"

Jack shook his head. "I'd rather not do this at the cabin. Nicki's here."

Trey touched his arm to get his attention. "If we don't do this here, we'll have to either split up or leave Nicki here alone."

Jack breathed in deep. He definitely wanted to be in on bringing down these two, but there was no way he was going too far from Nicki's side either. He had no choice but to agree to Jimmy's plan. "All right. Give us ten minutes and then lead them here."

"Great! See you then."

Jack could hear his brother's excitement through the cell phone. Shaking his head, he said, "See you. And be careful."

Trey was laying the spare weapons and flak jacket he'd brought for Jack out on the table when Matt closed his laptop triumphantly.

"Done. One mobster down, two to go." Matt slipped his arms through his own bulletproof vest and then began checking his weapon. "And for once, I get to be in on the real action instead of stuck in a van full of computers somewhere."

"So glad I could help entertain you, Matt." Jack scowled, getting pretty tired of everyone enjoying this so much when all he could do was worry about Nicki and wish this bullshit was over already. "Now here's the plan—we set up outside in the trees. We take these two down before they ever hit the front porch or set foot near Nicki."

"Take them down how, Jack? What are we aiming to end up with here, bodies or prisoners?" Trey asked.

Good question. What sort of force was warranted? Usually this kind of decision was the commander's, or Central Command's. Jack was just considering that when the sound of tires on the road had all three of their heads snapping up.

"Car," Matt announced, not that the rest of them hadn't already heard it.

Jack killed the kerosene lamp, grabbed the handgun and stood behind the door. "That was *not* ten minutes and that doesn't sound anything like my brother's truck."

Trey closed his flak jacket and turned to face Matt, whose weapon was already out. "You remember how to shoot that thing?"

Matt didn't have time to answer because Nicki chose that moment to sit straight up. "Jack? What's happening?"

"Darlin', I need you to get up, go into the bathroom and lay down in that old cast iron bathtub. Don't move until I come and get you. Okay?"

Trusting she'd do as she was told, Jack turned his attention back to the looming threat outside. Pressed against the wall, he snuck a quick glance out the window in time to see Bobby Barton getting out of his sheriff's vehicle.

"Dammit." Jack hadn't seen Bobby in years, and yet here he was for the second time in one night. Jack strode to the doorway, cracked it open and called out, "Bobby Barton, get your butt inside right this minute. We have a situation here."

Bobby glanced around him before approaching the cabin and slipping inside the doorway. He blinked in the darkness. "I got a call that a strange car was driving on the private road toward your cabin."

His eyes must have eventually gotten used to the dim moonlight that filtered into the cabin through the windows, because he looked from one black-clad figure to the next to the last. "Uh, Jack? What's going on here? You're not a member of one of those radical groups that wants to blow up the government or something, are you?"

Jack would have laughed at that if he weren't so wired. "No, Bobby. You know I'm military. We work *for* the government, not against it."

"I know that, Jack. But you have to admit this looks pretty strange." Bobby eyed Matt and Trey, suited up for battle, right down to night vision goggles.

Jack couldn't blame Bobby for being doubtful. It wasn't like this was an official operation by any stretch of the imagination.

"Deputy Bobby Barton, this here is Matt and Trey. They're a couple of my teammates. I called them because we've got two New York mobsters out to hurt Nicki. Right now they're following Jimmy and he's leading them here so we can ambush them."

And since local law enforcement was now on the scene, they all had the answer to the previous question. They'd have to take these guys alive.

The only remaining dilemma was what the hell were they going to do then? This wasn't a government-sanctioned mission, but it involved four special operatives who needed to stay off the radar and out of the local papers.

"Hey, Bobby. Wouldn't it look really good for your career if you took these two bad guys down all on your own?"

Bobby glanced again at the three. "Yeah, Jack, I suppose it would."

Jack smiled as a plan presented itself . . . right before all hell broke loose.

The sound of screeching tires cut through the night. Jack moved to the window as Jimmy's truck fishtailed around the corner. A big, black car followed shortly behind him.

Since this was by no means a road and they were in the marshlands, the car didn't stand a chance when the driver strayed too far off the path. Soon the car's tires were spinning in the mud, giving Jimmy just enough time to jump from his truck and dive into the front door of the cabin.

"Dammit, Jimmy! Be careful of your spleen," Jack yelled when Jimmy hit the floor with a tuck and roll.

"I'm fine. Hey, Trey, Matt. Bobby, how the hell are you?" Jimmy brushed himself off and pulled his weapon from the ankle holster.

"Good, Jimmy. You?" Bobby responded.

"Never felt better." Jimmy grinned.

Jack smothered a groan as he glanced from one to the other. "Everyone all caught up? Now who's got a plan? Because idiot number one and idiot number two just got out of the car."

The two mobsters ducked behind the hood of their vehicle until only the tops of their heads and their overly big and showy guns were visible.

Jack couldn't help but think what a perfect target they would make for a sniper's rifle. The idiots didn't even know enough to stay down. Duck and cover must have been in the mob handbook they didn't bother to read.

Through the night air, Jack heard their conversation clearly since they didn't seem to know enough to keep their voices down either.

"What do we do now?" one asked.

"Tell them we want Nicki," the other answered.

"But, Paulie, how do we know she's in there?"

"Use your brain, Vin. They must have her stashed in the shack. Why else would that hick from the farm come here after we showed up asking about her?"

"Hick?" Jimmy's unhappy sounding whisper filled the cabin.

Jack shushed him and strained to hear Vinnie's reply, though he liked them calling his family's cabin a shack about as little as Jimmy liked being called a hick.

"Yeah, I guess you're right, Paulie. Okay. I'll ask them to send her out."

"No, I'll ask. You'll probably fuck it up." At that point in the conversation, Paulie actually stood, leaving himself totally exposed. "Hey! Give us the girl and nobody gets hurt."

Jack sighed as their opponents' idiocy seemed to increase. His finger on the trigger itched as he longed to teach the man a lesson. Maybe he could give the guy's hair just a little trim on top with a well placed bullet.

He restrained himself and decided to answer their insane request instead. "Sure, hold on a sec. I'll go get her for you."

Vinnie stood too as Paulie yelled back, "Okay."

Jack glanced over his shoulder at his team. "Do these assholes really think we're gonna do that?"

Jimmy let out a short laugh. "I told you they're not the sharpest tools in the shed."

Bobby took a step forward. "I'm going to have to inform them I'm in here, Jack. I'm an officer of the law."

"Go ahead. They obviously didn't notice the big white sheriff's vehicle with the lights on top, so you'd better say something." Jack couldn't help but let out a laugh himself. This situation was absolutely surreal.

"Hey, do you have the cops in there with you?" the skinny one asked.

Trey snorted. "I guess they're not quite as dumb as you thought."

Jack shook his head at the sheer stupidity of their question. "What do you think?" he yelled back.

"I don' know. You tell me."

Trey outright laughed at Vinnie Don' Kno's response while Matt blew out a huff of air. "Shit. They're too dumb for me to even shoot. It wouldn't be a fair fight."

Bobby moved closer to the door. "I'm a local deputy sheriff. If you lay down your weapons and surrender peacefully, we'll go easy on you. But if you insist on firing upon an officer of the law, I will fire back. This is fair warning."

Jack was impressed. Bobby sounded very official. Much more imposing than in their youth. The memory of Bobby bent over, puking after a beer chugging contest at a graduation party briefly crossed Jack's mind.

There was silence for a moment, so Jack risked a quick peek out the window. "Uh, oh. The two idiots are whispering to each other about something."

"Jack?"

At the sound of Nicki's voice, Jack spun to see her standing in the doorway of the bathroom.

"Jesus. Darlin', get down. This ain't over yet."

"But—"

"Please." Jack wasn't above begging and pleading at this point. "I promise I'll get you when it's over."

Nicki planted both hands on her hips and Jack suspected she wasn't going without a fight. "Jack, I've been dealing with these guys for a lot longer than you have."

"I understand that, but you're not in New York anymore. You're in my town now. Let me handle this."

She hesitated with one hand poised on the doorknob. "Promise me you won't get hurt?"

Hurt? By these guys? Jack laughed. "I promise. Now go back in the bathroom, close the door and get inside that tub. Okay, darlin'?"

Finally she nodded and said, "Okay."

"Is that the looker you were parked naked with by the river tonight?" Bobby whispered after Nicki had disappeared into the bathroom.

Jack cringed. He could only imagine the reaction on the faces of Trey, Matt and especially Jimmy.

Jimmy muttered a cuss beneath his breath and said, "Now I owe Jared twenty bucks."

Knowing he shouldn't ask because he likely wouldn't like the answer, Jack said anyway, "Why?"

"Jared said you'd have her naked before week's end."

"We weren't naked." Jack ground his teeth.

"Well, no. Not totally, but from the waist up you both were," Bobby clarified.

"Really? Excellent. That might not count. Maybe I didn't lose after all." Jimmy sounded hopeful.

Feeling spiteful, Jack decided to burst his brother's bubble. "You lose anyway. We went skinny dipping in the pond this afternoon."

Jack smiled in victory at Jimmy's second cuss in the dark.

Trey moved closer. "Hey, so what's going on with you and Nicki?"

Good question. Bad timing. They had two idiots outside, still muttering to each other about what to do next, and Jack and his team were inside gossiping like this was the local hair salon.

"You think maybe we can talk when this is all over with?" Jack asked. Perhaps when there weren't two armed goons intent on getting to Nicki. Maybe by then, Jack would have an answer to Trey's question because he sure as hell didn't have one now.

Matt glanced out the window, then pulled back. "We appear to be at a standoff, boys."

"I could call for backup," Bobby suggested.

"This is gonna be hard enough to explain. I mean, all of us, here and armed." Jack nodded toward his teammates.

Bobby sighed. "You're right."

"Jack, I have an idea." It seemed Nicki was determined not to stay safe in the tub as he'd asked her to. She came out of the bathroom, squatted and crab-walked her way across the floor to him.

At least she hadn't stood in front of the window and made herself a nice target. He let out a patient sigh. "Okay, darlin'. What's your idea?"

"I want to talk to them."

"You aren't going outside." His voice sounded a bit more feral than he expected.

"I'll yell from here."

He let out another breath of frustration. "All right. Give it a try if you think it will help." He supposed it couldn't hurt.

"Hey, guys!" She yelled from the floor.

"Nicki, baby. Come on out. Tony misses you," Paulie the Pudge called back.

"Yeah, I really miss him too, but I got to tell you something. I wouldn't feel right if I didn't."

"What's that, Nicki baby?" Paulie asked.

Was Nicki's New York accent getting stronger just from talking to these two? Even so, Jack was happy to see they were responding well to her.

"Remember a few months back, when Tony was screwing around with Johnny Bag-o-Doughnuts' wife?"

"Johnny Bag-o-Doughnuts?" Jack whispered to Nicki.

She shrugged. "He likes doughnuts."

"Yeah," Paulie said.

"Well, when Johnny found out and accused Tony, Tony said it was you she was fooling around with. So Johnny told your wife and that's why she left you."

"What? My bitch wife got the house and half my money in that settlement. You sure about this, Nicki?"

"Paulie, I was Tony's hostage for a week. You hear things. Guards forget you're there and talk. I'm sure."

"Son of a bitch. But what am I supposed to do about this? I can't cross Tony. He'd kill me."

"You could both drive away from here and forget you ever found me," Nicki suggested. "You may not be able to confront him, but you sure don't want to make him happy by bringing me back, do you?"

Jack heard Paulie ask Vinnie, "What do you think?"

"I don' know," Vinnie answered predictably.

"I was wrong. This is *worse* than a really bad movie," Trey mumbled from a dark corner.

Paulie and Vinnie seemed to reach some decision and he yelled, "If we forget we saw you, will this here deputy forget he saw us?"

Jack raised a brow in question. "Bobby?"

Bobby shook his head. "I wouldn't know how to explain this in a report anyway." He moved closer to the window. "You drive straight out of here, cross my county line and don't look back and I'll pretend I never saw you."

Paulie nodded. "Deal. Stay safe, Nicki baby. Tony's not gonna stop looking for you, you know. You really pissed him off."

"I know. Thanks, guys. You stay safe too."

After a few minutes of flying mud and spinning tires during which Jack feared they'd all have to go out and give the two idiots a push, the car finally fishtailed its way back onto the path and down the road.

Jack slid down the wall and sank onto the floor next to Nicki. "It's over, darlin'."

"No it's not, Jack. They're right. He'll never stop looking for me. I'll be on the run for the rest of my life. I'll have to leave here . . ." Her voice broke.

Matt lit the kerosene lamp and the room came into view again. "I don't think he's going to have time to bother with you, Nicki. I think he'll be a little busy soon."

Jack slid his weapon back into its holster. That left his hand free to grab Nicki's. "We took care of him, Nick. Rather, Matt did. Either way, he's likely going to be locked up for a very long time. And there's no way he can connect it to you."

"Really?" Nicki's eyes widened.

He could almost see the weight lift from her shoulders. He squeezed her hand. "Really. Come on. Let's go home."

CHAPTER FOURTEEN

The sun hadn't been up for more than an hour, but Jack was already slumped at the kitchen table, both hands wrapped around a now cold cup of coffee.

"I have to say, this is a pretty pitiful sight."

He looked up and saw Trey standing in the kitchen doorway, looking far too chipper for Jack's taste. "Don't start with me, Trey."

"You're really going to let her fly back to New York and never see her again?" Trey asked.

"That's not how we left it. We agreed we'd stay in touch." Jack glanced at the clock on the stove.

By now, Nicki's plane had already taken off. His chest tightened as he pictured her speeding farther away from him with every passing minute.

So much of yesterday had been spent recovering from the events of the night before that he felt like they'd barely had any time together.

Nicki had immediately gotten in touch with her father to tell him she was all right. The man had chronic high blood pressure and she was afraid the stress of the last few weeks had taken a toll on his health. She wanted to see for herself he was okay and let him see she was fine too, so she'd found a direct flight to New York that left at zero-six-hundred this morning.

Jack had offered to get up early and drive her to the airport, but she'd insisted she could take a cab. Eventually he'd given in to her wishes.

It was better this way. They got their goodbyes over with here in private rather than on the curb in front of the airport.

Jack rubbed at the strange pain that had been in his chest since the night before when he'd kissed her cheek and left her alone in her apartment above the barn.

Trey dropped his gaze to the movement of Jack's hand. "What's wrong with your chest?"

"Heartburn or indigestion or something." Jack pushed the mug away. "It's probably the coffee."

"Your mother's coffee is as good as her pie, so I doubt it." Trey pulled out a chair and straddled it backward, a stupid-looking grin on his face. "What color are Nicki's eyes?"

Jack frowned. "What the hell kind of question is that?"

"Just answer it."

"Deep blue, like the color of the ocean when you see it from really high up in a plane. Why?"

"Ha! I knew you'd know." Trey broke out into a broad smile. "You love her."

Jack rolled his eyes. "Just because I know what color her eyes are doesn't mean I'm in love with her."

"Does your *heartburn* hurt worse every time you think about her leaving?"

Jack rubbed his chest again, wondering why his discomfort was making Trey so happy. "I don't know. Maybe. I guess. But so what? It's a coincidence. I hardly know her."

"In the short time you've known her, you've been through a whole lot of shit."

That was true, even if Jack refused to admit it.

Trey shook his head. "You once told me I was either too stupid or too stubborn to realize I was in love with Carly. Which one are you, Jack? Are you too stupid or too stubborn to admit you have feelings for Nicki?"

The truth of his own words being turned back on him hit

hard. Jack buried his face in both hands. "Both, I guess."

"Then do something about it."

"Do what?" Jack glared at Trey, who seemed full of love advice today but had offered no useful solution as yet.

Trey raised a brow. "Go after her, Jack. Get on a stand-by flight. Or get in that car of yours and start driving. You'll be there before nightfall."

"Then what?" Jack asked. "How's this gonna work, Trey? She's a New Yorker. She's not gonna move down here to Pigeon Hollow and continue to shovel manure for my brother now that she's not in hiding anymore."

Trey shook his head. "I'm betting after all that's happened to her up there, she's had enough of New York."

"Who's had enough of New York?" Jared wandered in the back door and joined the conversation uninvited. He walked over to the counter to pour a cup of coffee and then glanced back at Jack and Trey, waiting for an answer.

"Nicki. She flew back home to New York this morning to be with her father," Trey answered.

Jared took a sip from the mug and then shook his head. "No, she didn't. She's outside in the yard right now."

"What?" Jack sat bolt upright at that information.

Had Nicki missed her flight? As horrible as it seemed to be happy about that, he was still glad. All he cared about now was making sure she didn't leave.

Before Jared or Trey could say another word, Jack was up, out of his chair and heading through the door.

~ * ~

Nicki leaned against the rail of the fence, watching the mare with her colt and feeling totally at ease for the first time in a month.

She'd probably never been safer than at this very moment. Matt and Trey, the two mysterious black-clad, military-type friends of Jack and Jimmy, were still on the property. And Jared and his barn hands had proven they could also be armed and ready for anything.

Her father had called on the phone extension in the barn

late last night. Tony was all over the New York news. He'd been arrested for tax evasion and racketeering. All his files and computers had been seized. They'd denied his request for bail.

Tony had a heap of trouble to deal with now. Hopefully he'd be much too busy to remember her.

Even so, her father had said he'd feel safer with her out of New York for a little longer, so she'd happily agreed to remain where she was. Staying on the farm was no hardship. She'd come to really love it here.

Not to mention it was where Jack was.

What a difference a day made. She sighed, content. Now if only Jack would get out of bed so she could surprise him. He thought she'd flown back to New York.

"Hey, darlin'."

As usual, she didn't hear him until he was right behind her. She smiled as he slipped his arms around her and nuzzled her neck. She tilted her head to one side and let him kiss from her ear to her collarbone.

Groaning in pleasure, she finally managed to say, "Your family's going to see us if you're not careful."

Not that she really wanted him to stop.

"I don't care." Jack spun her around and she saw how serious his expression was. "I'm trying to convince you not to go back to New York. To stay here and be closer to me."

She opened her mouth to tell him she wasn't going back. In fact, her father was talking about selling his farm in New York and retiring down here, but Jack put one finger on her lips to silence her.

"Nicki, I can't promise you it'll be perfect. I'm away a lot, but I'll be with you every second I can if you'll let me."

She waited, and since he seemed to be done, she finally got to tell him what she'd been dying to.

"I'm not going back. I'm moving down here. My father's coming down next week to see me and we're going to look at a small horse property Jared told me about that's for sale in the next town. So it looks like I'll be around whenever you are." She smiled at the surprise on his face.

He whooped, picked her up and spun her around until she was dizzy. She was breathless from laughing when he finally stopped spinning.

Jack didn't put her down. She remained level with his gorgeous gold-flecked eyes.

She wrapped her legs around his waist and became very aware of the alignment of their anatomy. "Jack, I don't think I can wait until dark for the drive-in to open tonight. What do you say we go upstairs to my apartment right now?"

"Are you sure your papa's definitely not coming until next week?" Judging by the desire she saw in his eyes, he was tempted by her suggestion, even while trying to be respectful of her father.

She laughed. "I'm sure."

Jack grinned. "Then I think that's an excellent idea."

Leaning down to press a kiss to Jack's mouth, Nicki couldn't agree more.

JIMMY

CHAPTER ONE

6 months ago

Jimmy Gordon glanced down the length of the table packed nearly shoulder-to-shoulder with the bulk of the men seated there. All five of his teammates wore a similarly confused expression in reaction to their leader's vague orders to "suit up".

"Excuse me, sir." Jimmy raised his hand and got the attention of the commander. "Could you clarify? What exactly is our assignment?"

In the front of the room stood a rolling rack that held black trousers, white button-down shirts, short black jackets and bow ties. Six of each and all on hangers under clear plastic, the reason the team had the same baffled look on their faces.

They usually wore flak jackets and weapons, not waiters' jackets and bow ties.

The commander remained unfazed by the doubt-filled question. "You heard me, Gordon. Change into the black-and-whites. Tonight, you'll all be waiters. Except for Coleman, he'll be manning the communications equipment, and your brother, he'll be a bartender."

"Why do you get to tend bar?" Jimmy frowned at his brother, Jack, seated next to him.

"Because I'm so pretty, I need to be behind something

sturdy to keep the women off me?" Jack grinned.

Jimmy scowled at Jack's high opinion of himself while the commander continued with the instructions for their mission—if you could call it a mission.

"This party is being attended by some big shit VIPs, both domestic and foreign. Government and civilian. The chatter on the lines indicates there could possibly be an attempted attack. I say attempted because our team will be on-site replacing the wait staff. Anything goes down, we'll be ready for it."

BB Dalton raised his hand hesitantly. "Um . . . but I don't know how to be a waiter, sir."

"Yeah, and like *I* know how to be a waiter?" Bull snorted.

Bull had earned his nickname through sheer size. Jimmy conjured a mental image of Bull in a china shop and figured that was pretty much what it was going to be like tonight, except Bull would be carrying a silver tray in his big mitt-sized hands and wearing a bow tie.

Matt chimed in from behind his ever-present laptop. "It's easy. I waited tables at one of the catering halls on Long Island during high school and summers when I was in college. Just don't spill on anybody and you'll be fine."

Bull looked skeptical. "Then why aren't *you* playing a waiter, Coleman, if you know so much about it?"

"I'll tell you what, Bull. *You* learn how to do what *I* do by tonight and I will." Matt looked like he was feeling pretty damn confident when he made the offer. But he had every right to be cocky. Matt's technical skills had saved all their asses a time or two.

"No way that's going to happen." Trey chuckled. "I doubt Bull's fingers would even fit on the keys."

Laughing, Jimmy had to agree. They were all safer with Matt on the console, even if it meant Bull spilling things on the rich people tonight.

Watching the exchange with an expression of amused patience, the commander finally held up one hand to silence them. "If we're done bickering, ladies, grab your uniforms and weapons—leg holsters only—and let's go. I want you all as familiar with the layout of the venue tonight as you are with your own dicks. Got it?"

Jack smirked. "That will be pretty familiar for you, big brother, considering I haven't seen any women around lately volunteering to hold yours for you."

Jimmy frowned. He got laid plenty. He was just discreet. Although he had been experiencing a bit of a dry spell lately. He raised a brow in his brother's direction. "They're not exactly lined up for you either, little brother."

"That's because I'm holding out for the love of my life. That cute little thing who tends bar down the street."

He knew the one Jack was talking about. Word was she didn't date military guys. "If that's true, then I think you'll be holding your own for quite some time yet."

"Twenty bucks says I get a date with her before summer." Jack stuck out his hand to shake on the bet.

"You're on." Jimmy took it with pleasure. Easiest twenty bucks he'd ever make.

With the wager secured, they both rose from their seats as the table began to empty. Jimmy found the hanger marked with his name and grabbed his uniform from the rack.

Wondering what the hell the night would bring, he headed out of the meeting room with the rest of the team.

Two short hours later, Jimmy winced as he ran a finger under the incredibly stiff collar of his white tuxedo shirt. The damn thing felt like a noose around his neck.

There was a reason he'd joined the military instead of taking a corporate job. It was so he wouldn't have to wear a shirt and tie to work everyday.

, Yet here he was, not only in an overly starched shirt, but in a bow tie no less. Figuring the loaded .40 caliber handgun strapped to his leg balanced out the sissy bow tie on the testosterone scale, he still wasn't happy about the whole situation.

"Don't all you boys look cute." Matt's voice came through the communicator implanted in Jimmy's ear and interrupted his internal soliloquy about his hatred of the shirt and tie. The mocking only seemed to make the discomfort seem worse since Matt was safely locked away in the surveillance van wearing his own nice comfortable clothes. "I've got eyes and ears up and running. Talk to me."

"Gordon, Jimmy." In the usual, preset order, Jimmy checked in first and confirmed his receipt of Matt's communication, such as it was, about having audio and visual surveillance in place.

"Gordon, Jack."

"BB."

"Bull."

"Williams."

One by one, the rest of the team had verbally checked in, except for the commander.

"Commander?" Matt's question came through Jimmy's earpiece.

Jimmy could see the commander across the room in his own penguin suit, looking just as uncomfortable as he felt.

"Yeah, I'm here, Coleman. Let's get this show on the road. This tie is killing me."

At least rank didn't have its privileges on this op.

Enjoying the thought immensely, Jimmy smiled.

"You guys better go into the kitchen and find out what you'll be passing," Matt warned.

"You mean besides gas?" Obviously pleased with his own wit, Jack beamed.

Jack looked pretty comfortable in his position behind the bar. If only Jimmy had been lucky enough to be assigned the job of bartender instead of stuck out here trying to play waiter.

Jimmy heard a round of snickers through his earpiece in response to Jack's juvenile joke.

"Ha, ha, Jack. Very funny." Judging by his tone, Matt was not amused. "You're all lucky. Tonight is butler service, just passed hors d'oeuvres. But I'm serious about this. People are going to ask what's on your tray. Take it from me, you'll feel like an idiot if you don't know."

Jimmy had a feeling they might actually be better off with Bull on the communications console and Matt out here. He really was the only one who knew what the hell he was doing as a waiter.

All of their training for Task Force Zeta didn't prepare them one little bit for butler service.

Damn, did people even have butlers nowadays? Jimmy saw the first guest arrive, and judging by the look of him, these people did.

"Guests are arriving." He turned his head to face the wall as he spoke and kept his voice low as a few more people filtered into the room.

After turning back, Jimmy visually swept the space.

"I'm ready." Jack's voice came through the communicator at the same time Jimmy heard the sound of a champagne cork pop.

The commander nodded once. "Let's roll, boys."

Their leader looked impatient to get this assignment over and done with. Jimmy couldn't agree more.

Trey, Bull and BB all headed toward the entrance to the kitchen. Jimmy decided he better follow and see what the hell waited for them with this butler service crap.

When he arrived in the rapidly filling kitchen crowded with cooks and now his teammates, a counter covered in big silver trays containing tiny food greeted him. The team lined up.

Being in the military, they were all skilled at waiting in line. It was the next part Jimmy was concerned about as the chef shoved a tray at BB.

"Herb-encrusted goat cheese." The chef's words were spewed with every bit as much disdain and authority as a drill instructor barking orders to a new recruit at boot camp.

Maybe this wasn't going to be as far out of their realm of familiarity as Jimmy had anticipated.

BB picked up the tray with two slightly unsteady hands Turning in slow motion toward the door, he tenuously balanced the tray as if it held a nuclear bomb.

Trey stepped forward.

"Bruschetta," the chef barked with another shove.

"Bru-whatta?" Trey frowned down at the little red triangles laid out in an artful display in front of him.

The look the chef shot him could have wilted the green leafy things garnishing Trey's tray.

Trey's tray. That was funny. Jimmy laughed to himself at his own little joke. He'd have to find a way to use that later.

"It's chopped tomatoes with basil on garlic toast points," the chef explained none too patiently.

"Oh." Trey grabbed his tray with one hand, raised a brow and then left the kitchen.

"Don't piss off the chef, whatever you do. I had one throw a butcher knife at me once." Matt issued that warning to them all, unbeknownst to the chef in question.

Great. Now Jimmy had to worry about the chef throwing things at him on top of terrorists blowing up the rich guys who were going to be asses to them for not knowing what bruschetta was.

Bull stepped up as the chef shoved another tray forward.

"Wild mushrooms and brie on sourdough toast."

Hmm. Who knew toast was so high falutin'? It was in a bunch of these things already. Jimmy had been eating toast all his life. He hadn't known he was so classy.

Bull took the mushroom toast things and looked like a storybook giant carrying a doll-sized tray out of the kitchen.

Uh, oh. Jimmy was next. He stepped up to the stainless steel table.

"Hot parsnip soup." The tray slid toward him as the chef announced its contents.

Uh, oh, again. His silver and very slippery tray contained about twenty tall shot glasses filled with a whitish liquid that he thought looked too much like semen for him to even contemplate drinking, or eating or whatever.

But that wasn't the least of it. How the hell was he supposed to carry it without the shot glasses sliding all over the place?

The commander was behind him, so he stepped aside to magnanimously allow him to go first. "Sir?"

"Oh no, Gordon. That one's all yours. And don't call me sir."

Under the impatient scrutiny of the chef, Jimmy cringed a bit and picked up the tray with shaking hands.

He could shoot the bull's-eye out of a target with a hand so steady he could perform brain surgery with it, but carry a tray full of semen soup filled shot glasses and he was . . . well . . . shot.

Jimmy somehow got himself out the door without spilling, although the whole lot of glasses shifted slightly to the left, along with the white lace doily that might look nice, but did dick to help him keep from spilling.

He paused to scope out the situation in the rapidly filling room and nearly got knocked into by a guest as he did.

That was it. He couldn't keep his eye peeled for the bad guys if he was staring at this gross soup in a vain effort to not accidentally dump any.

Jimmy walked over to his brother at the bar. "I'm leaving this tray here with you before I spill it."

"What the hell is it?" Jack glanced at the contents of the glasses.

"Parsnip soup."

Jack winced. "Well, it looks like—"

Jimmy held up his hand to stop Jack before he went any further with his most likely X-rated description. "I know what it looks like. Just tell the guests what it is if they ask. I'm going to do a walk-through and see what's up."

"A'ight, but nobody's going to drink that shit—I mean stuff." Jack censored himself just as a couple walked up to the bar and into earshot.

Jimmy smiled. This gig might not be too bad. It would definitely be something to talk about over drinks later. Until then, he'd just keep dumping his trays with Jack so he wouldn't have to deal with them.

Proud of his stroke of genius, Jimmy was still congratulating himself when he saw one hot number walk into the room on the arm of one of the VIPs they were there to protect, an old dude he sincerely hoped was not her date.

That would be a shame, since she was hotter than that soup he'd ditched and a hell of a lot more attractive.

Her red hair was pulled up to reveal the sexiest porcelain neck and shoulders he'd ever seen.

Her legs seemed to stretch nearly up to her armpits. Her black, strapless dress slit up the side nearly hip-high was pretty nice to look at too.

Her eyes, as big and blue as the cool pond on his mama's farm, completed this vision of walking, talking sex that would fulfill any man's fantasy.

Wow. Good thing he'd ditched that tray. Otherwise, he definitely would have dropped it when he saw her.

She was gorgeous and she knew it. Head held high, she waved off BB and his tray with a flick of her wrist without even glancing at him.

Jimmy watched the commander sidle up to her. It looked as if he had teeny tiny lamb chops on his tray.

That figured. The commander not only got food easy to carry, but it was something the hot chick actually wanted. She grabbed a chop and a little white napkin and turned back to listen to something her companion was saying to another old guy in a tux.

Jimmy swallowed. His mouth started to water, and not only because the lamb looked really good and he hadn't eaten since lunch. It was because he was picturing her doing something else with that luscious mouth as he watched her suck on the delicate lamb bone.

Mmm, mmm.

"Gordon." Jimmy jumped at the unexpected and harsh sound of the commander's voice through his earpiece.

"What?" Jack's surprised response came through Jimmy's comm unit.

"Not you, Jack. The other Gordon." The commander

sounded annoyed.

Jimmy turned toward the wall so no one would wonder why he was talking to himself and whispered, "Sir?"

"Stop drooling over the redhead and do a sweep of the area, dammit. And don't think I didn't notice you *forget* your tray at the bar. Good job on that one, by the way."

Jimmy turned and saw the commander shaking his head but grinning across the room. He'd gotten caught ogling Red, but at least he wasn't in trouble over the cum-soup. He nodded once then headed off to do a lap around the public and staff areas.

CHAPTER TWO

Amelia Monroe-Carrington pasted on a sweet smile and feigned interest in what the senator and her father, the governor, were discussing.

They were deep into campaign season and if she had to attend one more party and pretend she was having a good time, Lia feared she'd lose her mind. Unfortunately, there were many more such parties on their schedule.

"Amelia. How is your mother feeling?"

Lia wrestled her wandering attention back and focused on the senator's question. "Better, though she wasn't quite up for tonight. Thank you for asking."

The explanation tasted bitter on her tongue. Her mother had been deemed fit by the doctors months ago, and yet here Lia was, still playing lady of the family.

Lia had been more than happy to fill in as her father's date when it was necessary during her mother's recovery from a bout with a bleeding ulcer, but now she was clearly being taken advantage of.

"Glad to hear she's on the mend. Please give her my regards." The senator's eyes dropped to take in the exposed cleavage of a passing woman and Lia smothered a scowl.

Instead, she pasted on her campaign-picture smile. "I will be sure to do that, Senator."

She supposed she shouldn't blame her mother for seeing a way to escape the political society's merry-go-round and taking it. It had most likely been both her father and his career that had given her mother the ulcer in the first place.

Lia only wished her father hadn't dumped the full responsibility of publicly supporting him on her shoulders so happily.

She knew exactly why her father had readily jumped on the opportunity to have her be his new social partner and the reason was standing before her now, holding his martini and looking down women's dresses.

Lia's father made no secret of his desire to see her married off to the senator's self-absorbed son. An *alliance of two of the greatest southern political families*, he'd called it.

The entire concept made her ill.

At least the senator's son, John Dickson III, wasn't here with his father tonight. He was as pompous as his name made him sound and she had no interest whatsoever in the man.

Lia wanted to be swept off her feet, fall head over heels in love and marry someone who would give her the *happily ever after* she'd always dreamed of.

That, however, didn't seem to matter to her father. He wanted her married not for love, not for compatibility, not because of overwhelming sexual chemistry, but for politics.

She'd seen what her father and mother's *alliance* was like. They'd had separate bedrooms for as long as she could remember. She was pretty sure they'd only had sex once and that was the night she was conceived.

However, the all-powerful families of the Monroes and the Carringtons had been united with their marriage, so everyone pretended they were happy. Even Lia.

She stifled the urge to sigh and glanced around the room, actually seeing it for the first time since her arrival.

All these parties were alike. She'd long ago stopped observing them, except maybe to see what horrendous fashions reared their ugly heads on some of the women who dared stray from the campaign semi-formal party circuit uniform of the basic black dress. Lia had an entire closet of black dresses, because heaven forbid you wore the same one twice.

Her gaze swept the room and landed on not one, not two, but half a dozen really buff male members of the wait staff.

Where in the world did the caterer find these guys? Had an all-male strip club gone out of business and all the dancers needed to start waiting tables?

Watching a huge guy trying to balance a tray in one hand while handing the mayor and his wife a cocktail napkin, Lia had to bite the inside of her lip to stop from laughing.

The server was concentrating so hard, the tip of his tongue stuck out between his lips as he frowned.

Lia glanced around some more and saw a cutie behind the bar smiling at the wife of one of the most powerful businessmen in town.

The object of his flirtation was absolutely eating up all the attention. She leaned over the bar, giving the bartender a clear view of her exposed cleavage, which he was shamelessly taking advantage of.

She took closer inventory of the staff. They all displayed varying levels of gorgeousness, incompetence and hilarity.

Her gaze landed on one guy across the room and she realized she was not the only one doing some observing. Bold as anything he was staring right at her, watching her as she watched all of them.

She raised a brow and met his stare head-on. Mirroring her, he lifted a brow back and treated her to a crooked smile.

Then his expression changed. He seemed to stand a little straighter. He broke his gaze from hers and was gone from the room before she could fully appreciate the rear view of his tight black pants pulling across tight butt cheeks.

That was a shame. He'd been a welcome distraction.

Lia snagged another lamb chop from a passing waiter. This one was a bit older than the rest, with silver streaks of grey in his hair, though he was just as built as the others. His arm muscles strained the seams of his jacket.

As she bit into the rosemary encrusted flesh and chewed, she considered how she'd like to nibble on the tall, dark and handsome waiter who'd disappeared. Hopefully he'd return soon.

CHAPTER THREE

Jimmy had been making some good progress in his visual flirting with the hot redhead when Matt's voice came across the comm unit. "Code Orange."

The commander's gaze immediately landed on Jimmy. He was the only man there not burdened by a serving tray, except for Jack, who couldn't leave the bar.

Jimmy nodded to the commander. The hot chick would have to wait. He had a job to do and he couldn't do it in the middle of a cocktail party where he was supposed to be nothing more than a waiter.

He slipped into the hallway where he could respond to Matt unobserved. "What's the Code Orange, Matt?"

"I ran the guest list through the computer again and got a hit. One of the last minute additions matches an alias used by a terrorist on our watch list."

It looked like the shit might be about to hit the fan. Jimmy felt his adrenaline begin to pump at the thought of some action. "Give me the name. I'll find him."

Matt did as requested and Jimmy headed to the entrance where the guests were being cleared through security.

The guard there pointed Jimmy in the direction of the guy who'd checked into the party under that name.

Jimmy nearly laughed when he saw him. He ducked

outside and around a corner to talk to Matt. "Uh, Matt. Unless your terrorist is a little old gray-haired man of about eighty who uses a walker, the name is just a coincidence."

Matt's laugh came through the earpiece. "Roger that."

"Anyone else?"

"Negative. The rest of the list looks good."

After reporting his findings, Jimmy went back inside the building to resume his post, but he knew the magical moment with Red had been broken.

That thought had him scowling as he made his way down the hallway toward the ballroom . . . until he smacked right into the redhead of his dreams coming out of the ladies' room.

Reflex had him reaching out with both hands to steady the incredibly sexy woman as she teetered on her high heels. "Sorry, darlin'."

Her brows shot up to her hairline and an amused smirk appeared. He realized he probably shouldn't be calling the guests *darlin'*, but what could he do? He'd been calling females not related to him that since puberty. It just slipped out.

Red didn't seem too upset about it though. As Jimmy reluctantly released his hold on her, she raised her hands and ran them up and down his lapels. "You're forgiven. What's your name?"

He breathed in the rich scent of her. Expensive-smelling perfume with an undertone of lamb.

"James." Entranced by her clear blue gaze, he somehow managed to supply his given name for her. Though even his mother didn't call him *James* unless she was mad, it seemed to fit better in this situation than *Jimmy* so he went with it.

The vision of sex on heels before him reached into her envelope-sized purse. Was everything rich people owned and ate tiny? She took out a pen and a scrap of paper. On it she scribbled something and then handed it to him.

"Nice to meet you, James."

The pleasure was all his, especially when she winked and

sashayed away and he got to drool over the rear view.

When she'd turned the corner—without looking back, he noted—Jimmy finally had the presence of mind to look down at what she'd written on the paper she'd given him.

Seven digits and a name—*Lia*.

She'd given him her phone number and he hadn't even asked. That was one hell of a woman. One he definitely would be happy to get to know better.

Jimmy suppressed the whoop of excitement threatening to bubble out of him, but since he was alone in the hall he figured he could ask the question uppermost in his mind out loud. "Hey, Matt. When is this gig scheduled to be over?"

Whenever it was, it wouldn't be soon enough for him.

A few hours later, Jimmy walked out of the back door alongside Jack and Trey.

In what would have looked like a coordinated effort to an outside observer, all three tugged at their collars simultaneously as they struggled to rip off their bow ties. Jimmy, for one, couldn't get his off fast enough.

"That was a waste of time," Trey grumbled.

Jimmy wouldn't exactly say that the fact no terrorists had blown up the place made it a waste of time, but it was frustrating to go to all the effort for a false alarm.

Nothing more exciting than Matt's early scare about the old dude with the suspicious name had happened all night, unless he counted the phone number he'd gotten.

Now *that* was something to get excited about.

He patted his breast pocket and assured himself the number was still safely tucked away. His fingers itched to grab for his phone and dial it right then and there. Instead, he controlled the impulse until he could get somewhere private.

"At least you didn't drop your *tray*, Trey." Jack grinned, obviously proud of his cleverness. "See what I did there?"

Jimmy frowned. "That was going to be my joke."

"Late again, big brother." Jack slapped him on the back. "So, what do y'all say we hit the bar after checking in on base? We can get a cold one and I can see how my hot bartender is doing."

Free from the tie now, Trey undid the top two buttons of his shirt. "Sure. As long as we can change out of these monkey suits first."

Jimmy thought again of the precious piece of paper tucked away in his pocket. It was already getting late. He had to either call now or not at all if he had any hope of meeting up with her tonight.

"You two go ahead. I'm, uh, a little tired."

Jack shot him a look. "Tired? From walking around a party picking up dirty napkins all night? Come on. We'll just go for one beer."

"It wasn't just playing waiter. We had to keep on alert in case anything did go down." That much was true, even though Jack was correct—Jimmy wasn't tired from the party. He was tired of being celibate and had every hope Lia would help him out in that area.

"But nothing went down," Jack reminded him.

Jimmy struggled to come up with an excuse not to go to the bar so he could see Lia, if she wanted to see him. "Yeah, but I'd have to stop by the bank and get some cash first."

"Yeah, and? So what? That'll take like a minute." Jack stared at him, waiting for a response.

"But then I'd need to get gas too." Jack was still frowning at him doubtfully, so Jimmy added, "Maybe I'll meet y'all there later."

Jack shook his head. "Whatever."

Trey stopped next to his truck. "See you guys back at the base."

They had each taken their own vehicles, thinking it would appear less suspicious arriving individually as waiters would, instead of piling out of one of the team vehicles as a group the way they usually traveled.

"Yeah, see you." Ignoring his brother's displeasure with him, Jimmy thankfully shut himself in his vehicle.

Grateful once again he had his own transportation, he sat in the driver's seat and waited for Jack to close the driver's door of his own car, then he punched Lia's number into his cell phone.

"Hello?" Her sexy voice sent a shiver right down from his ears to his toes and everywhere in between. "Hey, darlin'. It's Jim—uh, James."

"Hello there, James. Where are you?"

"In my car outside the party. We just got off."

Oh yeah. Judging by the sexy purr of her voice, he had a feeling he was about to *get off* all right.

"Meet me at the Hilton in ten minutes. Ask for the private elevator that leads to the presidential suite. I'll leave your name at the desk so they'll let you up."

Jimmy heard a click and she was gone.

Holy crap. He didn't know what to be amazed at more. The fact he was going to get lucky with the hottest woman he'd ever laid eyes on, or the invitation to the presidential suite at the Hilton.

Meanwhile, there was no way he could drive back to base, check in and then get to the hotel in ten minutes, and Jimmy had a feeling Lia was not the kind of woman who responded well to being kept waiting.

The mission had been uneventful. Maybe no one would notice if he didn't check in tonight. His decision made, he drove directly to the Hilton so fast it was a miracle he didn't get pulled over for speeding. He stopped only long enough to grab a box of condoms and breath mints at the twenty-four-hour convenience store across the street from the hotel.

Jimmy remembered to unstrap his leg holster and secure his weapon in the glove compartment. He even remembered to lock his parked car, but that was about the only time his mind strayed from thinking about what was about to happen up in that suite.

Inside the massive marble lobby, he gave his name to the man standing behind the concierge desk, thinking there was a good chance he'd be thrown out on his ass.

Lo and behold, he wasn't. Instead, he was ushered by another uniform-clad employee into a brass and mahogany elevator with only two buttons inside. They read *Lobby* and *Presidential Suite*.

As the valet, or whatever he was called, rode up the many floors to the top with him, Jimmy finally allowed himself to stop thinking this whole thing must be some kind of a joke. That was something he knew for sure when the elevator doors opened onto the eerily quiet, private hallway on the top floor of the building.

The hotel employee held the door open with one arm and dismissed him with a nod. "Have a good night, sir."

"Thanks." Intending to do just that, Jimmy stepped out onto a marble floor.

With a swish, the doors swept shut behind him and he was alone facing a single, massive white door.

Jimmy ignored the erratic pounding of his heart and raised his hand to knock. When the door swung wide a moment later, Lia stood before him wearing nothing but a black strapless bra, lacy thong underwear and mile-high heels.

He didn't question the state of her attire. Her intentions were clear enough, so he strode in and blindly slammed the door shut behind him.

Never a man to beat around the bush, he grabbed her head with one hand and her waist with the other and sank his tongue deep into her warm, welcoming mouth.

He explored down the silky warm flesh to land on her ass cheek and discovered she felt as good as she looked.

Lia let him enjoy both her mouth and body for long enough to make his hard-on start to throb as it pressed against the zipper of his pants. Then she pulled away.

"You don't waste any time, do you?" she asked.

A woman who answered the door half-naked shouldn't talk about how fast he was moving.

"Darlin', you ain't seen nothing yet." He ran his hands one more time over her curves with a groan.

Enough with the standing. Time to get horizontal. He glanced around the large space. It was decorated like a living room with a sofa and a huge flat-screen television that he might enjoy at another time when he didn't have a raging hard-on and a willing woman beneath his hands.

He swept his gaze over the kitchenette and dining area and landed on a partially closed door. Bingo.

She let out a small squeak as he scooped her up and headed for the adjoining room where he hoped to find a bed. A really large one if he was lucky. What he had in mind was going to take more than a little bit of time and a whole lot of space.

When he pushed the door open wider with one foot and saw the king-sized mattress with the bedding already turned down for the night, it looked as if he was blessed enough to get what he wanted.

He dropped her on the bed and began tearing off what remained of his uniform. He'd long since ditched the jacket back in the car, so all he had left was the button-down shirt and pants.

She watched each piece of clothing fall to the floor, including his underwear, and then stared at his naked body. "Nice."

Jimmy didn't miss the gleam in Lia's eye as she said that.

Damn right, it was nice. He worked hard to keep in shape. The whole team did. About time he put it to use for something other than practice maneuvers and fighting bad guys.

"Glad you approve, darlin'." He pulled her panties down with both hands and spread her legs.

He ignored her surprised intake of breath and settled himself eye level with her creamy thighs and a whole lot more.

She was totally bald down there except for a tiny neat strip of red curls. The rest was smooth and hair-free.

He must have been staring for quite a while, because she finally reached down and grabbed his head in both hands, raising his face so he could see hers.

"What's the matter, handsome? Don't your waitress girlfriends believe in laser hair removal?"

As hot as she was, and as incredible as the results of her laser hair removal looked, he didn't need any more of her smart-ass waiter comments.

He was betting she was a talker, and he wanted quiet during this so he could fully enjoy himself.

There was one sure-fire way to make sure she stopped talking. Jimmy spun himself around so quickly she let out a small squeak. He straddled her face and pressed his cock to her lips.

Since she opened her mouth and took him in without hesitation, he figured he hadn't offended her delicate, rich-girl sensibilities too badly. And damn, did her mouth feel good wrapped around him.

He lowered his head and began to enjoy a taste of her for himself. He slid his tongue between her folds and worked her over. Gently at first, then rougher.

"Gordon!" Just as Lia's hips had begun to rise from the bed in response to his efforts, the loud, angry voice sounded inside Jimmy's head.

Startled at the sound, Jimmy jumped.

"James Gordon, answer me! Where the hell are you?" the voice repeated when Jimmy didn't respond.

Visions of his mama's unhappy face as she used his full name while reprimanding him for something as a child threatened to deflate his very happy erection, but this angry voice wasn't his mama's. It was the commander's and he had obviously turned on Jimmy's two-way communications device.

"Mmm, James. Don't stop." With what had to be the worst timing ever, Lia chose that moment, while they were being monitored, to let Jimmy know how unhappy she was he'd stopped what he'd been doing.

As he worked her with his thumb to keep her from complaining, there was radio silence during which Jimmy vainly hoped communications had been lost.

"Who is that and what the *fuck* are you doing, Gordon?"

No such luck. Apparently he was still transmitting loud

and clear.

"Um, sir. I'm pretty sure fucking *is* what he's doing." The sound of Matt's amused voice, letting him know it wasn't only the commander listening in, made the entire situation worse.

Jimmy scowled at Matt's comment and silently cursed the communications implant one more time.

"Get a GPS reading on him, Coleman."

Damned tracking implant.

"He's at the Hilton, sir." It figured Matt could locate him so fast.

Jimmy guessed he was lucky Matt hadn't pinpointed his exact location as the presidential suite's bedroom.

"Dammit, Gordon. You check in on base after an op and get officially dismissed before you go and check into a hotel to get laid. You hear me?" The commander's order filled Jimmy's ear just as Lia kicked things into a higher gear.

She took him even deeper into her throat and sucked hard while working his balls with her hand.

A tingling, pleasure-filled shudder passed through him. Pissed-off commander or not, Jimmy couldn't maintain his control any longer. "Oh, yeah."

"Was that response for me or for her, Gordon?" With an edge of annoyance in his voice, the commander questioned the words that had escaped Jimmy's lips.

"I suppose it could be for both of you, sir," Matt supplied not so helpfully.

Jimmy could hear the laughter in Matt's voice and vowed to wipe the smile he knew was there right off his face at the next opportunity.

Meanwhile, Lia had begun using her teeth and he knew there was no way he'd be able to stay quiet. He bit his lip and tried anyway.

"Gordon, my office, zero-eight-hundred. Coleman, cut communications." If possible, the commander sounded even angrier than before, but then thankfully there was blissful silence.

Relieved, Jimmy went back to working Lia until she began to shudder beneath him. He filled her with his fingers while he circled her with his tongue and sent her directly into a hip-bucking orgasm.

Whoever said rich girls were cold hadn't been with this one. She was sweet and warm and wet, and he intended to experience all of her charms, including her incredibly sexy moans. He pulled himself out of her mouth so he could fully enjoy hearing her, loud and clear.

Longing to be inside her, Jimmy flipped back around and reached for his discarded pants with the condoms in the pocket. When he knee walked back to her across the large bed, he found her watching him with heavily lidded eyes.

Oh yeah, she wasn't near done yet, which was good, because neither was he. A quick tear of the wrapper and he was soon safely covered.

He sank himself inside her and felt exactly how *not* cold she was. Wet and ready for him, her body accepted his like they were made to fit together.

"Oh, darlin'. You feel so sweet."

He wanted the feeling to last a very long time, so he kept the pace nice and slow. Lia pulled her knees up and his next stroke sank him even deeper into her. He groaned his approval.

She threw her head back against the pillow and gripped his forearms. "Harder. Faster."

Yup, she was a talker all right and she liked to give orders.

Jimmy took orders all day at work. He wasn't about to have to follow them in bed too. With her knees pulled up and braced against his chest, he couldn't even lean down far enough to shut her up by kissing her. That didn't mean he couldn't teach her a lesson about being bossy.

He slowed his rhythm even more.

"I said faster, dammit." Her ice-blue eyes flashed.

That had really pissed her off. He smiled, having more fun than he'd had in a long time. Shaking his head, he slowed down further.

She frowned. There was a good chance no one had ever said no to her before, poor thing. Jimmy was proud to be the first.

He stopped the in-and-out motion totally, pushed in deeper and pressed himself against her, making small circles. He knew how to please a woman. She'd just have to shut up long enough to realize it.

Each rotation of his hips ground the base of him against her most sensitive spot. He watched her eyes drift closed, then heard her breath catch in her throat.

She started to shudder again and with one incredible cry, she shattered around him.

He did love hearing her come. He loved feeling it even better. Her muscles squeezed him and he enjoyed every pulse.

Only when the spasms slowed to a stop did he give in to her previous wish, purely for his own pleasure.

Jimmy took her deep and fast until he lost it himself, coming hard until he could barely support his own weight on his shaking arms.

He collapsed on top of her with a groan.

They both lay panting for he didn't know how long. Finally, he gathered enough energy to lift up on one elbow.

Jimmy gazed down at the satisfaction clear on Lia's face. "One word of advice, darlin'. Never tell me how to make love."

She seemed shocked for a second, and then pursed her lips. "I'll try and remember that."

He was still hard inside her, so he pulled out and stripped off the used condom. Quicker than she could say "Yes sir, may I have another?" he'd rolled on a fresh one.

Sitting up on his knees, erection pointing proudly at her like a divining rod, Jimmy slapped her hip. "Flip on over, darlin'. This time I wouldn't mind a view of that sweet ass of yours."

She raised one perfectly shaped brow at him, but rolled over without saying a word. He said a quick internal thanks for her silence and slid himself into her for round two.

Money or not, everybody was the same when they were naked and sweaty.

Sex. The great equalizer.

That should be a bumper sticker or something.

Jimmy smiled at his own cleverness. He was on fire tonight.

CHAPTER FOUR

The dim gray tint of dawn filtered through the blackout curtain covering the window in the suite's bedroom.

After years in the military of snapping awake and being ready for action, even that dusky light was enough to break into Jimmy's sex-induced sleep coma.

He came quickly back to consciousness and became aware of the warm, naked body pressed against him.

Memories of a long night of incredible sex flooded his mind and body.

True to form, one part of him in particular was ready for some action. He pressed his pelvis against the soft cleft of Lia's ass and let out a groan. There was no better way to wake up than with some nice, easy morning sex.

Lia apparently agreed with that sentiment. With a soft sigh, she snuggled closer. Giving his hard-on better access to her, she bent one knee before pushing back against him so just the tip of his morning erection entered her.

He basked in the incredible feel of her warmth and longed for more.

Before things went any further, he slipped out of Lia and into one of the condoms he'd left within reach on the nightstand last night. He rolled back to her waiting body and slid easily inside.

She purred out a groan—a soft, sleepy, contented sound. He liked that about her. She was a hellcat one moment and a kitten the next. A man would never get bored of a woman like that.

Knowing he wouldn't last long, Jimmy reached around, found Lia's sweet spot and began working it. Her muscles tightened around him and brought his impending orgasm dangerously close.

He clenched his teeth and held back with all his might when he felt himself losing control, but it was no use.

Clutching her close to him, he gave in. With no choice in the matter, he let loose, sorry he hadn't lasted longer for her sake.

"I'm sorry, darlin'. Mornings tend to be quick for me."

Lia groaned and rolled toward him. "That's okay. You have all day to make it up to me. Unless you have to work later."

"Work. Shit." Jimmy's gaze cut to the digital clock on the nightstand on Lia's side of the bed. He mouthed another cuss. "I'm more sorry than you can know, but I have to shower quick and get out of here."

She cocked one brow high. "Why? Is your girlfriend expecting you?"

Jimmy laughed as he sat up and swung his feet to the carpeting. "I don't have a girlfriend. I wouldn't be here with you if I did. It's my boss."

She frowned. "Do you have to serve at a morning event? Like a breakfast or something?"

Getting pretty damn tired of the waiter crap, Jimmy shook his head. "No. I've got a zero-eight—um, an eight o'clock meeting."

After all the years he'd spent referring to the time by a twenty-four-hour clock, the very military sounding zero-eight-hundred had nearly slipped out of him.

Leaving her to ponder that, he strode naked into the bathroom and flipped on the water. He had just stepped into the shower and was about to soap up Little Jimmy, who he'd already divested of his latex covering, when the bathroom door opened.

Jimmy felt the cool burst of air hit his skin as Lia slid open the sliding glass door. As naked as he, she stepped inside with a devilish smile. "I thought if you're in such a hurry, I'd help you wash. It'll go faster that way."

He seriously doubted that, but after she closed her fingers around him and delivered a few strokes, good sense fled and time lost all meaning.

When she rinsed the soap from his skin, bent over and took him in her mouth, he couldn't care where he was supposed to be or who was waiting for him there.

An hour later, dressed in the same black waiter's pants and white shirt he'd worn on the mission, Jimmy burst through the door of the meeting room with barely a minute to spare.

He hadn't had time to go home and change and his hair was still damp from his shower with Lia, but he was there. That would have to be good enough.

Taking a deep breath to steady himself, he knocked on the commander's closed door.

"Get your ass in here, Gordon."

It wasn't exactly a warm welcome, but Jimmy had no problem hearing the commander within the inner office.

He opened the door and slipped into the room.

Standing in front of the commander's cluttered desk, he tried to look contrite and waited for the ax to fall.

After what seemed like a long time, during which the commander shuffled papers and ignored him, he finally told Jimmy, none too nicely, to sit the hell down.

He had a feeling this wasn't going to be a fun meeting.

Even so, in spite of the fact he'd only gotten maybe a couple of hours of sleep in between bouts with Lia, Jimmy was in such a good mood that even the commander's scowl and unhappy tone couldn't break it.

"Of all the men on this team, you were the last one I expected to . . ."

Jimmy tried to pay attention as the commander laid into

him, but his mind kept drifting back to the suite and thoughts of Lia. His little hellcat.

It hadn't taken her long to lose the attitude and soften toward him. By the morning, she'd been as cuddly as a kitten when he'd woken up beside her.

While the lecture droned on, Jimmy's mind wandered back to the many times he and Lia had enjoyed that big king-sized bed, and then later the shower.

Mmm. He'd really liked the shower. Her body all soapy. Her hands and mouth all over him. His hands all over her.

Beneath that hot spray of water while they were both slick with soap, she'd even told him to slide in for a little backdoor action.

A tingle ran straight down his spine at the memory. That had been the only time she'd broken his rule and told him what to do, but he hadn't minded following *that* order one bit. Not at all.

Jimmy wrestled his attention back to the commander before he embarrassed himself and got a hard-on right there in the office.

The commander stood and started pacing the room while he ranted. That wasn't a good sign.

". . . in fact, after last night it would serve you right if I pulled you off this assignment."

Assignment. Shit. What assignment? Had he missed something during his daydreaming?

The commander had stopped the deluge of words and stood staring at Jimmy, so he decided this was a good time to make amends.

"Yes, sir. I apologize. It will never happen again."

Groveling out of the way, Jimmy hoped the commander would get back to the assignment and tell him what it was.

The commander scowled at him for another moment, sighed and then sat down behind his desk, which felt like an improvement over the pacing. Things were looking up.

"You're aware of the target CENTCOM has been tracking in Kosovo?"

Jimmy's heart pounded. He suddenly had no trouble keeping his tired eyes wide open or his attention completely on the commander's words. "Yes, sir."

"We're ready to move on him. You're going in deep undercover, Gordon."

His dream assignment. Deep undercover inside a terrorist's organization. Holy shit.

"You leave tomorrow. Here's the dossier. Memorize it then destroy it. Basically, you're an American who's been recruited by the target's organization."

Jimmy nodded, too excited to even speak.

The commander continued, "Coleman's been setting your cover up online for months. The team will know what your assignment is, but no one else. Communications will be minimal and only when necessary. You got me? Call your mama to say goodbye, but tell her you'll be training new recruits overseas for the next few months or so and won't have time to write or access to a phone. The same story goes for whoever the girl *du jour* is from last night. Now get out of here."

"Yes, sir. And thank you."

The assignment was what he'd been preparing for for years. But along with the excitement, Jimmy felt a tinge of regret deep down.

Lia's cell phone number was safely folded in his wallet. He'd been toying with the idea of calling her later today.

Who was he kidding? Even if he wasn't going to be playing with the bad guys in Kosovo for an indeterminate amount of time, he knew what last night had been about.

She was just some spoiled society chick getting her jollies diddling with the help. If anything, he'd been the boy toy *du jour* more than the other way around.

But she sure would give him plenty to think about on those long, lonely nights to come. For that, he was immensely grateful.

The meeting over, Jimmy was dismissed. Walking, actually nearly sprinting down the hall, Jimmy realized he was whistling.

He couldn't wait to tell Jack he'd landed the assignment. His brother was going to be so jealous.

CHAPTER FIVE

Six months later

Jimmy sat—or more accurately lay like an invalid—on his bed.

The same book he'd been trying to read for the last two weeks was open on his lap. He stared at the words on the page but they were just a meaningless jumble.

Why couldn't he concentrate? It wasn't like he had anything else to do. Or all that much else to think about.

Downstairs his mama was baking one of her famous pies. The smell wafted temptingly up the staircase to his room. He supposed he could limp downstairs and get some if he really wanted.

Jack was still home on furlough for another few days. Maybe he could sneak outside and see what his brother and his new girl, Nicki, were up to.

His other brother Jared had brought in a new stud stallion he was planning on breeding today. He could perhaps hobble over to the paddock and watch that.

Letting his head fall back against the pillow and roll to one side, he stared at the faded wallpaper he remembered so well from his childhood and decided all those ideas for diversions sounded like too much work.

Sighing, Jimmy considered taking a nap, but he doubted

he could fall asleep. A man had to actually do something to get tired enough to sleep in the middle of the day.

Instead he let his mind drift to Lia, like he did so often even if it was the most pointless exercise on earth.

He'd thought about her every day he was in Kosovo. He'd jerked off to visions of her each night. He didn't even feel like doing *that* anymore. In fact, he didn't think he'd had a hard-on since getting home from the military hospital in Germany.

The guards who'd taken him had worked him over pretty damn good before the team had rescued him. There'd been a time he'd wondered if he'd ever see home again. But he had made it home.

His body was healing but it seemed his spirit was a little slower in recovering.

Now that he was here, safe, why didn't he feel happier about it?

Maybe because there was probably something wrong with his dick too.

Great. Something new to worry about in addition to the bruises, broken bones and enlarged spleen.

He was just considering digging his teen stash of girlie magazines out of the back of his closet to test this new horrifying broken-dick theory when Jack knocked on his door.

"Hey, big brother." Jack was always so damn cheerful, but then why shouldn't he be? His dick worked just fine and all signs indicated that he was working it out day and night with Nicki.

"Hey." Jimmy couldn't muster a smile to go with the greeting.

Jack frowned. "You doing okay? You don't look so good."

"I'm fine. What's up?" Jimmy wasn't exactly in the mood for small talk today.

Unperturbed by Jimmy's short answer, Jack walked over to sit in the chair next to the bed. He shrugged. "Oh, not much, except that I was just talking to the commander."

"About what?" Jimmy wasn't sure if talking about the team would be a good diversion or just make him feel worse about being away from it, but he asked anyway.

Jack broke out into a wide grin. "He wants you to come back to base with me when I go in a few days."

Jimmy sat bolt upright. "Really?"

Jack nodded. "You have to call him though. There's a doctor sign-off or something you have to get before the big brass will let you back on active duty."

He'd get a note from his mama, the Surgeon General and the President of the US of A if it meant going back on active duty. "I'll call him now. Thanks, Jack."

Jack laughed. "I thought that news would cheer you up. I just hope it makes up for my bad news."

Jimmy paused as he reached for his cell phone on the night table. He knew it was too good to be true.

He narrowed his eyes at his brother. "What bad news?"

"The governor and that bastard senator who tried to shut down our base a few years back are coming here for sweet tea and pie tomorrow afternoon."

"What the hell? Why?"

His mama was having a senator and the governor over for sweet tea and pie? Was he having a really strange dream? He hadn't taken any painkillers in months. He couldn't be hallucinating from them still being in his system.

"You know that organization Jared belongs to? The one that lobbies for the small farmer? Well, the governor and the senator are coming to meet with the organization, along with a shitload of press."

Great. Nothing Jimmy loved more than the press. "So let Jared deal with them all. He planned this mess."

"Oh, I plan on it. I'm sending Nicki away for the day too. I don't want her face in the newspaper right now. And you and I shouldn't be posing for any photos ourselves. The commander would shit a brick and our undercover days would be over. I figure we can hang out at the barn and watch Jared's circus from a distance."

Circus was a good description. From what he knew of the senator, the man was pretty much a clown who'd do anything to get the most people to cheer him on and vote him into office again.

Jimmy would love watching his youngest brother Jared play gentleman farmer for the idiots, as long as *he* didn't have to do it with him.

He nodded in agreement with Jack's plan. "Sounds good."

But more important than worrying about the big wigs visiting tomorrow was the phone call he had to make to his commander today.

Back on active duty. That was enough to make Jimmy smile.

CHAPTER SIX

"So, Staff Sergeant Gordon. You're here for an evaluation." The doctor glanced down at the paper in his hand through glasses that hung just on the end of his nose.

When he raised his gaze again, he looked at Jimmy over the top of the frames.

Jimmy hadn't been referred to by his rank since he'd been recruited out of the Marines for the special task force. They didn't use ranks on Zeta. It sounded strange hearing his mentioned now, but he supposed it was still accurate so he didn't correct the man.

"Yes, sir, and call me Jimmy." He glanced at the nameplate on the desk.

Dr. Marvin Stein, PhD, MD. That was quite a mouthful. Absently, Jimmy wondered what the good doctor's friends called him for short. Marv, perhaps?

Doctor Marv took a pen from among the many lined up in his breast pocket and scribbled something on a pad of paper. "Okay, Jimmy. Tell me about yourself."

Jimmy raised a brow.

Much like the stages of grief, he'd gone through many emotions over the last twenty-four hours since the commander had ordered the psych evaluation.

First he'd been elated, followed closely by anger that he

didn't need some doctor's note to tell him if he was ready to go back to duty. Now, finally, he simply felt acceptance.

Whatever it took to get back on active duty, he'd do. Even put up with Freud here watching him over the top of his granny glasses while taking notes on everything he said and did.

"Um, about me. Okay. I was born in Pigeon Hollow thirty-four years ago on the horse farm that's been in my mama's family for three generations. Daddy was a drunk. He took off when I was fifteen, leaving Mama to raise us three boys. I'm the oldest so I helped as much as I could. I was all-state in football in high school—"

The doctor held up his hand. "This is all very interesting, Jimmy. But perhaps we could skip ahead to what happened on your mission and your recovery since then."

As a doctor, he should be more specific with his questions. Although it was just the local VA hospital, not the Mayo Clinic, so Jimmy didn't expect much.

"All right. Well, my family doc says I'm pretty much all recovered from the injuries I sustained. My ribs will be sore for a little bit more. Broken ribs seem to take forever to heal. But my spleen is just about back to normal now."

"I'm not talking about your body, Jimmy, although I'm happy to hear you're healing nicely. I'm talking about you emotionally."

Hmm. Muddier waters. "I'm fine there too, doc."

"Ah." The doctor nodded and scribbled something else.

Ah? What the hell did *ah* mean? Jimmy fought the urge to stand up and grab the pad right out of his hand.

"Tell me what you've been doing during your time home, Jimmy."

Wrestling his attention off the yellow paper, Jimmy managed to come up with an answer.

"Um, well I was totally laid up for a few weeks or so. The doc wouldn't let me move because of the spleen thing. My ankle had been busted too and the house is full of stairs, so it was easier to stay up in my room. Now I get around all right though. The ankle's practically good as new, though I bet I'll be able to predict when it's going to rain from now on." He laughed at his little joke.

The doctor didn't.

"And what do you do for fun?" he asked.

How was he going to explain the extremely fun but unauthorized and probably illegal op they'd recently staged under Jack's command? "Uh, well . . . I, uh, joined my brother and some members of my unit for a night at our old hunting cabin a few weeks back. That was fun. Oh, and my brother got a new girlfriend. She works with the horses at our farm. We all hang out together sometimes."

His life sounded pretty pitiful now that he thought about it. If it weren't for Nicki and her mob friends, he'd have nothing at all to talk about.

"I see. What about you? Is there a special woman in your life?"

Besides the girl he'd spent one night having unforgettable sex with six months ago and hadn't stopped thinking about since? "No. My job isn't exactly conducive to long-term relationships."

He could just picture the date-night conversation had he taken Lia out before he left for his mission. Having to tell her he wasn't a waiter and that he was leaving for a job he couldn't tell her about for he didn't know how long.

Oh, and he couldn't call, write or email for the undetermined duration of it either.

That would have gone over really well. About as well as if he could have told her the truth, that he would be pretending to be a terrorist recruit and if he was exposed they'd torture him before most likely killing him.

Marv nodded and scribbled some more. "Any trouble sleeping since you've been home? Nightmares?"

Jimmy shook his head while squinting at the upside-down writing on the pad. "No. Not really."

During his first few days in the German military hospital, he would wake up in a cold sweat with his heart pounding until he realized he was safe.

That was to be expected, he figured. It wasn't a bad dream. More like it took a minute to remember he'd been rescued from the real-life nightmare.

The doctor was giving him that probing stare again. "Anything you say here is confidential, Jimmy. So I want you to speak freely."

Yeah, sure. So the doc could tell the commander not to put him back on active duty? No way.

As Jimmy considered that, his new pal Marv continued, "I'm going to be honest with you. You're incredibly well adjusted considering what you've been through. I feel going back on active duty is the best thing for you at this point. I made that determination based upon the fact that the only thing you've shown any excitement over in this interview was the night you spent with the men from your unit."

It had been one hell of a night, but more importantly, this guy was going to let him get back to work. His heart rate kicked into high gear at the thought.

"However, I also think there are things you're not telling me. I really do want to help you. So . . ." The doctor took a white piece of paper out of his drawer, scribbled some more and then slid it across the desk.

"That is my recommendation you be put on active duty immediately. It's yours to give to your commander. Take it and put it away, then tell me what you're holding back."

"Thanks, doc." Jimmy took the paper, but still hesitated spilling his guts to this man. What good would it do? He just wanted to take his paper and go.

The doctor filled the silence. "Do you know why your commander sent you to me in particular and not to any of the other doctors here?"

Jimmy shook his head. "I guess I didn't think about it."

"I was a POW in Nam."

"Wow. I didn't know." Jimmy saw the man with new respect.

Dr. Stein waited expectantly. What was it about silence

that made a person want to fill it?

Jimmy shrugged. "I don't know what kind of revelation you're looking for here, doc. There's really nothing to tell."

"Isn't there?"

Jimmy thought his lying skills had been honed pretty well, but good old Marv obviously saw right through him.

Actually, maybe he wasn't all that great at lying. He'd apparently somehow messed up in Kosovo too and blown his cover. Maybe he needed some more training in the deception department.

He let out a deep sigh. "It's just that I don't seem to have much interest in anything anymore. I feel . . . Well that's just it. I don't feel anything at all. Not angry, not happy, not excited—except for that one time with my brother and teammates. I'm not even, um, horny."

The doc nodded but thankfully didn't reach for his notebook again. Jimmy was very happy he wasn't taking notes on any of that, particularly the last part.

"It sounds to me like depression, which is not surprising. You've been an operative so long it's become your identity. Being forced to sit on the sidelines has left you without purpose. The lack of sexual interest is typical of depression. I think all of the symptoms will pass when you get back to the base." He smiled. "In fact, you perked up the minute I gave you that paper. But if it doesn't get better, call me and I'll prescribe something for you."

Relief flooded through him. He hadn't realized how good it would feel to admit his fears to a stranger, someone he hadn't grown up with and who wouldn't judge him, try to cheer him up or reason away his feelings.

Jimmy stood and extended his arm to shake hands with the doctor. "That's great to hear, doc. I feel better already."

The doctor laughed. "I can see that. Good luck, Jimmy."

"Thanks, doc." He nodded and was out the door with the golden ticket back to active duty clutched in his hand.

Now all he had to do was make it through Jared's political circus this afternoon and he was home free.

CHAPTER SEVEN

Lia rode in the limo next to her father and stared out the window at the rural scenery speeding by.

Meeting with the Small Farmers Coalition at Gordon Equine was far preferable to some stuffy cocktail party.

Best of all, although the senator was coming, his son wasn't. Lia would gladly walk her three-hundred-dollar shoes through horse manure any day if it meant getting away from him.

The sun was shining. She was wearing a pantsuit instead of a dress that required a torturous strapless bra and stockings. All in all, it was a good day. It would have been a better day if her mother had agreed to come with them when Lia suggested the trip to the country might do her good.

Of course, as usual her mother had said she wasn't feeling up to the drive. It had become such habit for Lia to accompany her father she feared her mother would never take her rightful place again.

Lia mentally reviewed her schedule for the next week. There would be more of the aforementioned cocktail parties this weekend. The most ridiculous thing was she had to control her heartbeat each and every time she walked into one. Even after six months, she'd still search the wait staff to see if James was among them.

It was crazy. She needed help. Although perhaps he needed the help. What guy could have the amazing kind of night they had together and not call afterward?

She hadn't expected him to ask her out on a date or anything, but come on. Not even a midnight drunken booty call? Nothing. Nada. Zip. For six damn months.

The bigger question was why did it bother her so much?

She'd worked that one over in many a therapy session. Her therapist thought it was because he had rejected her first before she had a chance to reject him and that it particularly bothered her since he was from a lower station in life.

She knew it was more likely she was obsessed with him because, unlike all the men who fawned over her, this one hadn't taken any of her shit.

He was a real man, not a spoiled rich boy. He knew his mind and treated her like an equal, not the governor's daughter.

After the initial shock that she wasn't always going to get her way around James had worn off, she'd really liked that about him.

Her therapist also thought she'd slept with James as a rebellion against her father and the pressure he'd been putting on her regarding the senator's son.

The psychologist may be a little bit right about that. Lia nearly laughed out loud in the limo when she considered what her father would say if she ever brought James home.

Hello, father. I'd like you to meet my new boyfriend the waiter. I'm going to marry him and have his babies and they will likely all grow up to be waiters too.

Marry him. Sure. She hadn't even made enough of an impression for him to call her. But boy, had he made an impression on her. Unforgettable.

He knew how to please a woman—at least this woman. Every inch of her. All night long until morning when he had to rush off to an early meeting with his boss.

Wait . . . Early meeting? What kind of early meetings did waiters have?

That had obviously just been an excuse to get out of there and she'd been too blinded from the sex haze he'd left her in to see it then.

That was a demoralizing thought.

What was laughable was she had actually hesitated before inviting him to the hotel because she was worried he'd fall in love with her and become a stalker or something.

Humph. He most likely slept with a different woman at every party he worked. No wonder he was so well stocked with condoms. He probably bought them by the case.

Lia shook her head at her own foolishness. Six damn months and he was still on her mind and it still killed her he hadn't called.

She definitely needed help, or maybe some sex. But the only man she'd even gone to dinner with lately was the senator's son, at her father's insistence. No way was she going to encourage him with anything more than just a casual dinner and a peck on the cheek or she'd find herself married.

That was *not* going to happen. John III held zero appeal for her, as a life mate or a bed mate.

The limo pulled down a charming magnolia-lined drive and up to a white farmhouse that, in typical southern tradition, had columns in front.

The car came to a stop and the driver opened Lia's door. She stepped out into the sunlight, slipping her sunglasses on to shield her eyes from the glare.

At least today's event would be a distraction from her pitiful love life.

The scent of jasmine wafted to Lia's nose. She breathed in deep, perhaps for the first time in a long time. Running in the rat race in the city wasn't really conducive to breathing deeply. Not with the car fumes and all.

It was beautiful here and peaceful. Besides, she'd always wanted her own horse.

Maybe she'd move to the country. That would really give her father heart failure. How would he play matchmaker with her so far away?

It was a nice dream, but it was expected that a dutiful southern daughter did what was best for her family. She couldn't fight tradition, though she might have tried if things had turned out differently . . . Lia pushed the pointless thoughts of James out of her mind.

One day a man would sweep her off her feet and she'd forget all about her night with James. Hopefully, that day would come soon.

CHAPTER EIGHT

Jimmy stood in the shade of the barn, chewing on a piece of hay and watching the limos and trucks pull up.

What a joke. As if a politician who arrived in a chauffeur-driven limousine could really understand the views of a farmer who drove himself in a pickup truck hauling a horse trailer.

Yeah, good luck to Jared with this little powwow.

Jack stood next to him, acting like he was incognito with his old straw cowboy hat pulled low on his forehead. He needn't have worried about being photographed. So far the press only had eyes, or rather camera lenses, for the politicians.

To the reporters, Jimmy and Jack were just two farmhands loafing around when they should probably be shoveling manure instead.

Of course, a few of the farmers they'd grown up knowing had come over to welcome them home. But everyone went rushing back to the meeting tables set up under the big trees by the house when the politicians arrived.

"Mama's been baking for two days straight. I was fixin' to cut into one of her pies and got my butt smacked with a wooden spoon over it. I had memories of being ten again, when I cut into the pie before Christmas dinner the year

Grandma and Grandpa Gordon were coming." Jack shook his head as he reminisced.

Jimmy laughed. "You think you would have learned not to touch Mama's pies after that time. If I remember correctly, you couldn't sit down that Christmas."

Jack rubbed his butt with the memory. "I learned. I just thought that when I turned thirty Mama couldn't smack me anymore."

"Well then, boy, you still have a lot left to learn. Mama can smack you no matter how old you are."

Jack rolled his eyes, shadowed beneath the brim of his cowboy hat. "I never thought I'd say this, but going back to the commander will be an improvement over living with Mama for two weeks."

Jimmy snorted. "How do you think I feel? I've been here a hell of a lot longer than you. When I first got out of the hospital, she wouldn't even let me go to the toilet. She tried to make me use a bedpan. She was going to help me do it too. How would you like to be thirty-four and have your mama helping you take a piss or a dump?"

"All right, you win with the worst 'living with Mama' story. It'll be good to get back to base for both of us."

"Amen." Jimmy agreed wholeheartedly on that one.

"Ooo, eee. Look at the hot number getting out of that limo. I never had me a redhead."

Ignoring the object of Jack's attention, Jimmy turned to glare at his brother. "You've got yourself a pretty hot brunette. What the hell, Jack?"

Jack frowned. "Oh, don't get your panties in a bunch. I'm only looking. Nicki's the only girl I want. I'm just saying, I wonder if redheads are, you know, red all over." He waggled his eyebrows suggestively.

A horrible and wonderful image flashed through Jimmy's mind of smooth skin punctuated by red curls that he'd never see again.

"They are," Jimmy said.

Jack opened his eyes wide. "Whoa. Tell me everything."

"No." Jimmy turned away to make sure Jack knew he was serious. He wasn't going to kiss and tell.

While he was pointedly ignoring his brother, he let his gaze wonder to the parking area near the house. That's when he saw her and nearly choked on the piece of straw he'd been chewing on.

Next to one limo stood the redhead Jack had been ogling. *His* redhead. Lia.

Jimmy's mouth got so dry he had trouble swallowing. His pulse pounded so loud he wouldn't be surprised if Jack heard it.

Even though Jimmy's world had stopped dead at the sight of Lia, the rest of the universe kept on going. At that point, everyone who was expected must have arrived, because Jared walked up to the podium and began speaking into the microphone he'd borrowed from the Rotary Club.

Jimmy had no idea what his brother was saying. He only had eyes for Lia, who was escorted by the same VIP she'd been with at the party.

Was she his press secretary or something? He hoped so, because the thought that Lia could have been dating some older-than-dirt politician at the same time she'd had amazing sex with him made Jimmy ill.

Jared announced the names of a whole bunch of people Jimmy had no interest in. Finally, Jared got to the old guy and Lia and introduced them as *Governor Carrington and*—holy shit!—*his lovely daughter, Amelia.*

"Hey, doesn't the hot redhead look kind of familiar? Where have I seen her before?" Jack's attention was glued to the podium too. When Jimmy didn't answer, he turned to him. "Jimmy. Hey, you a'ight?"

Not trusting his voice, Jimmy nodded as his brother continued to frown until recognition set in.

Jack's eyes bulged. "The redhead was at that party. The night you went AWOL to get laid at the Hilton right before you left for Kosovo. Holy crap. Bro, you had sex with the governor's daughter?"

"Shhh," Jimmy hissed and glanced around to see if any of the farmhands were near enough to hear them. "And how the hell do you know about where I was that night? Damn gossiping Matt."

"Don't blame Matt. He's usually a vault when it comes to this kind of stuff. But I know the combination to Matt's vault. Bourbon." Jack smiled. "So *she's* how you know redheads are red all over. Did you know whose daughter she was when you were ah, you know?"

"No." Jimmy ran his hands over his face.

This was a mess. Of all the many, many times he'd imagined seeing Lia again, it was never like this.

Jack snorted. "As if you knowing would have stopped you. Who are you kidding? Look at her. She could have been the devil's own daughter and you still would have done it."

Jimmy certainly wasn't kidding himself about that. Jack was right. He wouldn't have cared who she was at that point.

In fact, it probably would have made it even more exciting since he had no love of the current administration. The question was what the hell was he going to do now?

Hiding came to mind. So did grabbing her behind the big-ass limo parked by the house and kissing the hell out of her.

He'd have to make up his mind between the two somehow and soon, because it appeared as if Jared was about to give the entire group a tour of the barns, and walking next to his youngest brother was none other than Amelia Carrington herself.

CHAPTER NINE

Lia walked toward one of the horse barns for the grand tour alongside Jared Gordon, heir apparent of Gordon Equine.

He was handsome, polite and he lived and breathed horses. She had learned that about him already. Although, after a few long boring dinners with the senator's son where he talked of nothing but his political aspirations, horses would be a nice change of topic.

She glanced sideways at the young Mr. Gordon. Too bad when she pictured getting hot and sweaty with a man, it was always James who came to mind.

Hmm. Now that she thought about it, this guy reminded her a bit of James. Same warm brown hair with golden highlights. Same hazel eyes swirled with flecks of gold and green. Same drawl in his speech.

But the one big dissimilarity, the deal-breaker, was the fact that when she looked at Jared, her heart didn't pump until she felt dizzy. Not like it did when she'd seen James standing in the hallway in front of the elevator that led to the presidential suite that night so many months ago.

She sighed at the memory.

How pitiful was she? In fact, it was all she could do to prevent herself from searching through her old cell-phone calls to try to find James's phone number so she could call him. Would an incoming number still be on there after six months? Maybe she should check.

Amelia Monroe-Carrington, calling a man. This must be what happened when a woman turned thirty.

What was that statistic she'd heard? Something like a woman was more likely to get hit by a truck than married after the age of thirty?

Humph. She could get married tomorrow to John Dickson if she wanted to, but thinking about who the candidate was, she'd rather get hit by a truck.

She brought her attention back to the tour of the farm. Jared was explaining something about his philosophies regarding natural breeding versus artificial insemination, all of which were going right over her head.

Lia smiled and nodded, a skill she'd perfected young. She was doing a good job of pretending she knew what he was talking about until she glanced up and spotted a man who literally knocked her right off her designer pumps.

Just as she was about to take a header in the dirt, James treated her to the crooked smile she remembered so well from that night and caught her by both arms.

"Easy there, darlin'."

"You all right, Miss Amelia?" Jared was next to her in an instant, glancing at the floor, probably to see what she'd tripped over besides her own feet and shock.

She managed to nod a response to his question as she began to tremble simply from being in James's presence again.

Lia stared up at him for what seemed like an eternity as Jared continued, "Miss Amelia. This is my oldest brother Jimmy, and my second oldest brother Jack."

Jared made the introductions that delivered the second shock of the day. James the waiter was really Jimmy Gordon, as in *Gordon Equine?*

She finally managed to break her gaze from him and see the man next to him. When she looked closer at the brother under the cowboy hat, she found he was actually the cleavage-gazing bartender from the party where she'd met James—make that Jimmy. She turned back to him.

Gathering her composure, she straightened her spine and extended her hand. "A pleasure to meet you, *Jimmy*."

Her voice may have been cordial, but she sincerely hoped her narrowed eyes said what she was really thinking. That being, what the hell were two successful horse breeders doing playing at being wait staff miles away and why hadn't James—or rather Jimmy, called her after their night together?

"The pleasure is all mine." He smirked, apparently unaffected by her subtle censure.

"We're taking a tour of the breeding barns. You two wanna tag along?" Jared invited his brothers, not knowing what their mere presence was doing to her.

Torn between wanting to never let him out of her sight again and wanting to be as far away from him as she could get, Lia waited for the answer.

"Sure. I'd love to tag along." His gaze never leaving her face, Jimmy smiled, which seemed to be the default expression for him. He offered his arm to her. "Miss Amelia?"

She only nodded. At the moment, she wasn't sure her voice would function. Swallowing hard, she placed her hand in the crook of his warm, muscular arm.

The group moved on and Jimmy made a show of following, but it wasn't long before she found herself pulled off into a deserted part of the barn.

When they were alone together, he grabbed her face with both hands.

"I've been waiting a long time to do this." He grinned and then kissed her.

Hard. Demanding. He took possession of her mouth and, to her horror, she responded.

She kissed him back until she was breathless and she enjoyed it, until the relief over seeing him again was replaced with the anger and hurt she'd been harboring for six months.

Pulling away, she punched him in the arm. "Stop that, you bastard. I'm mad at you. Why didn't you call me?"

Oh well, so much for her plan to act cool and aloof if she ever saw him again.

A fly probably would have bothered him more than her hitting him had. Smiling, he captured both her hands in his and kissed them, one by one.

Drawing in a deep breath, he let it out in a sigh. "Ah, darlin', I wanted to. Believe me. I hate to say it, but we both know what that night together was. You're the governor's daughter. If I had called, you probably would have changed your phone number and gotten a restraining order."

"That's not true." If it were, he'd never have been able to inflict six months of torture on her. Lia disengaged herself from his grasp and folded her arms. "You don't know me at all."

"Sure, I know you." Jimmy stepped closer and pinned her between his rock hard body and a wall of stacked hay bales. "I know the cute little way you snore when you fall asleep after making love."

He leaned down, rested his big hands on her waist and kissed his way down her neck before continuing, "I know you have a tiny tattoo of a heart on your right ass cheek, and now that I'm aware of who you are, I'm pretty sure Daddy knows nothing about it. And I know exactly how to touch you to make you come." His voice dipped lower and if possible, got even sexier.

Her insides rebelled against her mind and twisted with need, with want, for him. "Okay. Enough. I get it."

Jimmy smiled. "You're right, darlin'. Less talking, more kissing."

He leaned low and she let him kiss her again.

Let him. Who was she kidding? She loved him kissing her. There was no letting about it. It wasn't as if she was an unwilling participant.

Running her hands up under his shirt, she remembered exactly how good it felt to touch him. She couldn't stop the sound of pleasure that escaped her.

This kiss had affected him too. He groaned and pressed closer against her. She felt the bulge in his jeans and the need inside her grew.

"Oh, darlin'. You have no idea how good you feel."

As charming as this country setting was, she wished they were back at the Hilton on that big bed. She braced her hands against his chest, hoping to hold back both her desire and the advance of his head toward hers. "We can't do this here."

"Not true at all. *Here* in this very hay room is where I lost my virginity."

Jimmy's casually delivered revelation left Lia insanely jealous of whoever that lucky girl was, even though she was probably married with a minivan full of kids by now.

The sound of voices got louder as the group began moving back toward their hiding place.

Jimmy dropped one last kiss on her lips and released her. "You'd better get back."

She nodded but wasn't convinced her legs would work to get her back to where she was supposed to be.

Luckily, he wasn't ready to release her yet anyway. Jimmy curled his hand around the back of her neck. "When can I see you again?" he asked.

"Call me." Shocked at her own answer, Lia couldn't stop the bitter laugh that escaped her.

He treated her to a dimple-filled grin. "Don't worry, darlin'. This time I will."

"See that you do." Leaving him and his oh-so-tempting, hard-all-over body by the bales of hay, Lia moved to the doorway.

She waited and then slipped in behind the rear of the group unnoticed. Unnoticed that is, by everyone except for the other mysterious Gordon brother, Jack, who winked at her and treated her to the same crooked smile Jimmy wore so often.

Ignoring Jack, she tried not to appear too self-conscious as she ran a finger around the edge of her probably smeared lipstick.

Lipstick she could fix, but there was nothing she could do about the blush she felt creep into her cheeks or the Gordon man who'd crept into her heart.

The cell phone in her purse vibrated. She hung back behind the other visitors and hit to answer the call from the unidentified number. "Hello?"

"Hey, darlin'. See? I'm calling, as promised."

She shook her head but couldn't help feeling like a teenager again.

He'd kept her phone number all this time. For six long months. Somehow, that made up for the fact he hadn't called it for as long. "Yes, so I see. Thank you. I'll talk to you later."

"Count on it."

Maybe she was stupid or naïve but she did count on it—on him. Only time would prove whether she was right or wrong to do so.

CHAPTER TEN

Jimmy ended the call on his cell phone just as he saw Jack saunter into the hay room.

"Well, well, well." Jack folded his arms and leaned against the doorframe. "Before you go have pie with the governor, big brother, you might want to wipe his daughter's lipstick off your mouth."

Jimmy scowled and scrubbed one hand over his lips. A man couldn't even find privacy in the hay room anymore. But come to think of it, Jack had walked in on some pretty sticky situations a few times in their teen years too.

At least Jimmy was alone for this unwelcome interruption. He thought about how he hadn't been alone just a minute ago and smiled.

It seemed the doc had been right. His dick wasn't broken after all. It just needed the right motivation.

Lia sure filled that bill. He resisted the urge to adjust himself in his jeans until he was alone.

Jack shook his head. "Man-oh-man, you got it bad."

Jimmy didn't answer. He wiped one last time at his mouth to make sure there was no more lipstick and took a step toward the doorway. "Let's go get us some pie, little brother."

He couldn't wait to be near Lia again, even if they had to pretend in front of the others that they hadn't spent one hell of a night six months ago getting to know one another in the carnal manner.

"Uh, huh. Pie. Is that what you're calling it nowadays?" Jack smirked.

That smart-ass remark earned Jack a punch in the arm as Jimmy tried to remove the I-just-made-out-with-your-daughter-in-the-barn smile from his face before he had to sit down with the governor.

The press had taken all their shots and left so Jimmy didn't worry when he, Jack and Jared, being the three Gordon men, were seated at the same table as Governor Carrington, Lia and—as much as he dreaded it—Senator Dickson, the senator who had been referred to on base not so affectionately as *Dickhead* ever since he tried to shut them down in the name of budget cuts.

Asshole.

The man proved Jimmy's low opinion of him was well deserved when he said, "I have to stick to my assertion that if we could cut money from the defense budget, this administration would have the funds to support small farmers like yourselves."

As Dickhead spouted off about the state budget over pie, Jimmy tried to stay in his happy place so he wouldn't lose his cool and tell the senator exactly what he thought about him and his theory.

Even with all of his effort to distance himself, Jimmy felt his face getting hot. He glanced over to find Jack clenching a fork in his fist so tightly his knuckles were turning white.

"I have to disagree with you, Senator." The comment from Lia had Jimmy's ears perking up as he turned in his chair to hear what she had to say. She laid down her fork and continued, "Besides the importance of the US maintaining a strong military in today's volatile world, you know as well as I that you can't simply shuffle money from one budget line directly to that of another. It doesn't work that way."

Her speech had Jimmy's heart swelling with pride. Actually, after seeing her put the senator in his place, other parts of him were starting to swell too. He always had found intelligence in a woman sexy as hell.

The senator blanched at Lia's remarks, but being a scumbag politician he managed to pull himself together quickly. He pasted a phony smile on his lying face. "Such a charming naiveté. I'm sure once you and my son are married, you'll become more familiar with the complex inner workings of politics. Though I hope you'll be too busy giving me grandchildren instead."

Jimmy was barely aware of Jack choking on his iced tea next to him. He was too busy trying to not lose his own pie all over the table after what the senator had just said.

He looked at Lia, vainly hoping for her to deny what Dickhead had said. How could she have kissed him like that in the hay room and then told him to call her if she was engaged to the senator's son?

Her face turned bright red as she glanced at him then back to her future father-in-law.

Father-in-law. Jimmy's brain nearly exploded at that thought.

"Senator, I must remind you—" Lia began, but was cut off by her father the governor.

"Amelia, dear. We're not here to talk about the defense budget. Mr. Gordon, perhaps we should begin the agenda for our discussions so these very busy farmers can get back to their businesses."

Enough of this crap. One farmer was leaving now. Jimmy stood.

"I'll let y'all get to your meeting. Governor. Senator." He nodded and strode as fast as he could away from the woman he apparently was never destined to have in his life.

He heard footsteps and suddenly Jack was beside him, grabbing his arm as they reached the kitchen door of the house. "Jimmy."

Jimmy shook off his brother's hand. "Leave me alone, Jack."

At the warning in his tone, Jack was smart enough to back

off, but Jimmy's torture was not over yet. He'd barely gotten up the stairs to his room when his cell phone rang.

He looked at the display and recognized Lia's number. Cussing, he dropped the phone on the bed unanswered and pulled his duffle bag out of the closet.

Shoving clothes in, he made sure to tuck his precious doctor's note inside too before he zipped up the bag and flung it over his shoulder.

He'd find his mama, say goodbye and then grab one of the trucks. There was no way he could wait around for Jack to drive him back to the base when he left. All Jimmy knew was he couldn't get away from there—and her—fast enough.

If only he could run away from his feelings as easily.

CHAPTER ELEVEN

Lia kept seeing the horrified expression on Jimmy's face when he heard the senator, that pompous ass, say she was marrying his son. As if that was ever going to happen.

She couldn't even imagine what Jimmy thought of her for kissing him in the barn when he thought she was engaged to someone else.

Actually she could guess what he thought of her and it wasn't good.

If he'd only answer the damn phone and let her explain, everything would be fine, but he wasn't answering her calls.

There was one good thing that had come out of all this. Selfish as it was, Lia couldn't keep her spinning mind from returning to the thought that Jimmy must care a little bit for her if he was this upset over the thought of her with someone else.

In the meantime, this eternal meeting was still dragging on. She kept her eyes peeled for Jimmy around the farm for the next hour. She even pretended she needed to use the restroom and had almost searched the entire first floor of the house looking for him before she ran into Lois Gordon and had to feign being lost.

Now her father and the senator looked like they were wrapping this thing up, and she still had yet to find Jimmy to explain.

Fine, she'd just leave the explanation that she wasn't engaged in his voicemail if she had to. Of course, being a stubborn man, he would probably delete her message without listening to it.

Maybe she wouldn't have to leave a message after all because suddenly his brother Jack was in front of her.

"Looks like your *father-in-law* is itching to go. I guess there's a limit to how much slumming a man like that can handle in one day. Is that what you're doing with my brother, darlin'? Slumming? Because I gotta tell you, he deserves way better than that."

She bit the inside of her lip and took all of Jack's insults in silence until he finally shut up. "Are you done?"

He gazed at the sky for a moment as if thinking before focusing again on her. "Yup. I think that about covers it."

"Fine. Now it's my turn. First of all, it's not any of your business, but since you're Jimmy's brother I will tell you. I'm not engaged to the senator's son. The senator may want us together but it's not going to happen. I've had dinner with John alone a total of two times and that was because I couldn't think of a way to get out of it. And you know what, if your brother was so into me, he should have called me months ago."

Since the Gordon she wanted to yell at wasn't here at the moment, this one would have to do.

Lia's heart pounded as she wound up to continue her rant. "In addition, I've been calling your brother's phone for an hour now to explain all this to him and he won't answer. So go get him from wherever he's hiding and I'll tell him in person."

Jack watched her closely, as if deciding what to do with her. Finally, he shook his head. "No can do."

She sighed in frustration. "Why not?"

"Because he's gone." Jack delivered that news with such certainty that she couldn't doubt it was true.

"Gone where?" she asked.

Jimmy couldn't be too far. Where was there to go around there? The barn?

"He went back home." Jack's answer did nothing but confuse her.

Lia frowned. "What do you mean, home? Isn't this home?"

Jack hesitated just a bit before answering, "Not exactly."He scratched his head and screwed up his face as if the answer had been a hard one for him.

Where a person lived shouldn't be difficult to answer, unless there was something more than meets the eye.

"What's going on, Jack? Who are you two? It's pretty obvious you're not waiters. Now I'm starting to doubt you're farmers either."

"Shit." Jack shook his head. "This is something you have to discuss with him."She wanted to rip out her hair and scream from sheer frustration. "That's what I'm trying to tell you. He won't take my calls."

Jack huffed out a breath and then pulled his cell phone from his pocket. He scrolled a bit on the screen and then raised it to his ear. "Hey, it's me. I know you're in no mood to talk, but you might wanna listen. Your girl here says she's not engaged to Dickhead's son. She's here next to me and she wants to talk to you. Okay?"

Your girl. True or not, she kind of liked being referred to as Jimmy's girl. And *Dickhead?* Good name for the senator. She liked that too.

Jack thrust the phone at her. "Talk quick. He's not in a good mood."

She grabbed it and said fast before Jimmy hung up, "I'm not engaged to John Dickson. I'm not even dating him. The senator and my father have been trying to fix us up for years. I don't want to be with him, Jimmy. I don't even like him."

He was silent for a moment before he said, "Where do you live, Lia?"

"At the governor's mansion with my parents." She knew

that sounded pitiful. Thirty years old and still living with her parents.

No wonder her father still had so much control over her life. She made it easy for him.

Jimmy snorted out a bitter-sounding laugh. "That figures."

"Hey! I have my reasons."

She'd initially stayed living at home after college graduation because her grandfather was living with them. She was the apple of his eye and knew she wouldn't have long enough with him once they diagnosed the lung cancer. Then she'd stayed because her mother had been ill and her father needed her.

But somehow even though Granddad was gone and her mother was fine, Lia was still there.

Maybe Jimmy was right for judging her.

"Whatever. Call me when you get home later. Your *mansion* isn't too far from my hovel. Maybe we can meet somewhere." Jimmy's invitation was delivered in a voice that told her he may be talking to her, but he still wasn't happy.

Meeting him so they could talk was what she wanted, even if the way he had suggested it was not so great. Right now, she'd take anything she could get. "Okay. I'll call you when I get back."

"Fine."

The sudden dead air that met her ear told her he'd ended the call without even a goodbye. She really did feel like a teenager with a crush, and now she was remembering why she'd hated her teen years so much. They just plain sucked and her thirties weren't looking much better.

Lia handed the phone back to Jack. "Thanks."

Jack stashed the phone in his pocket, then leaned back against the pristine hood of the limo as the driver shot him a nasty look. "I just have one thing to say to you, darlin'. Don't you go to him if you're only going to hurt him later. Promise me that. He's been through too much already."

At least one of the Gordon brothers was still calling her darlin', since it seemed Jimmy wasn't any longer. But what was Jack referring to?

Curiosity got the better of her and she couldn't help but ask, "What has Jimmy been through, Jack?"

He shook his head. "That story's not mine to tell."

After tipping his hat to her, he strode away.

She watched him walk all the way to the barn where a woman had just driven up the driveway in a Gordon Equine truck. She parked near the barn and ran to him. Jack lifted the brunette up and kissed her while swinging her in a circle.

Lia's heart twisted with envy. She wanted that kind of love. A man had never greeted her that way, though she had a feeling Jimmy, like his brother, was the kind of man who would.

These guys were so much deeper than she'd given them credit for. Maybe she was the shallow bitch they thought she was.

She sighed and went to find her father. The quicker they got back to the city, the sooner she could get to Jimmy and work on smoothing things over.

It was time to move on with her life.

CHAPTER TWELVE

Jimmy hadn't been in his apartment since the day he'd left for Kosovo six months before.

Luckily he shared it with Jack, so except for the now-sour milk in the fridge that Jack had forgotten to pour out before he left on furlough two weeks ago, it was in pretty much the same shape Jimmy had left it. Comfy, sort of clean and home away from home.

He threw his duffle on the bed and then himself on the couch. TV remote in hand, he decided women were put on earth strictly to torture men.

One minute Lia was kissing him, the next she was engaged to Senator Dickhead's son and then an hour later she was telling him she wasn't. Now he was waiting at home like a damn high school girl for her to call. It was crazy.

He checked his cell phone to make sure it had a signal and was charged then shook his head at himself.

Frigging crazy.

The show on television held no appeal but he stared at it anyway. He guessed he dozed for a bit because the ringing of his cell phone startled him out of his sleep. Even while hating himself for being so anxious to speak with her, Jimmy jumped to answer it.

He fumbled with the phone until he swiped to answer the

call and said, "Hello."

"In the limo on the way home I told my father I'm never going to marry the senator's son, no matter how much he and Dickson push us together. I also told him I've met someone else. Someone I'm very interested in." She let out a short laugh. "Needless to say, it was a very long car ride home."

Jimmy swallowed the lump from his throat. "I can imagine it was. Did you tell him exactly who it was you met?"

He firmly tamped down his growing hope. This was a start, but he couldn't let himself think there could be a future for them. She was still the governor's daughter and he was the abandoned son of a drunken father.

"Not yet."

And there it was. She wanted him as long as he could remain a secret. He let out a bitter laugh. "Yeah, that's what I thought."

"No, Jimmy. You're wrong. I didn't tell him because I want you to meet him first."

He shook his head at her excuse. "I have met him, Lia."

"I mean meet him on equal footing, as my date. I have to attend a black-tie cocktail party tonight. Any chance you have a tux lying around?"

She was asking him on a date? An actual public, meet-my-daddy date. Maybe she was serious about trying to make this thing between them work. Though he had to laugh at her tuxedo question.

"Yeah, sure. My tux is hanging right next to my opera cape and ascot."

Lia ignored his joke. "You can just wear a suit then. Whatever you've got will be fine."

He sighed. There was nothing he could think of that he would enjoy less than being at this party with a bunch of rich guys in tuxes.

Even terrorist torture was looking good next to this thing, but he was starting to realize if he wanted to be with this woman he was going to have to work at it. This party tonight was just part of the dues he'd have to pay to be with Lia, but boy would he love to not go.

He'd have to suck it up and deal with it. Tonight would be the test, as least as far as her daddy was concerned. If he could make it through this party and survive the governor's scrutiny, they might have a chance together.

Though there were more people involved here than just the governor.

"Are Senator Dickhead and son going to be there?" he asked.

"Yes." She hesitated before asking, "Is that going to be a problem?"

Yes, but he'd be damned if he told Lia that.

This new bit of info changed everything. Now he wanted to go, if only to stake his claim for Lia. He'd knock any idea Dickhead and son had about her right out of their heads.

"Nope. No problem. I'll be there. Give me the address. I'll meet you."

After getting the time and address, he hung up with Lia and hoisted himself off the couch.

In his bedroom, Jimmy stood in front of the open closet. Inside, covered in a dry cleaning bag, were the dress blues he hadn't worn in a long time. He hadn't gained any weight so he figured they would still fit fine.

More importantly, he'd feel better wearing this than any tuxedo or suit. But seeing Lia while wearing his uniform also meant tonight was the night he'd have to confess to her who he really was.

After he'd slept with her while letting her believe he was just a waiter, and then kissed her when she believed he was a farmer, he had a feeling she wasn't going to be very happy about finally learning the truth.

CHAPTER THIRTEEN

Lia took her own car instead of riding with her father to the party. She made sure she arrived early so she could keep a vigilant watch for Jimmy's arrival.

Tonight was going to be challenging enough. She didn't want him to have to be alone and feel awkward for any amount of time.

Smoothing the fabric of her black dress one more time, she realized she was feeling pretty awkward herself. Her stomach fluttered with butterflies she hadn't felt in years, all from the thought of seeing Jimmy again. Not just seeing him, but declaring him her official date for this event to her father, the senator, John and pretty much the world as she knew it.

She prayed he'd come up with something decent to wear.

Second-guessing her suggestion he wear a suit to a black-tie event, she realized she really should have arranged for a tux to be dropped off at his house. Though it was doubtful he would have accepted it from her. James Gordon didn't seem the type to take handouts gracefully.

More than that, with his muscular build she doubted he would fit in anything off-the-rack anyway.

To still her jangling nerves, Lia grabbed a glass of champagne from a passing waiter's tray and downed a big swallow much too fast.

Reconsidering the wisdom of her idea of using alcohol to calm herself, she put the half-empty glass on a nearby table and glanced again at the doorway.

Maybe she should go out front and make sure that they had Jimmy's name on the guest list. She was about to do just that when she noticed everyone, the women in particular, staring at the entrance.

Through the crowd she saw a tall figure dressed in the unmistakable uniform of the Marine Corps.

As he paused in the doorway, he took off his hat and surveyed the room and that's when she got her first look at James Gordon in his dress blues.

He was in the military. Add one more mystery to all the rest already surrounding the man who took her breath away.

He spotted her and their gazes locked, him looking uncertain as his lips tipped up into a small smile, her trying to recover from the shock and from the fluttering of her heart.

She returned his smile and made her way across the room, dodging around guests in her path. When she finally stood directly in front of him, she raised a hand and touched one of the many ribbons pinned to his chest.

"Wow." Her voice sounded breathy to her own ears.

"Hey, darlin'." Jimmy took her hand in his and planted a light kiss on her fingertips.

She drew in a shaky breath, her gaze rising from the spectacular sight of the uniform to the face of the amazing man inside of it. "Well this raises about as many questions as it answers."

His expression turned contrite. "I'm sorry. I know I owe you a lot of explaining. Later, in private. Can you wait until then?"

Lia could wait for an explanation, but not for a kiss. The buildup of sexual frustration within her couldn't be denied any longer. She'd lived like a nun for months. Her body remembered too well what Jimmy could do to her and it demanded satisfaction.

The uniform had initially been a shock, but now the sight

of him in it was starting to make the woman in her stand up and take notice.

Who knew she had a thing for a man in uniform? Although maybe it was just this man in particular, uniform or not.

Feeling wicked she stepped closer and ran her hands up his chest.

"I'll wait for us to talk, but not for other things. Do you think there's a coat closet around here somewhere?" She glanced around them.

Grinning, he stilled her hands with his. "You'll have to wait for that too, darlin'. But I don't think I can wait for a drink. I'm such a bundle of nerves I'm practically shaking."

He hooked her arm through the crook of his elbow and led her toward the bar.

"Why are you nervous?" She glanced at him as they walked and her gaze caught on his ribbons. Judging by the number, he'd been in a while and seen a lot. Among the things he'd seen and done, some certainly had to be a lot more frightening than a black-tie cocktail party.

Jimmy covered her hand with his and gave it a small squeeze. "I'm officially meeting my girl's daddy. Something that monumental tends to make a man nervous."

Her heart melted right there in a little puddle on the floor and she fought to not tear up. "I like being your girl."

He treated her to his crooked smile. "Good."

As they paused near the bar, she took the opportunity to stand on tiptoe and kiss him.

Jimmy's eyes drifted closed for a second. He groaned and pulled back from her lips. "Don't get me started, darlin'. I'll embarrass myself and the uniform."

She liked knowing he couldn't resist her any more than she could him. She looked forward to them tempting each other much more in the future.

But besides the chemistry between them, so much more was becoming clear to her. Standing next to Jimmy, she realized that her continuing to plan her life around the incessant round of political cocktail parties to please her father was absurd.

This was not her place or her responsibility. Her mother was the other half in the Monroe-Carrington political dynasty, not Lia.

She was done. Starting right now.

The decision, as well as the enormity of the vow to herself hit her hard. Through misty eyes she noticed her lipstick smeared on Jimmy's mouth.

Reaching up, she wiped it from his lips and said, "Let's get out of here."

He opened his eyes wide. "Now? I didn't even speak with your daddy yet."

Frustrated, Lia sighed. He was right of course. She'd invited Jimmy here for a reason. Them sneaking out before meeting her father so she could jump him made no sense.

"Okay. We'll talk to my father. Then you're taking me to your place."

He laughed. "I'm warning you, darlin'. It's a cheap military rental. It's no mansion like you're used to."

"I don't care, as long as you're in it."

"That's good to hear." He brushed his fingers along her jawline, his eyes looking suspiciously misty as well. "Let's go find your daddy."

Lia dreaded this meeting with every fiber of her being, but with Jimmy next to her and the promise that they could leave and be alone together as soon as it was over, she could face just about anything.

All too soon she spotted her father in the crowd. Glancing at Jimmy, she asked, "You ready?"

Squeezing her hand, he tipped his head. "Yes, ma'am."

"All right. Here we go."

Her father's eyebrows couldn't have risen any higher toward his receding hairline when stepped in front of him on Jimmy's arm and said, "Father. You remember James Gordon from Gordon Equine."

"Um, yes."

"Sir." Jimmy extended his hand and her father had no choice but to grasp it.

Her father didn't have a chance to comment further since Senator Dickson walked up at the same moment. "Governor. Lia. And whom might this be?"

Lia smiled sweetly, enjoying it probably a bit too much as she said, "Senator, I'd like to introduce you to my date, actually my boyfriend, James Gordon. You might remember meeting him at his family's farm this afternoon."

The senator's mouth dropped open just as his son joined them.

With a soaring heart, Lia repeated the introduction for John Dickson III and watched him pale in reaction.

Taking control of her life and her future had been far easier and much more satisfying than she'd ever imagined.

CHAPTER FOURTEEN

Lia was still riding the adrenaline high when they arrived at Jimmy's apartment shortly after. Feeling like they were two kids who'd just snuck out of the prom to fool around, she jumped him just inside the front door, crashing her mouth against his.

Kissing was good, but she was bubbling over with too much energy thanks to her victory to remain quiet long.

She pulled back and said, "I still can't get out of my head the expression on the senator's face when I introduced you as my boyfriend."

He slid his hands down and gave her butt a squeeze. "You enjoyed telling him that, didn't you?"

"Yes, I did. Immensely. And so what?" She scowled. "He deserved that and more after he called me naïve today in front of all those men at your farm. And you should talk about enjoying things. You nearly crushed John's hand when you shook it. Tell me you didn't love doing that."

"Can I help it if I don't know my own strength?" Jimmy shrugged. "And in my own defense, he was trying and failing to crush my hand first."

She laughed as started to unbutton his jacket. "Why don't you show me how strong you are right now?"

"Gladly, darlin'." He groaned, deep and low in his throat.

Taking over with the buttons, he got his uniform jacket off and then scooped her up into his arms.

Jimmy carried her to the bedroom and laid her on the bed. Under the moonlight streaming through the window, he finished taking off his uniform, then moved on to undressing her.

Once they were naked on top of the covers he pulled her close and held her tight. She fit perfectly against him. It was strange. They'd only been together the one night, but being in his arms again felt like coming home.

Tempted to rush things thanks to the overwhelming need about to explode inside her, she reached for and grasped the hard length of him. He grabbed her hand with his. Raising it above her head, he held it there as he took his time exploring her face and throat with his mouth.

Admittedly, she enjoyed every sensation as he kissed her inch-by-inch, but she needed so much more.

"I want you now." She wrapped one leg around his hip and pulled him closer.

Jimmy nipped at her earlobe. His warm breath against her skin sent a tingle straight through her. "You'll get what you want, when I want."

"You are an extremely frustrating man, James Gordon."

He covered her pout with his lips, soothing her bad mood with the thrust of his tongue.

Angling her body, she managed to press just the tip of him against her entrance. She felt him laugh against her mouth as he kissed her, even as he pulled his pelvis away far enough to break contact.

Finally, he raised his mouth from hers. "I couldn't get you off my mind, not for even a day, the whole time we were apart all those months."

His confession brought tears to her eyes. She tried to joke them away. "Neither could I, and believe me I tried. It really pissed me off."

He released his hold on her hand and stroked her face. "You don't have to try anymore because I'm right here."

"Yes, you are, and do you think you could make love to me now? Please? I've waited a very long time for you, James Gordon, and I don't usually have to wait for anything."

He smiled. "I bet you don't. I guess I could see clear to giving in to your request, since you asked so nicely and all."

After donning a condom he got from the bedside table drawer, Jimmy slid inside her. They'd already had a night of wild, passion-filled sex six months before. She could honestly say this time felt even more wonderful.

His gaze stayed locked on hers as he loved her. They moved together as one. Slowly. Tenderly.

It was so different than their first time together. That had been sex. This was definitely making love. Lia hadn't truly known the difference before. She did now.

Her body tightened around him. Jimmy drew in a sharp breath in response and pressed closer against her.

She clung to him as she felt the climax coil within her until it snapped, sending spasms of pleasure through every part of her body.

Jimmy's breath and pace quickened as he came right after her. He shuddered with the last of his orgasm and with his face pressed against the pillow next to her head, he said, "I love you."

Her eyes flew open. She couldn't help the reaction. His unexpected post coital confession had come as a total shock. Jimmy looked as surprised that he'd said it as she was hearing it.

He groaned and tried to roll away. "I'm sorry. I didn't mean to say that. It just slipped out. Please, forget I said it. I take it back."

Tightening her arms like a vise around him, Lia prevented him from moving farther away.

"Don't you dare take it back." She squeezed him hard until he let out a pain-filled wheeze. "Oh, my God. I'm sorry. Did I hurt you? How could I hurt you? You're so big and strong."

He let out a short laugh and pulled her arms from around

his rib cage.

"It's all right, darlin'." He blew out a slow, controlled breath. "There's some stuff I have to tell you and I think now is as good a time as any."

Now that the time had come for him to clear up all the mysteries of the past six months, she wasn't sure she could handle hearing it.

She nodded anyway. "Okay."

As Jimmy talked, Lia lay silent next to him and listened. He told her everything that had happened over the past six months—at least everything he was allowed to. He explained there was a lot that was confidential, but she didn't care about that part.

It didn't matter to her exactly where in the world he'd been or why he'd been there. What was most important to her was that there was a very real reason why he hadn't been able to be with her before.

Even more touching was his confession that he had wanted to be with her each and every day they'd been apart. That thoughts of her kept him going when he thought he couldn't go on any longer.

Listening to his voice in the darkened room as he sat propped up against the headboard with his arm around her shoulders, she could barely comprehend all he said.

He talked about atrocities with a distance that belied the events that had happened to him. She was certain he was giving her only the tip of the iceberg.

For what he told her, for what she knew he still hid from her, her eyes brimmed with tears. She cried over how he'd been hurt and tortured. She cried out of guilt because she'd hated him for not contacting her even though he'd had no choice in the matter. And she cried that he hadn't felt he could call her when he'd finally come home to heal.

"That's pretty much all I can tell you. I didn't want to start off with secrets between us." He reached out and brushed a tear from her cheek.

More fell in its place as she said, "I'm so sorry."

He shook his head. "None of it's your fault, darlin'."

"But I wish I could have been there for you."

"You were. Every day. I thought about you constantly while I was there and afterward when I was home. I made love to you thousands of times in my mind." His laugh held a touch of embarrassment. "And quite a few of those times I imagined telling you I loved you."

"Which is why you said it before." Lia felt her heart ache.

He was in love with the image of her in his head, the one he had clung to during the horrors he'd been through. He wasn't in love with the real her.

Jimmy pulled her closer and touched his lips to each of her eyelids. "Maybe."

It didn't matter. He'd grow to love the real her. She'd make sure he did.

Lia moved over him, straddling his thighs with her own. She grabbed his face in both hands and kissed him hard. She felt his growing arousal beneath her. "Make love to me again."

Groaning, he rolled her onto her back. "My pleasure."

CHAPTER FIFTEEN

Jimmy opened his eyes and stretched. Judging by the sun it must be late morning. He'd actually slept really well once they'd gotten to sleep.

He looked down at Lia next to him and smiled. She was the reason they'd been up until the wee hours of the night, and she was also the reason he'd slept better than he had in months.

It felt good waking up next to her. Right. Perfect. He'd be happy to wake next to her every day for the rest of his life . . .

His blissful bubble was broken when he heard the front door open and voices in the living room.

A moment later, his bedroom door burst open and Jack flipped the light switch on.

"Jeez, Jack. Close the friggin' door. I'm not alone."

Lia, apparently not fast to wake, sat up sputtering. "Wha-what's going on?"

Jack's eyes bulged as the sheet fell away from Lia's naked breasts. Jimmy reached out and pulled it back up to cover her, but not before Nicki, who'd just walked in and taken stock of the scene, smacked Jack.

"God, Jack. Give them some privacy." She yanked him out by the arm and pulled the door shut behind them.

"You better get your naked butt out here, big brother."

Jack's voice came through the closed door. "You're in deep shit. Don't be surprised if the next person to come knocking is the commander."

"What? Why?" What now? He glanced down at the still-groggy Lia. "I better go out there and see what's up."

Sleepy and tousled and looking far too tempting, she nodded. Jimmy hopped out of bed before he lost interest in Jack and whatever bad news he had to deliver in favor of staying in bed with Lia.

He pulled on a pair of PT shorts and a T-shirt and went to investigate what the hell Jack was so flustered about.

He didn't have long to wait. The moment he entered the living room, Jack flung a newspaper on the table and pointed to the front page. "Good thing Mama still gets the newspaper delivered at the farm. Just imagine my surprise when over coffee this morning I see this."

The headline above the half-page photo of him and Lia kissing outside of the party last night read, *Mystery Military Man sMooches Miss Monroe-Carrington.*

Jimmy groaned "Aww, shit."

"You gotta give them credit for creativity, getting all those Ms lined up like that. The press will do anything for a witty headline, but yeah, *shit* is right. Good thing you had your hat on and it hid your face. They haven't figured out who you are yet, but you keep seeing her and they'll figure it out soon enough. Jesus, Jimmy. You gotta fall for the governor's daughter? The commander is going to flip. Dating her will mean your face will be in the paper all the time. You can forget about going undercover ever again. That part of your career will be over."

Jimmy shook his head. "I don't care. I'll leave the task force if they ask me to. I'm staying with Lia."

God, he hoped they wouldn't ask him to.

"No. I won't let you sacrifice your career for me, Jimmy."

At the sound of Lia's voice, he turned and saw her standing in the bedroom doorway wearing his shirt from last night. The sight only served to steel his stance. "It's not your decision, darlin'. My mind is made up. I'll change and go see the commander right now."

She shook her head and was about to protest when he walked to her, laid one finger over her lips and then kissed her. "I know what I'm doing. Please trust me."

"I do."

"Good."

She followed him into the bedroom and sat silently on the edge of the bed, watching him while he got changed into clothes appropriate for begging forgiveness from your commander.

Then that was it. He couldn't procrastinate any longer. "Guess I better get going. Will you be here when I get back?"

"Do you want me to be?" she asked.

He nodded. "Yes. Please."

Today and for every day after that.

Lia nodded. "Then I'll be here."

He led her to the bedroom door by the hand. Standing on tiptoe, she kissed him with tears in her eyes. "Good luck."

After seeing that, he didn't worry any more about the fact that he might be forced to leave Zeta. It would be worth it to have her in his life.

Jimmy glanced back into the living room at Jack sprawled on the couch while Nicki was in the kitchen filling the coffee pot with water.

"I'll see you two when I get back?" he asked his brother.

Jack sat up. "Um, maybe not. Shit, I know you got other things on your mind, but I was planning to start moving out today."

Jimmy groaned and ran a hand over his face. He couldn't deal with this now. "Jack. I'm sorry I snapped at you, but it's nothing to move out over."

Jack broke into a crooked grin.

"You know me better than that, bro. If I didn't want to go, you couldn't get me out of here with a bulldozer. I've been thinking about getting my own place so Nicki and I can be alone when she's visiting." Jack paused long enough to glance at Nicki in the kitchen. "Carly's moved in with Trey, so her old apartment above the bar is available. She said I can have it. And now that you're with Miss Monroe-Carrington in there, I figure you'll be wanting the extra privacy too."

What Jack said made sense, but it still seemed like a huge change in their lives just when things were changing too fast for Jimmy. Jack had lived with him since the day he'd joined the team.

Jimmy moved across the room and pulled Jack into a hug. "I'm gonna miss you, little brother."

Jack laughed. "Jeez, one near-death experience and he's all sappy. I'll miss you too, big brother. Good luck with the commander. Call me the minute you get out of the meeting."

"Will do." Jimmy nodded and with one final glance back at Lia, biting her lip and looking worried, he headed out the door.

CHAPTER SIXTEEN

All too soon, he was on base and standing in the commander's open doorway.

"Sir? May I speak with you?"

Jimmy had both the newspaper and his note from the doc rolled up in his hand. He only hoped he would need the second after he showed the commander the first.

"Gordon. Come on in. It's good to see you back, son."

The question remained, was he back to stay?

Jimmy swallowed and gathered his nerve. "Sir. I have to show you something. I want you to know, if you want my request for transfer after seeing it, I'll give it to you."He unrolled the paper and laid it on the desk facing the older man.

The commander read the headline then cocked one brow high. "Well, I have to say, *that* headline is far more creative than the one I read."

Reaching under his desk, he pulled a different paper out of the garbage and pushed it toward Jimmy.

Dickson's Fiancée and ???

Heart pounding, Jimmy shook his head. "She was never engaged to Senator Dickson's son, sir. I swear."

"Oh, good. That makes it all right then." The commander rolled his eyes. "Tell me this, why is it every time one of you

Gordons falls in love, it's a headache for me? First your brother is pummeling Williams over that bartender . . ."

Jimmy frowned at that revelation. Trey and Jack had fought over Carly?

The commander continued, "Then I'm hearing rumors about Jack's new girl being involved with the mob."

How the hell had the commander heard that?

While Jimmy pondered that, the commander kept ranting, "And now, you and the governor's daughter."

He leaned way back in his chair, leveled a stare on Jimmy and waited.

"I apologize, sir. I didn't know who she was the night of the party when we met—"

Jimmy's explanation was cut short by the commander's creative and colorful cussing. "*Now* I recognize her. She's the redhead from the party. The night you—"

"Yes, sir." No need to rehash that again. He'd already gotten enough of a reminder about his breaking protocol from the commander the morning after and from Jack yesterday when he'd recognized Lia. "I swear, sir, I hadn't contacted her at all after that night. We ran into each other purely by accident yesterday and that's when I found out who her daddy is. You need to know, I'm not willing to give her up. I realize undercover work is a major part of our missions and that dating a politician's daughter will put me in the spotlight no matter how hard I try to stay out of it, which is why I'm ready to transfer out of the unit if you ask."

The commander let out a frustrated sigh. "You're a stupid man, Gordon."

Uh, oh.

"You have the kind of night I heard over the comm unit with a girl who looks like that and you don't call her?"

Once he got over the surprise, Jimmy couldn't help but smile. "Yes, sir. She wasn't happy about it either."

"Listen, Gordon. Your undercover career was already over. You were compromised in Kosovo. You don't think your face hasn't been sent to every terrorist in the known world already?"

"I guess I hadn't thought about it. Yes, sir, you're right."

"But that doesn't mean I want you to leave. You're a valuable member of this team, with more skills than just the ability to go undercover with terrorists. And I'm thinking having you be the heartthrob who's dating the governor's daughter will make you kind of the poster boy representing all the brave, red-blooded troops on this base. That would make it look really bad if the governor allowed Senator Dickhead to shut us down."

"Yes, sir. It would." Jimmy smiled.

The commander chuckled at that idea before turning serious again. "I'd watch my back for a while, if I were you. Dickhead Junior isn't going to be too happy about being made a fool of on the front page."

Jimmy nodded.

"Go on home, Gordon. I'll see you tomorrow with the rest of the team for a zero-seven-thirty, end-of-this-fucking-furlough briefing. Oh, and if you want to marry her and pop out a few cute babies, I wouldn't be opposed to that either. The press loves babies."

Jimmy wouldn't be opposed to that himself, in time. "Yes, sir. Thank you."

He arrived home feeling far lighter than when he'd left.

Dressed in a pair of his navy cotton sweatpants and a grey USMC T-shirt, Lia greeted him at the door.

He lifted her in his arms and kissed her hard.

She pulled away and he saw the concern on her face. "Tell me what happened. I've been going crazy."

He smiled, going a little crazy himself at the sight of her wearing his clothes. "Everything's fine. Move in with me, Lia."

"What?" She frowned and laughed at the same time.

"It felt really good waking up next to you. And coming home to you just now. I want you here every time I walk in that door. I know this place isn't much. If you want we can move into a better one, but live with me, wherever we end up."

A smile lit her face as she nodded. "Okay."

"Really?"

She laughed. "Yes, really."

He squeezed her hard and then realized he was hard too. Lifting her off her feet, he headed for the bedroom. "Let's go celebrate."

"James Gordon, is this what my life is going to be like when I live with you? Nothing but sex day and night?"she asked.

"Yup." He grinned at the thought.

She pursed her lips as if considering the idea. "I can live with that. It's one of the many reasons why I love you."

He stopped mid-step. "You love me?"

"Yes."

Lia loved him. With a whoop, Jimmy spun her in a circle while she laughed and kissed him.

He stopped their motion so he could stare into her sky-blue eyes. "That's a very good thing, darlin', because I'm completely and absolutely in love with you."

Since he still held her in the air, Lia was eye level with him. He saw the emotion in her eyes when she said, "I believe you really are."

"Of course I am, woman. I wouldn't have said it if I didn't mean it. Now can we go to bed?" he asked, trying to lighten the mood before he teared up.

"Yes, unless you'd rather take me directly to the shower instead." She raised one red eyebrow prettily.

"Damn, I'm going to really like living with you." He carried her toward the bathroom, and this time he was locking the door behind them.

ABOUT THE AUTHOR

A top 10 *New York Times* bestselling author, Cat Johnson writes the *USA Today* bestselling Hot SEALs series, as well as contemporary romance featuring sexy alpha heroes who often wear cowboy or combat boots. Known for her creative marketing, Cat has sponsored bull-riding cowboys, used bologna to promote her romance novels, and owns a collection of camouflage and cowboy boots for book signings. She writes both full length and shorter works.

For more visit CatJohnson.net
Join the mailing list at catjohnson.net/news

Made in the USA
Coppell, TX
10 January 2023